THEIR LAST WORDS

An absolutely gripping serial killer thriller with a huge twist

STEVE PARKER

JOFFE BOOKS

Published 2018 by Joffe Books, London.

FIRST PUBLISHED AS "THE SKY IS CRYING." THIS IS A HEAVILY REVISED EDITION.

www.joffebooks.com

This book is a work of fiction. Names, characters, businesses, organizations, places and events are either the product of the author's imagination or are used fictitiously. Any resemblance to actual persons, living or dead, events or locales is entirely coincidental. The spelling is British English.

ISBN-13: 978-1-78931-022-1

To my special three. Weebles all.
To my father who left me with his love of reading.
And to the men and women of the Thin Blue Line wherever and however far it stretches to. Thank you for facing the dark.

CHAPTER ONE

Detective Superintendent Paterson was running late. He'd kept her waiting, but she'd wait a bit longer. The dead are good like that. Patient. With a clunk he shut the door of his Aston, flicked his umbrella open and hoisted it above his head. The heavy rain had been falling for the best part of a week now.

Any murder scene in the first few hours is chaotic, and this one was no different. Police cars and vans were parked anyhow, yellow crime scene tape was strewn across various junctions, each with a PC in attendance, and a control point was being established.

Paterson scanned the street for his DS, and quickly spotted him standing outside the white tent with the uniformed duty inspector, both in their paper suits. He could see that DS Jordan was wearing a serious face. Never a good sign. Stepping carefully around the puddles of water that threatened to engulf his Guccis, Paterson made his way over to them. They nodded.

'Evening,' guv,' said Jordan. 'Glad you made it.'

Paterson gave him a quick glance, unsure if he detected some of that famous sarcasm. He decided to give him the benefit of the doubt. Jordan handed him a paper suit, took his umbrella and held it over him while Paterson hopped about, trying to keep his balance while he pulled it on.

'Sir,' Jordan said, 'this is Inspector Steve Goodman. He's the night duty inspector. Mr Goodman, Detective Superintendent Ray Paterson. He'll be the SIO on this one.' Paterson was busy trying to keep his hair as neat as possible while he pulled the paper hood over his head. Goodman rolled his eyes. The two men shook hands, and Paterson noticed his ashen face.

'What we got then?' he said.

'A soaking wet detective sergeant out here and a right fuckin' mess in there.' Jordan jerked his head toward the tent. 'Young girl. In her twenties maybe. Stark naked. Butchered.' He paused for effect. 'Never seen anything quite like this before.'

Paterson frowned. If Jordan hadn't seen the like, he knew he was in for a rare old treat.

'Explain "butchered" for me, Dave.'

Jordan shot him a look. 'Her throat's been cut. Deep. Almost took her head off. He's removed her insides and dumped them on the pavement. Above her breasts he's carved the word "Don't" into her flesh.' Paterson grimaced, swayed a little. Jordan caught it. 'Not finished yet, guv. He's also cut out her vagina.'

Paterson closed his eyes momentarily. 'He's done *what*?' Maybe he was hearing things.

'Yep. Swear to God, he's cut out her vagina.' Inspector Goodman, his head down, nodded silently. Paterson looked at Jordon. All he could think of to say was, 'Dear God . . .'

'I think God's given this poor little cow a bit of a swerve tonight, guv. Certainly wasn't around when she needed him, that's for sure.' Paterson said nothing. Jordan, getting wetter by the minute, tried to edge his way under Paterson's umbrella. He pointed toward a uniformed female PC sitting in the back of a van, swaddled in a heavy blanket.

'That plonk found her while she was doing a quick roundup, looking for break-ins on her way back to the nick. Apparently she was busting for a piss and decided to cut through this side alley as it's quicker. I'm guessing she's pissed herself by now though.' Goodman shot him a look. Not funny.

Paterson turned his attention to Goodman. 'Make sure she's looked after properly. Get her to hospital as quick as, and make sure someone's with her at all times. Poor kid's in a right mess by the look of it and she's going to need someone when it hits her.' He shook his head, remembering the first dead body he'd seen on the job. Never quite leaves you.

Goodman nodded and dialled a number on his radio phone. 'My team preserved the scene as best we could, sir, until we could get a plastic over her.' He waited for someone to answer. 'They're all pretty good. They know not to go tramping about over crime scenes. That said, she was absolutely drenched when she was found, so it's very possible we may have lost some evidence, washed away like.'

Paterson grunted, looked around and spotted a drain, some five feet away from where they were. 'Inspector, get someone down there. It's doubtful but anything unusual, I want it out and bagged.' Goodman nodded, gave up with the phone call and got on the radio.

Paterson turned to Jordan. 'Any chance of witnesses?'

'No, guv, not at the moment. Apparently the street was empty when the WPC found her. There's some CCTV cameras around the sides of these buildings though. We've called the mobile security firms that take care of them. When they arrive, we'll pull the footage and see what we've got. We might touch lucky, but I doubt it.'

Paterson nodded. 'Best I go take a look then.'

Jordan put his hand on Paterson's shoulder. 'I know you have to, guv, but be prepared. It's not a pretty sight, I promise you. I've called the rest of the team. They're on their way in.'

'Thanks, Dave,' said Paterson, shoring himself up before he went in. The three men gave their details and signed in with a rain-soaked, thoroughly miserable looking PC. He had obviously drawn the short straw on this one, and was in for a long wretched night. Paterson noted that Jock Hudson, the borough pathologist, had signed in and out. Could have done without that.

Within five seconds of stepping into the tent, Ray Paterson wanted out of the tent.

'Fucking hell,' he said, turning his head away from both the smell and the sight. 'Oh Jesus Christ. What the hell did this?' Nobody answered. 'Anyone know who she is?'

'No idea, guv.' Despite this being his second visit, and maybe because of it, DS Jordan had turned a bit greenish.

'Have the togs been in?' asked Paterson.

'Been and gone, sir,' Goodman said. 'You'll probably be able to see all the photos on your iPad by now.'

'Right. I've seen enough. That should stay with me for the rest of my life.' Paterson turned sharply on his heels. 'Let's go.'

They stepped out into the cold night air, and the rain-soaked uniformed PC thrust a clipboard at him. 'Sign out, please, sir.'

Flicking open his umbrella again, Paterson took the board, and scribbled his signature. A quick check of his Rolex, and he jotted down the time. Two forty-four. He pulled down the hood of his paper suit and passed the board to Jordan. While his mind was busy with all the things he now had to do, someone shouted to him.

'Superintendent!' Paterson turned to see Jock Hudson, the senior pathologist, hurrying towards him. Hudson was struggling to hold an umbrella and an obviously weighty briefcase in one hand and carrying what Paterson guessed was a heavily scotched-up coffee in the other. Hudson,

Scottish *and* gay and with that surname, was a piss taker's wet dream come true. It helped even more that he looked absolutely nothing like the man himself, being a small red-haired, red faced chap covered in so many freckles he looked like he'd spent a month in Ibiza sunbathing under a tea strainer.

Paterson didn't have a lot of time for Alan Hudson, despite his professional reputation. Jock was a drinker, a scruff, full of his own piss and importance, and with a sense of humour that was dark even by pathologists' standards. Plus, he was Scottish. The drink he could forgive him for, considering his line of work. Couldn't be easy. The self-importance could be tolerated. Just. It was the sense of humour that didn't sit right with Paterson. It was disrespectful, and Paterson wasn't a big fan of that. He'd have to put up with him being Scottish.

'Jock,' he said flatly. He held out his hand, knowing that Hudson would struggle to shake it with both his full. 'What the hell happened here?' Hudson dropped the case, swapped the umbrella and clamped it under his armpit with ease and shook his hand. Paterson was just a little impressed.

'What kind of savage does this?' asked Jordan.

Hudson turned his attention to the soaking wet, dishevelled DS Jordan and smirked. 'Did you no bring an umbrella wi' ya, laddie?'

Jordan sighed. Here we go. 'Yep. It's one of those new invisible ones everyone's raving about. Turns out mine's sprung a leak.'

Hudson nodded. 'Lucky for you the paper suit is soaking it all up.' He turned back to Paterson. Jordan scowled at him. *Prick.*

'Jock,' said Paterson, 'What have we got?'

'Shall we step back inside the tent, Superintendent?'

'No thanks. We're fine where we are.'

'I'm sorry, sir. Back we go. I prefer to show and tell.'

'You don't need me back in there, sir,' said Inspector Goodman quickly, and checked his watch. 'I've got things to do.' He turned and began to walk away. 'I'll be over there if you need me,' he called back, pointing toward the makeshift control point. Paterson nodded. *Well played that man.* Just for an instant, he considered ordering him back inside.

Again, they signed in. Inside, Hudson went straight over to a corner of the tent and pulled a big tin of Vick's vapour rub from his bag. 'Under the nose, gents.' He wiped two thick gobs of the stuff over the top of his lip and offered the tin to Paterson. The vapour brought tears to Paterson's eyes but it was a whole lot better to be crying than to be smelling that again. He passed the tin to Jordan.

'Who the fuck does something like this?' Jordan repeated.

Hudson's demeanour changed. Pure professional now, he dropped to one knee, took off his horn-rimmed glasses and ran his eyes over the body. 'Someone who's bloody serious. Her throat's been cut down to the bone. That was most likely the cause of death but with the amount of blood around her body, I can't say for sure at this stage. Assuming she was dead, he set about cutting her up.' His broad accent made it sound like 'did.' 'He removed her innards by making two incisions in a crisscross shape. He opened her up like an envelope and, having looked inside myself, I can say that this procedure was not surgically exact. It was hurried, but would still have taken some time. He then shoved his hands inside and dumped her internals on the pavement. The removal of her fanny, however, was a bit different.'

Paterson winced. 'Bit of respect, please, Jock.'

Hudson shrugged off the mild rebuke and carried on. 'There is a level of precision here. Not surgical, but knowledgeable. I would say he's done this before.' The detectives exchanged a look and frowned. 'It's been cut out in a triangular shape, as you would expect, and the removal was made by severing the perineum.'

'The what?' Jordan said.

Hudson shot him a look. He couldn't let this one go. 'The perineum, Sergeant. It's a small area between the vulva and the anus. Just so you're aware, the vulva is not a car, Sergeant.'

'Knock it off, Jock,' said Paterson. 'I mean it.'

Jordan's scowl was now a death stare, but he rose above the slight. 'Sounds bloody painful to me.'

'It most certainly would have been, Sergeant,' Hudson said, 'but given that she was dead, it's unlikely she noticed too much.' He looked up at Paterson. 'Sorry.' His look said, "But he's walking right into them."

'How do you know she was dead?' Paterson asked.

'Have you had any reports of a screaming girl?'

'No.'

'Believe me, Superintendent, if she'd been alive when he did this, you'd have heard the screams all the way to Dundee and back.'

OK, Paterson conceded. Hudson had a good point. 'What about the word carved into her?'

'Can't be sure without a proper exam but again, from the lack of bleeding, I'd say it was done post-mortem.'

'How long before your report?' Paterson said.

'Give me a few hours. I have some more to do here. Seven, maybe eight o'clock.'

Paterson checked his Rolex. It was getting on for half three. 'Fine. I appreciate your help. Good work.'

Back outside, Paterson took a deep breath, closed his eyes and turned his face towards the pouring rain.

A PC appeared at his side and held out a plastic exhibits bag. 'Sir,' he said. 'If you're done?' Procedure demanded that as he'd been inside a crime scene, his paper suit would need to be examined and treated as a possible exhibit. He was more than happy to get out of it. White really wasn't his colour.

'Something you should see round the back in Holyrood Street, sir.'

Paterson exhaled sharply and brought himself back to the here and now. 'What is it?' he said, and turned to face yet another PC. This one was young and ridiculously fresh faced.

'PC Harrison, sir.' The youngster snapped to attention. For a second, Paterson wondered if he was ex-military but dismissed the thought based on his baby face. Not a face that had ever seen action.

'I've found some writing on a roller shutter, sir. I'm not sure what it means, but I'll lay a tenner that it's very much connected to that young girl. I got the photographer to take some shots. He's there now.'

Paterson followed him into a small alley a few streets away. The photographer, a grey-haired man in his fifties, was crouched down, busily packing away his digital SLR cameras and equipment into a large aluminium flight case.

'Morning,' Paterson said. 'What we got then?'

Barely lifting his head, the man grunted, 'Morning,' and pointed towards the shutter. 'It's exactly fourteen inches high at the highest point and twenty-one and a half inches wide.' With no idea what he was talking about, Paterson peered at the blind. In the dim orange glow of a nearby streetlight, he could just about make out a single word scrawled across the slats in what looked to him like black paint. It dawned on him that the photographer was talking about the dimensions of the word.

Wishing he'd brought his glasses out of the car, Paterson moved closer to the wall and squinted hard. 'What does that say?'

'It says, "Don't",' said the photographer. 'Same as what's on her tits.' Paterson glared at him.

'You also need to look a bit closer, sir.' PC Harrison stepped forward, snapped on a small Maglite and shone it onto the word. The letters changed from black to a deep, burgundy colour.

Paterson stared at the writing. 'Is that blood? Tell me that's not fucking blood.'

The photographer dropped the lid of his case and snapped the two silver catches into place. 'It's definitely fucking blood.'

'You got this?' Paterson pointed at the wall.

'Course I have. It's my job. And I've just sent them over the net to the blood splatter boys for analysis. They can get a head start and hopefully give you some info by breakfast time. Can't guarantee it though. Not my department. I'll send them over to you when I get in the car and out of this bloody rain.'

When Paterson first joined up, ten years ago, a lot of work still had to be done the long way round. These days, digital cameras and wifi made short work of it all. Even though he was a child of the tech age, he still shook his head in wonderment. He snapped a few with his own iPhone, checked the preview and called Jordan.

'We're lucky in some respects, sir,' said the PC. 'It's out of the rain. The forensics team are on their way over to take a sample now.'

'Good man,' said Paterson, genuinely impressed, then held up his finger. Jordan was on the line.

'Dave,' he said. 'I'm in Holyrood Street. Something you need to see. Soon as you can.' He turned back to PC Harrison. 'I'm afraid you're going to have to wait it out in the rain until forensics have been and done their bit. When you're finished, tell your guv'nor and give him a copy of your notes before you book off. Go get yourself a cup of tea and be back here in fifteen minutes. I'll hold the fort.' PC Harrison nodded gratefully, and scurried off into the rain. Paterson stood in the cold night wind and pulled his collar in tighter. Jordan hove into view.

Paterson watched his bald, overweight sergeant friend duck in and out of doorways in a pointless attempt to keep the rain off. The bald head was new, and Paterson wasn't sure he liked it. Jordan hadn't had a good head of hair to start with, but it kind of suited him. He remembered Jordan telling him that his elder brother had cancer, and he wondered if it was a show of support, a charity thing maybe. He'd ask him later. Paterson gave a little smile, hearing Jordan mutter curses to himself as he picked his way in and out of the puddles. He couldn't quite remember how they'd become friends, given their age difference and service level, but it just seemed to morph from a work pairing to a genuine friendship. Jordan was a genuinely likeable man, rough round the edges and a dinosaur in policing terms, but he'd forgotten more than Paterson would ever know, and he was grateful to have him on his team.

'Sorry, guv,' said Jordan. 'Just dug out a security guard from one of the nearby offices. Seems they have cameras and, believe it or not, twenty-four-hour recording. Might get a break. I'll pop back later and have a look.'

'Good stuff,' said Paterson, and pointed toward the shutter. 'Have a look at this.'

Jordan screwed up his eyes. 'What does that say?'

'"Don't". Same as on the girl. I have no idea what it means.'

Jordan took a step forward. 'Oh, fuck. I'm guessing that's her claret he's used then?'

'Should think so. Forensics are on their way. Pictures've been taken and will be with us soon.' Paterson peered up and down the street, looking for CCTV and more blood, although he guessed that PC Harrison would most likely have already done that.

'Let's bat this about, Dave.'

Jordan grinned. 'Maybe he killed her here, dipped his brush in and then moved her round the corner.'

Paterson frowned at him. 'If he'd "dipped his brush in" as you so delicately put it, there'd be splatter on the street. I can't see any. Plus, if he did reposition her, there'd be blood everywhere, a trail. There isn't.'

Jordan scratched his head.

'Maybe,' Paterson said, 'he used some sort of container to transport the blood.'

Jordan snorted. 'That should narrow it down, guv. Can't be too many psychopathic milkmaids in Bermondsey, eh?'

Paterson chortled. 'It's possible, right?'

Jordan weighed it up for a second or two. 'Possible, but not probable, guv. If this was a pre-planned strike, I just don't see him bringing a container with him. Again, if it was an opportunist, why would you be out in the early hours with a container?'

'Maybe,' Paterson said after a few seconds, 'he ran out of petrol.'

Jordan inclined his head. 'Good thinking, boss. So you're not just a pretty face then. I'll check the all-night garages to see if anyone bought a can tonight and check their CCTVs. Still don't think that's what happened though.'

Paterson glanced at his watch again. 'Dave, hang on here for the woodentop to come back. I'm going to head back to the nick and cheer up Commander Kelly with a rise 'n' shine.'

* * *

Dave Jordan turned his gaze away from the little black and white monitor that he'd been watching studiously for the past ten minutes, and looked out of the window onto the petrol station forecourt. Detective Constable Adam Walker was just getting out of his car when Jordan's voice boomed out over the public address system.

'Where the fuck have you been?'

DC Walker jumped, and cast his eyes around the forecourt. Inside the shop, he caught sight of a fat, middle-aged bald man standing on the wrong side of the counter and leaning in a bit too close to the middle-aged Asian man he assumed to be the night cashier. It took him a few seconds to recognise the bald man as his sergeant. He looked different somehow. He quickly figured that the Asian man was holding down the speak button and Jordan was leaning over the microphone in order to bollock him.

Grateful that there wasn't anyone around to share his embarrassment, Walker waved, pointed toward the door and headed toward it. He watched Jordan wriggle to shift his considerable bulk around from behind the counter and then struggle his way through the narrow aisles, obviously trying not to drag any of the stock onto the floor with his gut. The expression 'bull in a china shop' sprang to mind. Jordan pulled on the door a few times without a result. He looked back at the cashier, who grinned, waved and pressed the buzzer. The door opened.

Jordan glared at Walker. 'Fuck have you been? I've been trying to get hold of you on the radio and your phone.' He stood aside, and Walker dodged past him and made his way straight to the refrigerator section. 'Oi!' Jordan said. 'What d'you think you're doing?'

Walker opened the door to one of the fridges and pulled out a steak slice. 'Sorry, skipper,' he said. 'I'm starving. Sorry, I never heard you call. There was a huge punch up in the Old Kent Road again. Pubs v pubs. I thought I might need both hands free to wallop someone, so I stuck the radio inside my coat to keep the rain off of it.'

Jordan scowled at his DC. 'Did you?' he said flatly. 'And while I was waiting around for you and the car, I had to walk over here and I got absolutely fucking saturated.' Walker could see that was true. Even though Jordan had been inside for a while, there were still a few little rivulets of rain running off of his shiny dome and down his ruddy face before his collar soaked them up. For some reason, Walker was reminded of a Buddha statue that he and his wife Trish used to have in the garden. He remembered how that used to sit, inscrutably, in the rain. Jordan was not inscrutable but definitely on the Buddha side of Weightwatchers.

'Sorry, Sarge. What could I do? It was all going off as I drove past. Urgent assistance shouts went up and I figured the living were more important.' Biting the cellophane wrapper open, Walker tossed the steak slice into a microwave, set it for three minutes and reached for a bottle of water. 'What's with the haircut?'

'Never mind the haircut, son.' Walker bristled. He hated being called 'son.' 'We've got things to do. Go pay the man and let's get to work.' Jordan bumped and jostled his way past Walker and made his way back to the cashier. He thanked him, handed him his business card and left instructions for him to call if he remembered anything at all. The microwave pinged, and Walker gingerly lifted out the steaming steak with a handful of paper towels. Just then, Jordan barrelled his way down the aisle, banged into Walker and sent the slice flying to the floor.

'Oh, for Christ's sake, Sarge!'

With his back to him and a beaming grin on his face, Jordan headed for the door. 'Sorry, son. My fault. Bit tight in there.' The door buzzed open and Jordan strolled out onto the forecourt toward the Astra.

Walker picked up the steak slice and lobbed it onto the counter, before turning on his heels and making for the door. He looked back at the startled cashier and said, 'Sorry about that, Mo. Stick it on the slate and I'll square you up later.'

The cashier nodded. 'Thanking you, Mr Walker, sir. Thank you.'

Walker jumped into the driver's seat, started the engine and drove toward the exit. 'Where we going, Sarge?'

'One more petrol station to visit. Do a quick check of their CCTV and then back to the nick. The guv'nor's already gone back. We need an early start on this. I'll fill you in on the way.'

'Cheers,' said Walker. 'Appreciate that. Got to ask again, Sarge. The short back and shine you got there. Charity?' He pointed to Jordan's head. 'Or a bet? Or pissed?' He pulled out of the forecourt and into the main road.

* * *

Adam Walker, coming in at just under six foot, was a solidly built man in his thirties, could handle himself if he had to and hadn't long joined the squad. He was bright, no question of that, and came highly recommended. So far, he'd proved to be a good copper, being methodical, sensible. Jordan thought him a bit flash, too full of himself. Young. Like Paterson, he was going places. That narked Jordan a bit. He wondered why he'd never really gelled with him, and put it down to the fact that it was probably because Walker was twenty odd years younger than him. He was also nice looking, fit as a fiddle, got on with pretty much everyone on the team and was happily married. Plus, he had his own hair. Pretty much everything he wasn't.

'Fuck yourself,' Jordan said, with only a half grin. Although he wasn't Walker's biggest fan, he did like his sense of humour. They could at least have a banter if not meaningful conversation. Looking out of the side window, he broke with his own tradition of keeping things bottled up. He sighed and said, 'My younger brother's got the Big C. He's undergoing treatment but it's not looking too clever. Thought I'd show a bit of brotherly support and take my barnet off too.' Walker pulled up at a red light and ratcheted up the handbrake. Jordan winced at the noise. 'Press the button in,' he said.

'Fuck the button.' Walker turned to face him. 'I'm so sorry, Dave —Sarge. I didn't know. I—'

'It's okay, don't worry about it. I haven't told anyone yet, well, Paterson. I've told him. Y'know how it is.' He shrugged resignedly.

'What's his prognosis?'

'As I said, not good. He's just started intense chemo and radio. It's in his brain, mate. Sounds to me like all they can do is prolong his life a bit. Maybe six months. Who knows?'

'Why are you here? What are you doing at work, for God's sake? You don't need this shit.'

Jordan looked at him, touched by his concern.

'Nothing I can do about it, Adam. It is what it is. And let's face it, none of us are getting out of here alive, are we?' Walker shook his head slowly. Jordan said, 'Do me a favour and take the long way round. It's already been a long day and I'm knackered. I need to grab a quick ten minutes.'

He pressed the side of his forehead against the cold glass of the window and closed his eyes.

CHAPTER TWO

Seated at the large walnut topped desk in his office, Paterson reached down into a drawer and came up holding a half full bottle of Glenfiddich and two whiskey glasses. 'I take it you want a drop?'

'Is the Pope a Catholic?' Now fully dry and wearing a change of clothes, Jordan was just coming to the end of Jock Hudson's preliminary report.

Paterson poured a generous measure and pushed it across the desk.

'Cheers, guv'nor!' Jordan raised the glass.

Pushing aside a pile of papers, Paterson sank back into his leather chair and swung his feet up onto the desk. 'So what else we got? Anything from the CCTVs?' He sipped at his whiskey and grimaced slightly as the liquid burned its way down.

Jordan took a swig, screwed up his face and shivered. 'Christ, that's strong.'

'Make a man of you, Davey boy,' said Paterson.

Jordan was more of a lager drinker himself, but Paterson didn't keep cans of Tennants in his drawer. He wasn't that sort of person.

Jordan drained the glass. 'I visited three petrol stations on the off-chance your idea might have had legs. It didn't. Not a whiff of him. Inspector Goodman sent a couple of his boys into those offices that had night security and they had a quick viewing of their tapes. Nothing on them either, apparently. We'll need someone to collect and view the authorised copies properly later this morning. Whoever did this kept himself just out of sight of all the cameras. He's either the world's luckiest butcher or he knew where they were.'

'Meaning?' said Paterson.

'My money's on him being a local boy. Might even work in one of the offices nearby.' Jordan stared at Paterson and tapped his glass on the desk.

Paterson took the hint and poured out another, smaller amount. Jordan shrugged and leaned back in his chair.

'Why's that?' said Paterson.

'It's the layout of it, guv. Two people walking down an alleyway in the dead of night. The cameras are stuck on the wall in plain view, but judging by the size of them, they wouldn't have been too obvious to a casual passer-by at ground level. In a street that wide, if either of them were pissed up, the chances of them not staggering in front of the cameras would be slim. I'd go with astronomical. But, it's possible.' He took a small sip.

Paterson listened carefully to the seasoned policeman, nodding every so often. It embarrassed him that he would never be the copper that Jordan was. He'd probably be a superintendent-commander soon, one of the youngest ever, but that was by virtue of his education, the accelerated promotion system — the Met loves a degree — connections and money. He was well aware that he was ill-equipped professionally to oversee such an enquiry as this one. He'd need the full cooperation of his junior officers if he was not to fall spectacularly from grace, and it made him feel uncomfortable and vulnerable, which he didn't like at all.

'Then there's the kill itself,' Jordan said. 'She died just outside of the sightline of two cameras. I don't think that was luck. He then wanders off toward Holyrood Street, a good two-minute walk from where she was found, and sets about painting his message before buggering off. Not once, not fuckin' once, did he step in front of a camera. Never even put his big toe into the frame.' Jordan sat forward now, pressing his point home.

'There are no obvious signs of a struggle, and my best guess at the moment is that they knew each other somehow and he guided her to that exact spot. It was quiet, dark. He knew exactly where he was going.'

Paterson rubbed the back of his neck to relieve the tension that was beginning to build. Everything Jordan said made sense to him, but the SIO courses he'd attended told him to be open minded and warned of the dangers of following one particular line of thought.

'Why write the word "Don't" twice?'

Jordan shrugged. 'No idea. Drive the point home, whatever that is?'

'In two minutes,' Paterson said, 'I have to go out there and brief everyone. What the hell do I have to tell them, other than some mad bastard's on the loose and best to lock up your daughters for a while?'

'Probably should be doing that with you around anyway, guv.' Jordan winked, acknowledging that he knew Paterson was a bit of a ladies' man. Paterson ignored him.

'If I was you, guv, I'd start with the basics. Old-fashioned door to door knocking first off. Someone in the flats around Tooley Street may have seen or heard them heading to the arches. I know it was late, but someone might have got up for a piss in the night or a glass of milk and cookies. Worth a try. Then we'll do a spin of the local pubs, clubs and wine bars, see if they're on CCTV anywhere at all.' Making notes as he listened, Paterson was thankful that for all of his bluster and sarcasm, Jordan was willing to help and discreet enough not to embarrass him outright.

'And, guv, don't worry about them. They're a good bunch. Experienced. They all know you're new to the role. Treat this like any other briefing. Give them what we know and then give them things to do. They'll nod and agree and go off and do their own thing anyway. Set a time for a debrief this evening, and it's done.' Jordan pushed his glass across the table and stood up.

'Hang on, Dave. I just want to go through the team sheet quickly.' Jordan plonked himself back down.

'My DCI, Roy Singh Carr. Is that a joke?'

Jordan grinned. 'Nope. That's his name. Roy Carr. His dad had a wicked sense of humour and thought it'd be funny to give him the middle name of Singh. We call him F1.' Paterson smiled and shook his head. 'Good senior officer though,' Jordan added.

'Where is he then?'

'Sends his apologies. He's got three cases on the go. Two domestic murders. Husband v wife, wife v husband and a serious sexual assault on a fifteen-year-old boy. He'll be in touch soon as.'

Fair enough, Paterson thought. Man's busy. 'I see there's a DS Kane here with his name crossed out.' Jordan looked away. 'And a DS Johnny Clocks in his place. What's the score with Kane?'

'Called in sick last minute, guv. Apparently he's got the flu.'

'And DS Clocks? I've heard of him. Hasn't been good. Temper problems. Didn't he assault a superior officer a while back?'

'Yep, he did. An inspector who got a bit too shouty with him in front of his team. Timex, sorry, that's his polite nickname, isn't a particular fan of authority, and if I were you I'd think carefully about referring to yourself or any senior officer as 'superior.' He'll tolerate 'senior' because the rank dictates that, but he doesn't consider anyone to be 'superior' to him. As far as he's concerned, that's an arrogant wanker's point of view. That really will piss him off.' Paterson frowned. 'I've known him for years, guv. Worked together a few times. His biggest problem is his childish sense of humour. If you ever saw the film *Big* where a young boy is trapped in a man's body — that's Johnny Clocks to a T.'

'Not sure we want someone like that, Dave. We haven't got time to play babysitters with anyone.'

Jordan nodded. 'I know, guv, but underneath it all, he's one of the best thief takers I've ever met. Get on his right side and he'll take a bullet for you. He's solid. You want him in, guv.'

Paterson placed the team list back into its folder and closed it. 'What's his other nickname?'

'Thrush.'

'Go on,' Paterson said, 'I'll bite. Why's he called Thrush?'

'Cause he's an irritating cunt,' Jordan deadpanned.

Paterson grinned and shook his head. He drained his glass, stood up and pulled out a small pack of Tic-Tacs he had pocketed before leaving his house. Ten or twelve might be enough to take the edge off their whiskey breath.

* * *

A few of the team were stretched out uncomfortably on plastic chairs, trying their best to grab a bit more sleep while they waited. Dotted around the room, a few more lay their heads on their arms in a scene reminiscent of long ago Friday afternoon maths lessons. DCs Gedmine and Tressom were nursing cardboard cups from Starbucks, buying in to the idea that strong coffee would see them through the day ahead. Adam Walker was engaged in a game of heads up poker with at least fifty pounds sitting on the table.

Paterson stopped outside the door to the briefing room, pulled at the knot in his tie until it felt straight, ran his fingers through his hair and opened the door. A quick glance around the room showed a good number, but not as many as he expected. He figured that Jordan had already sent some out to do a bit of door knocking.

'Morning, everyone.' Paterson's tone, matter of fact, was pitched at just the right level to pierce through the half sleep of most of the people in the room. They shook themselves awake. Walker raked in the money from the final bluff of the night and wheeled around. In the middle of the room, a digital projector connected to a laptop balanced on a hi-tech tripod.

Paterson picked up the remote and turned to his audience. 'For those of you who don't know me, my name is Detective Superintendent Paterson. Welcome to Operation Stammer. I have no idea why it's called that, it's just the way the name came out of the computer. I am the SIO in charge of this case, and let's get a few things out of the way first. Yes, I am young. Yes, I am a flyer. And yes, this is my first posting as an SIO to a murder enquiry team. However, please don't take that to mean I'm a fucking retard.' He flashed them a smile. 'I imagine a few of you probably think I am. I'll be honest and say that I certainly don't know everything, but I do learn quick.' A few of the older detectives nodded in approval and understanding for the new boy. With that out of the way, he said, 'Do the lights for me, Dave.'

A full colour digital image of the dead girl's face flashed on to the five-foot screen from top to bottom. From the condition and cleanliness of the body, the detectives knew they were looking at the post-mortem photographs. Two cherry red stripes were visible across her throat.

'Female. White. aged between twenty and twenty-five. No ID on her, no obvious identifying marks. Found in Shand Street this morning by a probationary WPC. Two deep cuts to the throat. The first cut was most likely the cause of death, having severed the carotid artery. The second cut was most likely made after death. This wound is much deeper and may have been designed to sever the head from the body. If it was, it was a fail.' Paterson paused briefly to let his words sink in then clicked the button again. Several officers turned their heads away, disgusted at the sudden switch from post-mortem to crime scene images.

'She also suffered extensive wounding to the stomach area. The lower part of her abdomen was literally ripped open, and her insides dumped on the pavement.' *Click*. 'Carved into her chest just above the breast is the word "Don't," and if that wasn't bad enough,' he looked at his audience, 'he cut out her vagina.' He clicked again just as the image appeared on screen. That raised a few eyebrows and wrinkled a few noses. 'Why he did this, we have no idea. We will find out. I want full searches made of all of our indexes to see if this kind of thing has happened elsewhere—'

'Guv, I don't mean to be indelicate, but has anyone found her fanny?' Paterson could just about make out a dark haired man seated at the back of the room, hidden in the shadows with his hand up in the air. He looked to be around fortyish, muscular.

'You must be DS Clocks,' Paterson said. Dave Jordan visibly cringed. 'No, it wasn't found at the scene or nearby. We think it's most likely been taken as a trophy.' Clocks grinned to himself, but Paterson was in now. 'Something funny, DC Clocks?'

Johnny Clocks shrugged. 'I was just thinking where you'd keep a cut-out fanny, guv. It's going to smell a bit, isn't it? They generally do.'

'Guv'nor! For Christ's sake!' said Carrie Gedmine. 'Have a word with this fucking idiot, will you?' She glared across the room at Clocks.

Paterson did likewise. 'That will do, Clocks. You can give me your comedy routine after the briefing. In my office. Understood?' Clocks frowned.

Paterson moved on. *Click*. 'We also found the word "Don't" written on a steel shutter at one of the businesses in Holyrood Street. Initial testing confirms it was written in our vic's blood. Why he's written the word twice, or even why he's written it at all, we have no idea at this stage.' Paterson paused, watching several officers scribble in their notebooks, and allowed them to catch up. 'At the moment I need to know just two things. Who she is and who the fuck did this to her.' He moved so that he could just about be seen in the light reflected from the screen. 'Anyone got anything?'

DC Gedmine was seated just to the left of the projector. 'Sir, I think that's Kerry Donovan. Local slapper. Likes a drink and a leg-over on a Friday night and, if memory serves, she's got previous for indecent exposure. Shagging behind the bins, doorways, that sort of thing. Does a bit of tomming too. Lives in Devon Mansions I think. If it is her, she'll be in the system.'

'Ok,' said Paterson, 'might be the first part of my question answered.'

'Carrie, find out if she's pimped,' said Jordan. Paterson grimaced. He hadn't thought to ask the question. 'And keep me posted.'

'According to the initial forensic report, she has bruises around her throat consistent with having her throat grabbed. It would seem she was strangled into unconsciousness,' Paterson said, 'and once she was down our unknown began his work. If anybody has any ideas on this, or has seen anything like it before, I want to know. Now.' Jordan flicked on the lights.

'The time of death has been put at between two and two-thirty this morning,' said Paterson. 'There won't have been too many people around at that time and in that area, but,' he shot a glance at Jordan, 'someone in the surrounding flats might have got up for a piss and seen or heard something. Door knocking and statements, please.' Jordan gave a wry smile. 'Right then,' Paterson said, 'you all know what to do. DS Jordan will split you into your teams in a moment. I want all known sex offenders on this manor looked into initially. Young or old. Shake a few trees and let's see what shit falls out. Get warrants, make it up, do what you have to do but find me something. Understood?'

With grunts and nods, the team dispersed.

* * *

Back in his office, Paterson let out a barely audible sigh of relief before closing the door firmly behind him. Despite the childish behaviour of Johnny Clocks, he was pleased at how the briefing had gone. He made a mental note to talk to Jordan about Clocks, but was going to square him up now — as soon as he'd finished the call he had to make. He pulled his iPhone from a drawer and jabbed at the speed dial.

'Hello?' said a sleepy female voice.

'Hello, babe. It's me,' he said. 'Sorry I never made it over last night. The shit's hit the fan up here and we have to work through. I don't know when I'll be done. I'll give you a call when I'm finished . . . Yeah, I know . . . I'm sorry.' He hung up, poured himself another whiskey and sat down heavily in the leather chair. Hearing the sound of voices bantering in the station yard below his window, he was just in time to see Johnny Clocks looking up at him, and getting into a car.

* * *

Dave Jordan crammed himself behind the wheel of the unmarked Astra and opened the bag holding his McDonalds big breakfast. He pulled out the styrofoam container, chucked the empty bag onto the dashboard and popped the straw into his large sized Coke. Then he shoved the cardboard cup into a holder and set about piling the contents of his breakfast into the two toasted buns. Walker had seen Dave Jordan eat once before in the canteen of Southwark nick. Spaghetti Bolognese was on the menu, and it wasn't a pretty sight.

'Any reason you didn't just get yourself a sausage and egg McMuffin?' Walker asked him, shaking his head.

Jordan glanced sideways and took a big bite out of his makeshift McMuffin. 'Yep. This way I feel like I've made my own breakfast.' Much to Walker's disgust, he spat out little flecks of food and spittle.

'You want to be careful you don't have a heart attack, skipper,' he said.

Jordan took a large suck on his straw and let out a large, satisfying burp. 'Oh, that's just lovely.'

Walker wrinkled his nose. It was going to be a long day. He looked out across the car park, watching the mass of people going about their daily business blissfully unaware, as yet, of the savagery that had been committed in their midst. They'd know soon enough. The local press had picked it up, and given the nature of the crime the nationals wouldn't be far behind.

'What'd you think then, Sarge?' he asked, almost absentmindedly.

'About what?' replied Jordan, brushing at the crumbs on his lap.

'Our killer. How does someone do a thing like that?'

'The fuck am I supposed to know?' Jordan growled. A bit of egg had disappeared under his legs and would most likely leave yet another grease stain on his trousers. Walker bristled slightly at this response but checked himself. He knew Jordan could be, well, blunt.

'Sorry. Just asking. Thought you might have a few ideas to share with the junior. My mistake.' He turned away, and looked out of the side window.

Jordan sighed heavily. 'Sorry,' he said. 'It's just that I'm tired and a bit uptight. Always get this way when I'm running a squad.'

'What do you mean? Paterson's running it, isn't he?'

Jordan thought about this for a second or two, then shook his head. 'On paper he is, but he's not running it. See, he's new to all of this — not the CID itself, just the SIO bit. He joined straight after finishing his probation but he's got more degrees than a thermometer. He's on the fast track upwards, mate, and as you know, fast tracking means that with each new rank, he spends some time back in uniform. Has to learn the ropes of that particular rank, then he transfers back to CID, gets promoted, back to uniform and so on all the way to where he is now. He's been back in a suit about a month now, and this is his first post as an SIO. Being in charge of a murder squad is good for the CV.' He chewed his rapidly diminishing breakfast and glanced at Walker, searching his face. 'Surprised you didn't know.'

Walker shook his head. 'I'm not particularly interested to be honest.' Then, after a second, he said, 'So he's not a detective, then?'

'Not a real one,' said Jordan. 'He's got the rank and the posting but not a whole lot of experience in the trenches. He's a nice enough bloke. I've known him for years and he means well, but with the best will in the world, if he put both hands behind his back he'd struggle to find his arse. He's sharp though, learns bloody quick.' Walker nodded.

Jordan burped, thumped his chest and looked harder at Walker, the only officer he hadn't spent any significant time mentoring since his transfer into the squad five months ago. Today was a stab at putting that right.

'I heard he's got a few bob. That true, Sarge?'

Jordan took another slurp from his straw. 'Yep. He's got a few bob, and then some.'

'How much we talking about then?'

'Don't know for sure, don't think he does, but if you imagine the Euro lottery hasn't been won for a few months, you'll be in the ballpark.'

Walker let out a thin whistle. 'So why the fuck's he doing this job then?'

Jordan shrugged. 'Prove himself in his own right, I guess. His family were land barons back in the day. Land everywhere. Everything got handed down through the generations, but when it got to his dad he had a few tricks up his sleeve. From what I can make out, he flogged off a load of land to developers. That land happened to be along the Thames Embankment, and with the truckload of cash he had he became a property developer himself and turned shitloads of money into even more shitloads of money. Got himself wiped out in a car crash when the guv was in his late teens. He was divorced long before he died, so the missus had already been weighed off. Paterson and his sister copped the whole empire. She's more business minded than him so she took over the companies and he took off doing whatever the fuck he wanted. Cars, women, houses . . . Christ, he could fly a bleedin' helicopter before he was twenty-two. Swimming, boxing, that Kung-fu shit. You name it, he's done it. Fuckin' James Bond, mate, I'm telling yer.' Jordan pushed the empty container back into the paper bag. 'Fucking sure I wouldn't be a copper with that much dough. I'd have shagged meself to death with it.' Walker didn't disagree with any of that.

Jordan tossed his rubbish out of the window and wheel spun the Astra out of the car park, straight through a puddle, drenching a group of commuters.

CHAPTER THREE

He had nearly made it all the way to the top when his foot slipped out from under him and sent him spinning through the air for a split second before he went thudding cheek first onto the hard fibreglass. The second his foot slid, panic kicked in. A shot of pure adrenaline spurted through his system and sent him grabbing frantically at the air, desperate to regain a grip on something, anything, to stop him falling. Only he wouldn't fall.

The rope had him safe. Logically, he knew that, but right now, nine metres above the ground, logic had left him to his own devices. His heart jumped against his chest and his brain fogged over, blinding him to any thought but survival. Bouncing off the wall and unable to grab onto anything, he began spinning. The world turning uneasily in front of his eyes only increased his distress. His body, jerking wildly at the end of the nylon rope, betrayed him by moving him further and further away from the wall and safety.

Through the blood pumping in his ears, he could barely make out the shouts from the rest of his climbing companions who were desperately trying to get through to him, knowing that a full blown panic attack was well on its way.

Seeing him fall, two of them darted out of the group and began climbing the wall to get to him, hoping that he'd faint and dangle before they got to him. Danglers were a lot easier to bring down than someone in hysterics. They moved fast, their hands and feet confidently picking out the grips, both shouting instructions to him as they scaled the wall like demented Mexican black bears searching for their mother. In seconds they were level with him, reaching out, trying to avoid his flailing arms and feet, shouting at him to calm down, until suddenly, without warning, Ray Paterson lost consciousness and dangled.

* * *

Sitting on a small wooden bench some ten minutes later, Paterson held his overly sweetened tea in one hand and rested his head in the other, rubbing his forehead and breathing deeply to ward off a further undignified faint. A twenty-foot fall from a tree house when he was seven had left him with an unhealthy respect for heights. He had no problem with helicopters and aeroplanes, but things like bridges and tall buildings freaked him out.

'I'm sorry.' His voice was weak and carried a hint of a tremor. 'I don't know what happened. I felt myself go, panicked, couldn't stop myself . . . sorry.'

Mark Stone, a small, wiry man with dark shoulder length hair, had seen this all before. One of the world's most accomplished urban climbers, panic attacks and fainting were nothing new to him, but he could never really understand it. Ever since he first discovered what his feet and hands could do he put them to use by climbing out of his cot and down the stairs, much to the surprise of his parents, who were curled up on the sofa. Garden fences did little to contain him, and his mother had lost count of the telephone calls from bemused neighbours, asking if she would come and collect little Mark from their house. His father heightened the fence, but it just became a challenge. A couple of years back, Stone made headlines around the world by climbing the Shanghai Tower, at six hundred and thirty metres, the second tallest building in the world. He had done it without any form of safety equipment or ropes, giving his folks heart palpitations and sleepless nights when they saw the video on YouTube.

'Don't worry about it, Ray,' he said. 'Shit happens, mate. I say good on you for doing it. The fact you keep coming back week after week shows you're getting a bit better at controlling it.'

'I've made a right mug of myself again. I just don't—'

'You need to get your head straight, Ray,' Stone interrupted. 'You have to stop beating yourself up every time you make a mistake or . . . faint. Climbing's a mental game just as much as a physical one.'

'I've been seeing a therapist for about a month or so now and he's given me some techniques to use that seem to be working.' Paterson shrugged. 'But obviously not enough. I've been out on a few rooftops and had a day out at the Shard.' He started to feel a bit queasy at the memory of it and shook his head. 'He tells me that phobias are just mind fucks, and I have to make him right on that one.'

He took a sip of his tea and in his mind, watched a replay of Stone climbing the Shanghai Tower. How could a man bring himself to climb so high without any form of equipment save good rubber shoes and a pouch full of powder? He shuddered. What possesses someone to do that kind of thing in the first place? Why the hell didn't he faint past two or three metres or so, like any normal person? He concluded that Stone must be mentally ill but had been fortunate enough to find a creative outlet for it.

'That's a good thing,' said Stone, breaking Paterson out of his daydream. 'If you keep using the techniques and keep going out to higher and higher places, you'll soon get past this.'

Paterson nodded, stood up and looked round for the bin. 'Thanks, Mark. I appreciate it.' He glanced at his watch. 'Shit! Big challenge number two coming up. Off to see the missus, sorry, ex-missus and her new boyfriend now. Got to sign the divorce papers. I'll probably faint there too,' he said with a grin, and headed for the door.

* * *

Paterson checked the time on the dash. Nine forty in the evening. He was forty minutes late, but didn't feel under any pressure to be on time. Couldn't give a toss, if the truth be known. He pressed the remote on his keyring and sat and waited while two ornate iron gates swung lazily inwards. It always irked him that they were so slow, but Lisa thought there was something rather grand about the way they swept open, and so he left it as was.

The mansion they had bought together when they married seven years ago was a stunning Grade Two listed Georgian building set at the end of a long gravel path. The house, nestled comfortably in five acres of rolling Sussex countryside, once belonged to an Arab sheik who'd bought it on a whim. According to the estate agent, he'd never set foot in it, had eventually lost interest and sold it well under market. Lisa fell in love with the place the second she set eyes on it and the golden couple bought it there and then.

The Patersons seemed to have it all. Supermodel Lisa had the fame and the looks, the business, the TV career, connections and money. Ray had more money than her, than God some people said, the high-flying police career and the good sense to keep out of her way. The mansion, houses in Florida and Switzerland, a yacht and a privately owned Wessex helicopter were only a few of their many toys. Tatler magazine once said they were one step down from William and Kate.

Surface wise, everything was good for a few years but Ray Paterson's one big weakness was women. Lisa knew this, never tried to tame it, and generally turned a blind eye, provided he was discreet. But one night, discretion went out of the window and he slept with her younger sister, Leanna. There are some things you just don't do in life and your wife's sister is one of them. An unwritten rule but an eminently sensible one. Another unwritten rule and again, eminently sensible, is don't tell your big sister you've shagged her old man. Leanna did and it cost her a few tufts of hair and two enamels in a vicious cat fight not seen this side of Taylor Swift and Kim Kardashian.

He lost the one woman he truly loved, plus the house and yacht. Not legally of course, but he thought giving her the house was the least he should do for the woman he had betrayed. After tonight, it would be a done deal anyway. The boyfriend was a divorce lawyer par excellence.

He ran his hand through his tousled hair, checked his inside pocket for the papers he had signed earlier that evening, took a deep breath and rang the bell. After a few minutes, Lisa opened the door, a scowl etched on her face that did nothing to diminish her looks. 'You're late,' she said flatly.

He made a show of checking his watch. 'You're not wrong, Leese. Sorry. Work's a real bitch at the moment, hon.' He made to step inside and she moved backwards slightly.

'Come in, Ray. D'you want a coffee?' She wandered off toward the kitchen.

'Please.' He followed her in.

'Hello, Ray. Good to see you again. Helluva view, isn't it?' Lisa's new partner, Sebastian Harrison, was sitting at the counter with a small plate bearing the remnants of a crustless salmon sandwich.

Paterson saw a box file of papers at his side. 'Someone's getting royally shafted then?' he said, nodding toward the file, not really interested in the answer. Then it crossed his mind that the file might be his.

Senior partner at Harrison Law Associates, Sebastian Harrison was considered to be one of London's finest divorce lawyers. He had a fearsome reputation for uncovering whatever dirt he needed to thoroughly destroy the opposition and for finding whatever assets his clients' spouses had tucked away. He was ruthless in his determination and feared by the wealthy. Everyone that knew him considered him a prick.

Paterson gave him the once over. He was a tall, well-built man, decent looking for his age, with a perma-tan and teeth so bright they gave the sun a run for its money. Paterson had him down for a smug, pompous dick from the moment he first laid eyes on him. As he crossed the kitchen, he saw that Harrison was wearing a heavyweight towelling dressing gown over a blue striped shirt and a pair of trousers that were obviously part of a suit. He shook his head in disbelief. *Who the fuck puts a dressing gown on over their suit?*

'Evening, Seb,' he said, putting on a pleasant voice that was more for Lisa's benefit than his. 'Nice view indeed. Didn't see you skulking away in the corner. What brings you here? Apart from banging my wife, that is.'

Lisa rounded on him. 'Ray! Don't start!' She banged an empty coffee cup down on the granite countertop.

'You know how it is, Ray.' Harrison smirked.

'And don't you start either, Seb. I'm really not in the mood for this silly little pissing contest between you two.' She spooned in a couple of heaps of coffee and flicked the switch on the kettle. 'Did you bring the papers, Ray?' Paterson glowered at Harrison's smug face, ignoring her. 'Ray!' she said more forcefully. 'Did you bring the papers over?'

He tore himself away from Harrison and looked her straight in the eye. 'Sorry, Leese, I forgot. It's been a busy day y'know?' She threw her hands up in the air and clicked the kettle off. No coffee for him. Harrison shook his head, the smirk wiped away. Paterson was wearing it now.

'Jesus, Ray. That's what, the third time now? What is wrong with you?'

'I've had enough of this,' said Harrison. He slammed both hands on the table, scraping his chair on the tiles as he stood up.

Paterson wheeled around and jabbed a finger toward him. 'Shut up and sit yourself down. This is nothing to do with you. Stay out of it.' Harrison's face turned red. He started to come around the table and Paterson squared up, confident he could put him on his arse.

'That's enough!' screamed Lisa. Both men froze. 'Ray. Go. Go home.' She put herself between the two men.

'But, Leese . . .' Paterson looked down at her, realising he'd gone too far. Lying was one thing, but goading the boyfriend was something else.

'I said "go", Ray. I meant it. If you haven't got the papers, then there's no reason to be here. C'mon.' She nudged him toward the door. He went, glancing back at Sebastian Harrison, who was sitting himself back down. Paterson swore he saw a sneer on his face. For a second, he thought about starting again. Then thought better of it.

'Why did you come here tonight if you didn't have the papers, Ray?' Lisa walked him across the marble hallway and opened the front door.

'I'm sorry,' he said, looking down at his feet, embarrassed now at lying. For a second, he thought about giving her the damn papers. Fuck it. 'I thought I had them. I must have left them in the office. It's been busy, Leese. I meant to.'

'Sure you did, Ray. Like the other two times, huh?' She gave a deep sigh. 'You can't keep putting it off, you know. I want to move on with my life. You have to accept that it's over between us.' She put a hand on his back, gently, guiding him out of the door and back out into the rain.

'I can't, Leese. I'm sorry. Sorry for so many things. If you just give . . .'

She shook her head. 'No, Ray. No more chances. It's done. Now go home.' She peered out at the rain, now pouring down. 'Drive safe, won't you?' He looked at her beautiful, elfin face and his heart broke all over again. *Stupid, stupid man.*

'Why him, Leese? Of all the people, why him? He's a pompous, arrogant prick of a man.'

'He's a good man, Ray. He treats me well and I lov—'

'Ah, ah, ah!' Paterson held his palms to her face, trying to block out what was coming. 'Don't. Please don't, Leese.' She nodded.

'I treated you well, didn't I?' he said, trying desperately not to look at her nipples straining against the silk of the robe that the wind battled to rip open.

She folded her arms tightly across her chest. 'Yes, you did treat me well — for the most part. But, along with all the others, you also fucked my kid sister. I can't forgive that. Not ever. Goodnight, Ray.' She pushed the door closed and left him standing in the wind and rain.

He stood looking at the door for a few seconds. Then he turned his collar up, pulled his head down into his shoulders and walked slowly back to the car.

CHAPTER FOUR

He had his next victim. He squinted through the rays of multi-coloured light that stung his eyes. There she was, perfect. Carrying two drinks, he threaded his way through the bobbing sea of entranced bodies, back to the booth where he had left her . . .

Lynn Farrow was twenty-two years old and already a mother of two teenage mistakes, soon corrected once she realised the full commercial potential of her exceptionally well designed body. She was shrewd enough to know that her marketability relied heavily upon her schoolgirl looks, and tonight she played the role to perfection. Her blonde hair was tied in bunches that stuck out from either side of her head like nodding antennas. Her tight, white blouse was open just enough to expose the swell of her breasts, the tiny black micro skirt scarcely wider than a belt. Topped off with white socks and high heels, she was the ultimate fantasy of a certain type of buyer with plenty of cash and a weakness that could one day lead to prison. It was not unusual for her to make upwards of £1000 for a night's work, and she had earlier judged the man weaving his way through the crowd towards her as the sort who would be both willing and able to pay that kind of money.

Her eyes never left him as he slipped easily into the seat next to her. Raising his voice above the thump-thump-thump of the bass, he handed her one of the glasses and shifted toward her. 'Your drink.' She took a small sip of the electric blue liquid, and raised her thumb in approval. She moved closer. The game had begun.

'So tell me a bit about yourself,' she said, tilting her head to one side.

'Not much to tell, really. Usual story I suppose. Single man looking for a good time and,' he pulled back to take in the view, 'I think I may just have found it.'

She brushed a few strands of hair from her eyes and looked directly at him. 'You can count on that.' She threw him a cheeky little wink and demurely took another sip.

The next few hours were spent flirting backwards and forwards with each other. The alcohol plied its trade enough to relax them, but not so much that either forgot what line of business they were in. Settling on an agreed price for the evening, he handed her a wedge of twenty-pound notes as evidence of his integrity. She pulled open her blouse, made sure he caught an eyeful, and tucked the money inside her lacy bra. Expensive, but he was happy to agree to any price she demanded. She was never going to keep it.

He was ready now.

Picking up his overcoat they began to half walk, half sway across the vast dance floor towards the exit. His ears rang, and he was more than glad to be leaving the place.

He led her across the car park, empty save for the odd Porsche and Mercedes dotted here and there, and took her directly to the spot he had chosen for his work. The line of hedges made for a near perfect barrier from any stray eyes. 'Over there,' he said, his voice firm, hard.

'What? Here? I thought we were going back to my place!' He put his hand on the back of her neck and pushed her forward, the pressure sufficient to indicate she should continue walking but not enough to concern her.

'Here is good,' he told her. 'I prefer to work outside.' She could have done without this. It was both raining *and* freezing and she wasn't exactly dressed for the conditions.

'Whatever floats your boat, mister, but nothing changes pricewise. Understood?'

'Of course.'

Lynn Farrow began to raise her minuscule skirt in readiness for him. Easy money. Except he pushed her. Hard. She stumbled, hitting her head against the rough brickwork of a wall. Stunned from the impact, she rounded violently on him. Like most working girls, she had been in situations before with punters who got off on hitting her up. She had either managed to talk her way out of the situation or resorted to violence herself. On one occasion she had nearly blinded a guy with pepper spray, another she had striped across the face with a kitchen knife. There were only so many liberties you could take with Lynn Farrow's body, and she set the rules.

'You dumb fuck!' she shouted at him, and raised her hand to feel the spot where she had hit her head. Blood. Not much, but enough. 'I don't do that rough shit. Understand? Do that again, and you're on your own, pal. Fuck your money.'

He held both hands in the air in a gesture of surrender. 'My apologies.' Slowly, gracefully, he bowed low, mocking her.

'Oh that's it then, mate. We're done. Not taking the piss out of me.'

As she moved to barge past him, he gripped her throat like a vice, instantly pumping a massive shot of adrenaline through her system. Her eyes widened in terror and she instinctively, urgently, clawed at his hands, fighting desperately to breathe. He squeezed harder. Her clawing became frantic and she scrabbled for his face, his eyes, anything to make him let go. He turned his head aside, avoiding her flailing arms and razor-sharp nails, and felt her grow limp. Her legs began to fail her and his arms burned with the effort of holding her suddenly heavy weight. Her arms dropped and he looked at her. Soon she would fade. This was the part he most enjoyed. Even now, after all this time, he never tired of the sight of their faces as they began to leave this world. Faces flushed, turning first red, then purple. Flecks of spittle collecting at the corners of the mouth. Eyes bulging near to bursting. Tears welling up. Sometimes they made it to the cheeks.

They say the eyes are the window to the soul. Then he was watching the blinds being drawn on Lynn Farrow. She'd be seeing a final burst of colour, before the darkness rushed in to take her twitching body.

She was down now.

No screams. No threats of violence from some misguided hero-man. He'd picked just the right spot for tonight's work. Standing over her, he placed two fingers on the side of her neck and checked for a pulse. He found one — feeble, but it was there. A smile played across his lips. He stepped away from her, over the low wall, and reached into the bushes. After a few seconds of grabbing at air, his fingers found the handles of his sports bag. He unzipped it and pulled out a small nylon tool wrap. He laid this on the ground and carefully unrolled it.

The blade he chose was antique — nine inches in length, surgically sharp on both sides and curved upwards at the tip. The handle was exquisitely crafted mother of pearl, inlaid in a delicate silver filigree. It was perfectly weighted and balanced easily on the tip of a finger. A thing of beauty.

Gently, he took her chin between his thumb and forefinger and turned her head to one side. She murmured almost imperceptibly, but he heard it. Good. He rested the blade on her throat with one hand and shook her lightly to rouse her. This was the part that excited him, gave him purpose. He could almost feel her pulse along the blade. He pressed down slightly. A small thin line of blood rose in welcome. 'Hey, c'mon sleepy, wake up.' His voice was soft and comforting.

Out of the dark recess where her consciousness lay sleeping, Lynn Farrow began to respond. She struggled to open her eyes. He felt her move. Her foot twitched. He waited, hardly able to bear the tension.

'Baby, it's time to wake up, c'mon now.' Her eyelids began to flicker. She muttered something unintelligible. He smiled. Nearly . . .

'Wake up, sweetie,' he whispered. 'C'mon.' Suddenly her eyes flew open, and she instinctively jerked her body in a futile attempt at escape. His moment.

She watched, uncomprehending, the dark jet of fluid that inscribed an arc through the cold night air and splashed onto the ground a few feet away. A second later, another jet spurted forth. Everything began to blur, and the edges of her vision began to darken. Another jet, not so strong this time. Her legs and arms twitched violently as her life bailed out of her body, and gradually slowed.

He stood over her, his breath coming in quick, deep bursts, his body shuddering violently. When Lynn Farrow had finished her business of dying, he bent over her and drew the knife across her throat for a second time, pressing down harder, slicing through her dead skin, almost severing her neck. He stopped to breathe in the cold night air. Its sharpness burned his nostrils. There was more to do.

He ran the knife slowly along the front of her blouse and the fabric fell away easily. He stared at her chest. Impressive. He lifted the front of her bra, cut the thin piece of fabric holding her breasts together and watched them spill out. He retrieved his money from the right cup and tucked it back inside his coat pocket.

'Thank you.' He examined her chest for a moment or two, thinking. He stuck the blade into her right breast. Holding it in his left hand, he began to carve.

When he was finished, he stood up, looked down at his handiwork and cocked his head. 'Isn't.' It was readable. He looked down. Her skirt was raised in readiness.

* * *

Paterson decided to skip going home and made his way back to the office. He was surprised to see Adam Walker still at his desk, typing away at his computer, his face flickering in the blue-grey light from the screen. And there, in the gloom, tucked away in the corner, feet up on his desk, fingers knitted together on his lap and snoring gently, was Dave Jordan. 'Why're you still here, Adam? It's late.' He glanced up at the office clock. A quarter to midnight.

'Just topping and tailing a few things, sir. Nothing major I'm afraid. Just wanted to get it done while it's quiet.'

Paterson yawned hugely. 'Go home. If it's not important, do it tomorrow. I need you rested.' He nodded toward Jordan. 'How long's he been like that?'

Walker looked over at the slumbering giant. 'Only about ten minutes or so, sir. He was wandering about when I came in about an hour ago.' He turned back to his computer and logged off, stuffed a few papers into his bag and headed off.

Paterson crept past Jordan as quietly as he could and stepped into his office. Inside, he flicked on his desk lamp and shut the door softly behind him. He looked around for his Key Decision Log. This is an essential document for every SIO, containing a record of all decisions made and lines of enquiry followed. Paterson was a stickler for ensuring that this was up to date and the relevant sections correctly filled in. He'd once watched an aggressive defence barrister in the dock of the Old Bailey crucify an SIO by hacking and clawing away at a few incomplete entries that cast doubt on their veracity. They were simple mistakes made with no dishonest intent, but the defence was sharp enough to leverage it and gain an acquittal for their client. In the game of law, the devil really was in the detail, and Paterson's KDL was detailed. It was usually left lying on his desk, but someone had decided it would be safer in his bottom drawer. Fortunately, whoever put it there had had the good sense to file it next to the bottle of Glenfiddich, along with a crystal tumbler.

Pouring himself a good slug, Paterson opened the book and began to flip through the pages. It didn't make for good reading. Since Kerry Donovan's murder a week ago, there had been few developments. As he'd suspected, door knocking had produced nothing and the local CCTVs had drawn a blank. The murder had made it onto the national news with the BBC running it as their lead. The phones in the incident room were busy on the day the story broke. This had tailed off over the last few days but of the one hundred and thirty calls received, not one gave any information that could be usefully actioned. They did, however, tie up a lot of his manpower in following up dead-end information from well-meaning members of the public.

He spotted an entry for Daft Jack Lemmon. Yep, there he was as usual. Mr Lemmon had confessed to every murder in the country since 1974, but he had to be spoken to just in case this was the one time he wasn't crying wolf. He was lying of course, but he was very excited to be spoken to by a real live detective again, and one as pretty as Carrie Gedmine would keep his greasy little fantasies alive for a good while. What bothered Paterson most was the lack of forensic evidence. Locard's Exchange Principle, drummed into every detective at training school, states that every contact leaves a trace. Not, it seemed, in the murder of Kerry Donovan. Jock Hudson was adamant that she died where she was found, so where were her clothes? In his experience, young girls tended not to walk naked down side streets at two in the morning. They had to be somewhere.

Tired now, he kicked his shoes off, swung his legs up onto his desk and settled down into his deep leather chair. He picked up the copy of Hudson's report, took a big gulp of whiskey and read through it again. Hudson concluded that the only thing of any forensic note were small traces of a type of talcum powder commonly found in surgical rubber gloves. Paterson reckoned that the killer would have worn gloves, but it troubled him that there was nothing else — no hairs, no fibres, no skin flecks, no saliva, nothing. It didn't make sense. None of it did. He drained his scotch, tossed the report onto his desk and closed his eyes. His last thought before he nodded off was that Kerry's killer must have been the world's first forensically aware ghost.

The sudden trill of his mobile rudely jerked him from his slumber and he sat bolt upright, nearly dropping the tumbler that rested empty in his lap. It was pitch dark, and for a second or two he couldn't make out where he was. Fumbling inside his suit pocket, he pulled out the offending object and stared at the screen. Unknown number. He was half inclined to hit the 'off' button. He threw a quick glance at his watch. Three twenty. He'd managed to get about three hours' sleep. He punched the answer button and barked, 'Paterson.'

A well-spoken voice greeted him. 'Sir. Good morning. It's Inspector Newman, the duty officer.' Paterson rubbed the overnight stubble on his chin and struggled to focus on the large shape lying on his sofa.

'Yeah? What can I do for you?' Paterson caught sight of himself, ghosted in the large plate glass window at the far end of his office, overlooking the station yard. He was not pleased. He looked like a wreck. He looked like . . . a cop. Sleeping at his desk was never going to do his Armani suit any favours. He was slightly irritated at how easily it had creased, considering what it had cost. The top button of his shirt was undone and his tie was loose, allowing a small cluster of chest hair to escape. One side of his shirt was untucked and he was having trouble remembering where his shoes had gone.

'You could start by getting some of your chaps down to the car park of the Hedonism,' Newman said.

Paterson started to come to. Squinting into the gloom, he finally recognised the shape on the sofa as Dave Jordan, comfortably curled up in the foetal position with a blanket over him. Cheeky bastard.

'What's the problem?'

'We have a murder here, sir. Another young girl. The only way I can describe it is, well, slaughtered.' Paterson was up on his feet now, fighting off the ensuing head rush but completely focussed on Newman's voice. 'Sir, I can't explain this over the phone. What's your ETA?'

Paterson shot a glance at his watch again, then at Jordan. 'Give me twenty. Make sure the area's secure and wait for us. We're on our way.' He ended the call and snapped the light on, then picked up his grab bag. Jordan growled.

'Dave! Get up. C'mon, move yourself!' Jordan stirred, while Paterson slipped on his shoes and smoothed himself down as best he could. He darted into his en suite and threw handfuls of cold water over his face, catching sight of himself in the shaving mirror. Not good, but it would have to do.

'Dave! Up. Now.'

Squinting an eye against the bright light, Jordan started to move himself. 'Oh fuck. What's the matter now, boss?' The words came out slurred and mostly incoherent, but Paterson understood him.

'We've got another dead girl. Messy.'

Paterson watched his words register. Jordan sat up, graceful as a paraplegic rhino. 'Where?'

Paterson had to think for a second. 'The night club. Hedonism. The night duty inspector just called me. Him and his band of plods are on scene waiting for us. We need to get down there before they stamp all over the forensics.

Call everyone in. Get them into the office. Sharpish.' He yawned as he headed out of the door, patting himself for his car keys. Jordan, struggling to stand, fell backward onto the sofa, arms flailing frantically.

* * *

The car excited Jordan right through to his bones. Ever since he could remember he'd had a thing for cars, instilled no doubt by his dad's passion for buying old wrecks, restoring them and selling them on for a few quid profit. Ford Cortinas were always a nice little earner, they could be picked up dirt cheap and turned around quickly. Whenever his dad tinkered around under the bonnet of the car he had that week, little Davey boy was there at his side, handing out spanners and screwdrivers like a six-year-old surgeon's assistant. An Aston Martin V8 was fairly well placed outside of his pay-scale, and unless he won the lottery, Jordan would have to make do with ownership by proxy. He loved everything about it. The sleek lines, the smell of the leather interior, the way the seats hugged his body, the warm glow from the dashboard lights . . . every god-damned thing was just so beautiful.

Looking out of the tinted windows, he suppressed a smug little grin as the early morning traffic respectfully moved aside for them to glide their way through. If this car was a woman, he'd definitely have a crack at her. Sheer class, no doubt about it.

* * *

Inspector Newman, a straight laced, no-nonsense old-school copper had been playing by the rules for years. He had attended enough serious crime scenes to ensure the crime scene itself and the surrounding area remained as sterile as possible. Experience had taught him that the bananas — police slang for CID: bent and yellow — would look for every excuse to blame the uniforms for any fuck ups, and Newman wasn't about to give them the satisfaction. In addition to using every man he had available, he had requisitioned officers from nearby 'P' division to assist. Several of their officers now stood behind yellow tape, guarding the entrance to their assigned street while his own men spoke to several early morning office cleaners and a newspaper delivery van crew dropping off the daily papers to a nearby W H Smith.

DC Walker parked up and checked for his notebook and pen before stepping out into the rain. Through the gloom and the rain, the number of uniforms clustered about showed where the centre of attention was. Some sort of object lay over by the wall at the back of the car park. Pulling his collar up around him, Walker sprinted over to the group, scanning the street for the duty officer. The group turned to face him as he approached, and he reached into his back pocket for his warrant card to show them.

'Morning, boys,' he said, somewhat too cheerily for the night duty officers. 'DC Walker. Anybody know where the duty offi—'

Inspector Newman stopped him in his tracks. 'Hold on, you. Where's Superintendent Paterson?' His tone said loud and clear that he wasn't about to let a junior suit go trampling all over the scene he had so carefully preserved. Walker looked unhappily at the hand on his chest, and glared back at him. His face impassive, he said flatly, 'Get that off me.'

Inspector Newman bristled at being given an order by a junior rank, but realised he had overstepped the mark by manhandling him. He dropped the hand. 'Where's Paterson? You're not crossing into my crime scene until your boss arrives.'

Walker nodded, then turned his head to one side. 'Hear that?' he said and turned to face the car park entrance. Paterson gunned the Aston and shot through the entrance. Newman raised an eyebrow. Walker turned back to face him. 'That'll be him now.'

Paterson slid out of the car, flicked the umbrella up and headed toward Walker. Jordan, not so gracefully, half stumbled out of the door, ruining the image he had in his head of a really cool Starsky and Hutch type entrance. A couple of uniforms sniggered. Slightly red in the face, Jordan shouted at them, 'The fuck are you laughing at, you pair of pricks?' He held a copy of the *Daily Mirror* over his head. Knowing his temper, the uniforms turned away before he could get going. He caught up with Paterson as he shook hands with Inspector Newman.

'Morning, sir.' Newman eyed up the rumpled senior officer. Walker stood close by, watching Newman. His lip curled.

'What do we have, Inspector?' said Paterson.

'A white female. Young. Twenty something, I'd guess. Throat's been cut a couple of times. There's blood everywhere. I'm no expert, but I'd say that her carotid was severed.' He shuddered at what was coming next. Paterson started to speak, but Newman raised his hand. 'There's more, sir. It would appear that the bastard has also removed her vagina, and carved into her skin on her right breast is a single word: 'Isn't.'' Paterson and Jordan exchanged a look. Fuck. Serial-killer.

'We have the scene secure and the CSIs are on their way, as is the pathologist. Since our arrival, nobody has gone anywhere near the body so it's as sterile as I can get it.'

Paterson nodded. 'Thanks. Good job.'

The thought of having to go and look at her body filled him with dread, but he knew he must, and if he was going, so were Jordan and Walker. He gestured for them to follow him, and after giving their details to the PC, they slipped under the ribbon and began the long walk to meet Lynn Farrow.

Paterson stood over her, hit with a wave of revulsion and sorrow. Jordan shook his head, and turned away. Walker stood quietly, looked at her carefully, then bowed his head, as if in respect. Paterson wiped his mouth with the back of his hand. 'Has to be the same sick bastard that did Donovan.'

'I don't get this at all,' Jordan said. 'Killing them is one thing, but what's the deal with cutting out their girl parts and writing words on their bodies?'

Paterson looked around him. No CCTV anywhere. 'I don't know, Dave,' he said, 'but there has to be a damn good reason for it.' Walker crouched down and leaned over the dead girl, peering intently at the carved word. Paterson and Jordan were grateful that he blocked their view, if only for a moment.

'There's a significance to it all, a message.' Walker stood up and turned to face them.

'What fucking message?' said Jordan, and swallowed.

'The removal of the vagina is highly symbolic. Many cultures, particularly ancient ones, consider the vagina to be a gateway between heaven and earth, a giver of life. To remove it, and in such a brutal fashion, tells me that our killer struggles with women and has likely had a very unhealthy relationship with his mother as an adole—'

'Hang on a minute.' Jordan held up his hand. 'What's all this symbolism shit you're coming out with? Where's this come from? When the fuck did you become our resident behavioural analyst?'

Walker gave him a little half-smile, looked over at Paterson, who was watching him intently, and said, 'I'm not, Sarge. Just giving my opinion based on study. I have a degree in forensic psychology and I've made a point of educating myself. I find that working up thumbnail sketches of the offender at the scene helps me to be a better policeman.' Jordan caught the sarcasm in his voice. It helped *him* decide that on reflection, Walker really was a cocky little bastard, jokes or no jokes.

'Yeah, whatever. You kept this quiet though, didn't you?'

'It's all in my file. I mentioned it at my interview board.'

Jordan shrugged, looking awkward. He really had neglected this one. 'Come on then, Sherlock,' he said, 'let's see what else you've got.' Walker fixed him with a cutting stare, and the half-smile crept back across his lips, long enough for Jordan to see it and become annoyed by it. He turned back toward Lynn Farrow.

'We now have two words. "Isn't" and "Don't". In and of themselves they make no sense. I think he's writing a message of some kind, a sentence. It's my guess he's going to carry on killing and carving words into people until he's said what he has to say. Then,' he waved his arm around the scene, 'it'll all become clear.' Jordan and Paterson looked at each other. Some logic in it.

After a few seconds, Jordan said, 'The problem we have as I see it then is, how many words are in this fucking sentence?' The sound of vehicles driving into the car park broke up the conversation. Paterson recognised the small white van as belonging to the path lab, and the little red transit was the CSIs.' Two Ford Transits emptied themselves of more uniformed policemen, who immediately made their way over to Inspector Newman for deployment. Walking quickly past the uniforms, and already kitted out in his paper suit, Jock Hudson, bag in hand and sarcasm at the ready, headed toward Paterson and the others. Behind him, an assistant began offloading the van. Tent, portable chemical lab, various sizes of plastic bag, cameras and numerous other items used in the examination of death. It would take very little time to get the show on the road.

Hudson nodded curtly at Paterson. 'Sir.'

Paterson scratched his head. 'Mr Hudson. It seems we got off on the wrong foot before. I apologise. Spare me the ropey jokes, and I reckon we'll get on just fine, ok?'

Hudson thought about that for a moment. 'Aye, sir. Fair enough.'

'My officer here thinks this is the same man at work. Any chance you agree with him on the strength of a quick look?' Paterson said.

Hudson walked over to the body, seemingly unmoved by what he saw. Twenty-five years as a forensic pathologist hardens a man to anything. In his time, he had witnessed first-hand that Death, when he came calling, arrived in many guises, and was rarely dressed in his best Sunday clothes. Babies, oldies, shootings, stabbings, bomb victims, there wasn't much he hadn't seen, but even he would have admitted over a drink that Lynn Farrow's death was as bad as any of them. Not quite Kerry Donovan bad, but bad enough.

'Can't say for certain without a full exam, but I'd say your man was right.' He moved in for a closer look. 'Her fanny's gone too,' he said flatly.

'Delicately put, Doctor, but, yep,' said Paterson, 'it sure has.'

Hudson peered inside the dead girl. 'Jesus,' he said, and let out a low whistle. 'Same rough work as before too.'

'So we can rule out a doctor or a surgeon?' Paterson asked.

'Difficult to say. As before, it could be someone with medical knowledge or it could also be that the man who did this has done it before a good few times.' Hudson paused for a moment, staring off into space. 'Bearing in mind that all the time he was working he ran the risk of exposure and possible capture, I'd have to say he possessed some degree of skill and had to complete his work quickly.' Paterson looked across at Walker, hoping he could supply some sort of an insight.

Walker looked thoughtful. 'I'd have said "trophy". I'd guess that was his main prize. I can only speculate that he removed her vagina to humiliate, degrade her in some way. He's taken it away with him for some purpose.' Nobody wanted to ask what that purpose might be.

Paterson thanked Hudson for his help and, after requesting a full report, headed back to his car, telling Jordan and Walker to meet him at the office. Jordan's face dropped in disappointment.

Paterson started the engine and pulled away, feeling that the weight of the world was about to drop right down on his shoulders. Having one murder was testing enough, but two was a definite problem. In the seven days since Kerry Donovan was murdered he was no nearer to capturing her killer. With no useful forensic evidence left at the first scene and no witnesses, he had precisely — nothing. He guessed it would be exactly the same with this one. With a second murder, the big brass would be all over him like a rash. The similarity between the two kills was too much of a coincidence not to have been committed by the same person, and Paterson knew he was now in serial-killer territory. How he handled this case from here on would most likely make or break his career. The thought made him distinctly uneasy.

CHAPTER FIVE

The room was small and cramped, and a faint smell of drains seeped in through the single vent. Save for the faint flickering glow of the fifty-inch plasma TV suspended from one of the sound proofed walls, and the laptop on the desk, the basement was pitch dark. A single bulb hung by a frayed cord from the ceiling in the centre of the room, but it wouldn't be needed for this gig.

The stadium in his mind was ablaze with spotlights arching high over the crowd. I-pod jammed tightly into the Bose docking station and racked up to full blast, the butcher of two young girls was lost in the music, pulling hard at imaginary strings and a non-existent whammy bar, playing along with Jimi Hendrix, as the legendary guitarist launched into his four-minute solo. The double layered acoustic panels, expensive to buy and difficult to fit, had been a godsend. Now the noise was hidden from the neighbours and he could act out his fantasies, musical and otherwise.

The grainy black and white television screen flickered, but never once changed its point of view. A single hidden, unblinking eye, impassively recording the frenetic lovemaking of its two unwitting stars. His face, flickering in the blue-grey light of the TV screen, contorted. He stretched the invisible strings and rocked backwards and forwards in time to the thumping blues beat. His naked body shimmered in the faint light as he fingered an invisible fret board and played his heart out for the fifty thousand imaginary adoring fans that filled the stadium in his head. They loved him. Everybody loved him. *Why not you, mama? Why did you do those dirty things to me?*

With perfect timing he fell backwards onto the grimy, unmade bed at the exact moment the track reached its climax. It was over. *Thank you and goodnight.*

The silence seemed to crowd the darkness.

Exhausted and breathing heavily, he looked toward the screen. Very shortly his favourite part would show. His body was hot and damp from playing the imaginary guitar. He liked it this way.

The couple on the bed grew more and more frenzied, ever closer to their finish, and his anticipation grew. Soon he would see his own face there. The long legs splayed beneath his hips suddenly rose and gripped his lower back. Her fingers dug into his shoulders and his whole body stiffened. Here it comes. The best bit.

I know you.

On screen, the man rolled away and took his weight on his elbow.

I see you.

* * *

Ray Paterson was sitting behind his desk, flipping idly through brochures advertising the Land's End Hotel in Cornwall. He was pleased to see that, from the photographs at least, the place still looked the same. The peninsula itself is composed of a granite rock, a bleak, dramatic feature of the landscape and the shattered cliffs along its windward face. Looking out to the west beyond the rocky islands is the unmanned Longships Lighthouse. Past the lighthouse and visible on a clear day, lie the Scilly

Isles and beyond that nothing, until the vast expanse of ocean laps the shores of America.

Much of his childhood memories were steeped in the summers spent there with his parents, and whenever he found himself under stress, he would picture himself sitting on his favourite rock. There, away from the tourists, he would sit with his eyes closed against the biting wind, and listen to the crashing of the waves below him and the cries of the seagulls as they soared above.

The rocks were his place of solitude. He went there, always alone, to touch the face of his memories and escape when the world became too much to bear. He liked to sit there during the storms that frequently battered the coastline. The beat of the rain on his face and the roar of the wind combined to transport him back to a safer time. No need, in that place, for the company of others or the troubles of the world. His father would chide him, warning of lightning strikes. Even as a child, Paterson knew the risk was minuscule, and if it did happen, what a way to go! He sighed and glanced at his watch. Time to make a move. Rubbing his temples, he picked up a sheaf of papers, popped a few orange Tic-Tacs and walked off to the crowded briefing room.

He scanned the room for familiar faces, uneasy because Jordan was not at his side to guide him. Then he caught sight of him at the back of the room with Walker and Clocks, and straightened slightly.

'Ok, folks, settle down, please.' Paterson was in no mood to dance around with anybody at the moment. The earlier call from Assistant Commissioner Young had done nothing to assuage his concerns. Events were indeed being monitored closely, and an arrest was expected sooner, much sooner, than later. The press had now got hold of both murders and were having themselves a field day. They were baying for the full grisly story. It was down to Joanna Meacher, the team's media liaison officer, to hold them off, and she was doing a pretty decent job so far. He really didn't want to have to talk to them.

Paterson rubbed his neck. He was tired and stressed, and it showed on his face. 'Our second victim is a Lynn, er, Farrow, twenty-four years old — just. Two kids. She was killed in a similar, although slightly less savage manner than Kerry Donovan. From the state of her body, I'm confident that it was the same man on both occasions and unless I get any evidence to the contrary, that's our current line of thought. I'm hoping that someone here has made some inroads into this.' He looked out hopefully at the faces of detectives that had nothing to give him but disappointment. The knot of tension in his gut began to rise. From the back, Johnny Clocks raised his hand. Since their initial meeting, Paterson had done his homework and dug around into Clocks's record. Jordan's description of him as a quality detective was correct, but he was concerned that Clocks relied on instinct first and facts second, and that his behaviour had let him down in the past. There were a few entries that cast doubt on his honesty, but there was nothing serious or substantiated. The trouble was his mouth. He ran it too often and had upset too many people to ever rise beyond the rank of detective sergeant. An earlier bout of insubordination had arisen when Clocks claimed he'd forgotten a meeting. He'd let it slide, but it was unfinished business that would need to be dealt with.

Paterson nodded at him. 'Timex?' he said pleasantly, hoping that the nickname would be seen as a friendly gesture.

'I've done all the indexes, guv. Not a fucking carrot.' It was his tone that aggravated Paterson. He took a deep breath. Here we go, he thought.

'Thanks for that, Johnny.' He turned away, back to the board. 'If you ever manage to get anything useful, do let me know. Anybody else, please?'

‘I thought that was useful, guv. We now know that the indexes ain’t got a fucking carrot in ’em.’ He gave a huge Cheshire cat grin and beamed it around the room, which duly erupted in laughter. Jordan’s head retreated into his shoulders.

Paterson stepped forward a pace or two, putting the death stare on Johnny Clocks. ‘Knock the funny stuff off for a start, ok? I’m not in the mood. Tell me something worthwhile, Clocks, or shut the fuck up.’ His anger was visible in the muscles of his jaw. His face flushed. ‘Tell me why he cuts their throats. Tell me why he disembowelled Kerry Donovan but not Lynn Farrow. Tell me why he cuts out their vaginas. Tell me why he’s carving words into them. Tell me why he repeated the word on a wall for Donovan but not Farrow. If you can’t tell me any of that, then get the fuck off this squad, ’cause you’re no good to me. You’re supposed to be a detective not a fucking stand up.’ The laughter turned to stunned silence. This wasn’t going well.

Clocks’s face turned to stone. The knuckles of his balled fists were white. ‘All right, guv,’ he said, dark eyes flashing. ‘Fuck’s sake, calm down, will you? I was just trying to lighten the mood a bit.’

‘Well, you failed, Clocks, and don’t bloody tell me to calm down. We’ve got two down and no one has any idea, no idea at all, who did them. I’ll calm down when this mad bastard is banged up and eating his own shit for breakfast. Fair enough?’

Clocks stared at him for a second or two. Finally, he nodded. ‘Sorry, guv.’

‘Apology accepted.’ Paterson turned back to the screen, ‘Let’s move on. Anybody? Anything? Anything at all?’ Apart from a couple of follow ups to last night’s Crime Watch appeal, and a possible sighting on a very grainy CCTV, there was nothing.

‘Alright everybody. Back to work. Back on the streets. Find me something.’ There were a few sighs. ‘And don’t moan,' said Paterson. 'You're earning a bloody fortune in overtime, so I want to see happy little policemen. The commissioner can afford it.'

Clocks visibly struggled with himself but failed. 'Not if he keeps paying out to all these bloody Muslim coppers that sue him every five minutes.' Paterson couldn't help smiling.

* * *

As the detectives filed out of the room, Jordan and Walker remained behind and sat themselves down. 'What are we missing, boys?' Paterson asked, looking at one then the other. Both men shrugged and shook their heads. Jordan rubbed his eyes.

'You alright, Dave?' said Paterson. 'You look knackered. You coming down with something?'

Jordan sat up straight and shook his head. 'Nope. I'm fine.'

'You sure? You look exhausted.' Paterson searched his friend's face. Of late, Jordan always seemed to be tired and he wondered if carrying all that weight around was finally taking a toll. Diabetes wouldn't surprise him.

'Dark circles under your eyes, mate. You sleeping properly?'

'I said I'm fine, guv. Had a ropey night is all.' He turned to Walker. 'What you looking at?'

'Sorry, Sarge. He's right though. You do look a bit rough. No offence.'

Jordan shifted uncomfortably in his seat. 'Well, son, offence taken. Now can we forget about me and crack on with work?' He looked at them in turn, clearly not happy at being questioned.

Paterson nodded. 'All of our checks have thrown a blank so far, and that I don't understand. Someone like this rarely appears fully formed. They work up to this level of depravation and yet we have nothing.'

'Look, guv, don't get your hopes up but I *migh*t have something,' said Jordan. 'I wanted to run it past you first rather than broadcast it out there.' Paterson stared at him.

'I've been liaising with the NIDs and they may have something.' Paterson quickly scanned his memory for the acronym, and came up with the National Injuries Database. A large part of their work consisted of supporting serious crime investigations and liaising nationally with police and forensic practitioners in the analysis of weapons and wounds.

'It's a long shot, but there have been reports of two similar killings. Both in the US of course. Land of the nutter. But these were about ten years ago. Mutilations were similar but there's no report of words being carved into the victims' bodies. So, we have a few scenarios. One, it's our bloke and for some reason he's surfaced this side of the pond. Two, it's our bloke and he's changed his style a bit. Why, we don't know. Three, it's some sort of copycat. Not unusual. Or four, none of the above and he's just a flat out lunatic who thinks he's being original.' Jordan frowned.

'Seems to me like he's being original,' Walker said.

Jordan rounded on him. 'Trust me, son, he's not. You don't really think he's the only person ever to disembowel a victim? Or cut out their bits? No, matey. History is full of cowardly, vicious, sadistic bastards who can only beat up on women.'

Jordan turned back to Paterson. 'Coward's way. He cuts off the air supply by force. Both were throttled. Speed and surprise, minimum contact. On the ground he cuts their throats, writes his word, takes his bits and bobs and leaves. We know he didn't shag 'em or have a wank over either of them. Not a drop of sperm anywhere, so sex wasn't the motive. Probably can't get a boner anyway.' Paterson frowned now.

'Hold on, skipper,' Walker interrupted. 'He may not have done the obvious but how do you explain the removal of the vaginas? If that's not sexual, I don't know what is.'

Paterson reached over for his Tic-Tacs, popped the lid and dropped a few into his hand before offering them around. Jordan scooped them all. 'Fair point, Adam,' he said. 'Listen, we're going to have to call in a BIA.' Jordan groaned. Prettying them up by calling them Behavioural Intelligence Analysts didn't take away from the fact that they were basically profilers, and he wasn't a fan of those. He'd worked with a few before and as far as he was concerned they were, at best, good at guessing. The TV show *Criminal Minds* had seriously given the public the wrong impression of what these people could do.

'No point shaking your head, Dave. Order comes from Commander Kelly. We have to be seen to be using all of our resources on this. They're a resource.' He turned back to Walker. 'So, before we do that, you're a resource, Adam. What can you tell us from all your psychological training then? You have two now. Does anything jump out at you?'

'A few things,' Walker said. 'I would need to look more deeply into Doctor Hudson's report on the state of the bodies and any evidence I'm not aware of before I can build a useful working profile. Everything you have will tell me something about this man. I can give you the standard basic profile for now, if you want?' Both officers nodded. Jordan was more amused than interested.

'What I'm about to tell you is not written in stone. It's based on a huge amount of data gathered and analysed over many years. It's a reliable but not a precise science. I think it's reasonable to presume this man is a serial-killer, even though we only have two. I'm basing that on the similarities of the assaults. A serial-killer is normally categorised as a person who murders three or more people with a "cooling off" period between each murder.' He shifted in his seat, warming to his subject. 'Harold

Shipman was a prime example, so are the Wests. There's often a sexual element to the murders, but not always.'

'So he's a psycho then?' said Jordan.

'No, guv. Most serial killers are not psychotic in the sense that you're thinking of them. Your spree killer, the guy who goes apeshit in McDonalds with a twelve bore, is likely to have had a psychotic breakdown either temporarily or permanently, and for a brief period of time, sanity as we know it, deserts them. The way this bloke killed the two girls is indicative of a longstanding character disorder.'

Jordan leaned back in his chair, put his hands behind his head and closed his eyes. He was sure he could squeeze in a quick five minutes kip while his junior officer prattled on. Before he got too comfortable, he said, 'Fucking right, a character disorder. How much of a disorder has this prick got, for Christ's sake?'

'I'm getting to the good bit now. This one is more of a sociopath. They have a complete lack of empathy and feel absolutely no guilt for their actions. They are highly egocentric and impulsive. If they want it, they take it, and they don't conform to any social, moral and legal norms. These are cunning bastards. They live right here with us and appear to be quite normal. They have families, hold down jobs and drive Fords. You'd never know until you crossed one. Sociopaths tend to go one of two ways, low-life or high-life. Criminal or CEO.' Walker stopped to let his words sink in. This was the part that most people had difficulty understanding. Paterson looked over at Jordan, irked at his apparent lack of interest.

'The trait is found in some big businessmen. A number of millionaires all exhibit similar mental characteristics to the criminal and aren't so far apart on the scale. The only difference is in how they channel their energies. The same lack of empathy or guilt is often present. They tend not to give a fuck about anyone or anything. Top level politicians, for example. I mean, you've got be off your head to sanction wars and stuff. To be able to nod your head and send hundreds, possibly thousands, off to die and still sleep soundly at night isn't normal, is it?'

'Make you right there,' said Jordan, suddenly sitting up and leaving his seat for the coffee machine in the corner. 'So we know he's a heartless bastard. Anything else?'

'You're almost certainly looking for a white man, late twenties early thirties, highly intelligent. Most likely he'll have been nicked for some form of sexual offence, moving up the scale each time. Might have been done for rape.'

Jordan sat back down with his coffee, which spilled, and scratched his head.

'See, guv.' He nodded at Walker. 'That's why I've got no time for profilers. Same old shit trotted out every time. I blame *Criminal Minds*, I really do.'

Paterson pressed the heels of his palms into his eyes.

'So,' Jordan turned to Walker, 'apart from the "highly intelligent" bit, you've just described half the scumbags of Bermondsey.'

Paterson gave Walker a wry smile. 'I was hoping for a bit more really, Adam. I appreciate the effort though.'

Looking offended, Walker pressed on. 'That's just the basic thumbnail. As I said, I need to know much more about the two cases to get inside his head. It'll help me categorise him properly — organised, disorganised or mixed.'

Jordan, mopping up his coffee spill, shook his head. 'You know what we know, son. Nothing's being hidden here.' It wasn't strictly the truth, but protocol doesn't let junior officers know all the intimate details of a murder. Right now though, Paterson was desperate and Walker was his only hope of solving these two, at least until he met with the official BIA. Comparing notes would probably be a better way to go.

'Ok,' he said. 'I'll make the arrangements. Dave will brief you more fully. I want a full written profile on my desk by nine tomorrow morning.' Walker smiled.

Jordan frowned at Paterson's decision. Despite all of his apparent knowledge, Walker was still relatively young in service and an unknown quantity when it came to practicalities. Despite his misgivings, he said nothing.

Walker rose from his seat and nodded at the two officers. 'Thank you, sir. I'll do the best I can to get inside this guy's head.' He headed out of the room. Paterson too got up to leave.

'Let's hope he does us proud, Dave,' he said.

'Nah. He's a dick.'

* * *

Back in his office, Paterson pulled out his mobile phone and was about to make a call when his desk phone rang.

'Paterson.'

The person on the other end sounded Oxford educated. He spoke in precise, clipped tones. 'Good morning to you, sir. My name is Peter Reichenbach. I'm your assigned BIA. I was hoping we could meet later today to go over the details of this particular case.'

The name sounded German. Not so the accent. Paterson glanced at his watch. 'Sure. One o'clock this afternoon, my office. I'll have everything ready for you.'

Jordan strolled in as Paterson ended the call. 'Who was that?'

'The BIA. A Mr Reichenbach. Coming over this afternoon.'

'Reichenbach? Is he a German?'

Paterson shrugged. 'Didn't sound it.'

'They never do,' said Jordan. 'Listen, guv, I'm meeting my brother at Guy's this morning, then off following up on a couple of bits. Should be back by about quarter to one but if I'm not, make sure you save my seat. Chuck a towel over my chair. They understand that.' Paterson shook his head slowly. Jordan grinned and breezed out of the office.

CHAPTER SIX

Dave Jordan pulled his battered Toyota into the nearest disabled bay at Guy's Hospital just before nine. He fumbled behind the passenger seat, pulled out a laminated card that identified the car as being on police business and tossed it onto the dashboard. That should warn off anyone who questioned the absence of a blue badge. He hauled himself out of the car. After the heated interior, the sharp November wind hit him hard. Above, a number of builders were working on the scaffolding that snaked around the lower three floors of Guy's Tower, and he stood for a moment, fascinated by the brilliant flashes of light from the arc welders dotted about.

Pulling his scarf across his mouth, he made his way across the car park toward the main entrance, nervous and in dire need of a coffee. The enormous glass doors sucked him in and he wandered across the foyer, revelling in the sudden blast of warm air. An elderly man, dressed in a beige cable knit cardigan and brown trousers pounced on him with a cheery smile and asked if he needed any help with directions. Jordan politely declined his offer. He knew this place well enough by now. Catching a glance at the clock above the toilet doors, and with his brother Mark not due for another fifteen minutes, he headed off toward the canteen to grab a takeaway coffee for himself and a tea for Mark.

Armed with a scalding hot drink in each hand and a greasy paper bag containing an apple Danish clamped between his teeth, Jordan made his way along the corridor asking himself why, with all the money thrown at the National Health Service, they couldn't provide cardboard cup holders. McDonalds never had this problem. Jordan scurried forward to try and catch the lift, and a young nurse held the door open for him. He nodded gratefully. 'Fiffteenf floor, pleash.' He removed the Danish, set the two cups down on the floor and shook his hands vigorously. She gave him a smile.

'Bloody nuclear they are,' he said to the amused nurse. 'Don't suppose you've got a couple of tissues on you, have you?'

'Not on me,' she said, 'but I'm going to the same floor as you, so put them on a window sill when we get off and I'll go get you some.'

'Thanks, love. You're a life saver.'

She gave a wry smile. 'Funny you should say that.'

Arriving at the fifteenth, Jordan picked up the cups and made his way over to the nearest window while the young nurse punched the security key pad to her ward. A couple of minutes later she came back out, holding a thick bundle of tissues. He squashed the Danish into one of his pockets and carefully wrapped the tissues around the cups before thanking his life saving nurse and heading off along yet another endless corridor.

The last bit of the walk was the one he hated most. He'd done this a few times now and knew he'd probably only get to do it a few more. The thought filled him with both anger and sadness, but he'd dug deep and somehow made his peace with it. Standing at the entrance to the Macmillan clinic was his brother Mark.

A couple of years older than Dave, Mark was his polar opposite. Rake thin and smartly dressed, Mark owned his own building firm, was happily married to his childhood sweetheart and had three children of work age and his first grandchild on the way. Dave Jordan was dangerously fat, looked like he'd fallen out of bed most days, had three failed marriages behind him and one son that he never saw anymore. The only thing the two brothers had in common were their parents, bald heads and the same sense of humour — dark and disrespectful.

'Alright, fat boy!' Mark called out, a little too loudly given the nature of this particular clinic. The receptionist frowned at him.

Just as loudly, Mark said, 'I hope that cake hanging out of your pocket is for me! You could do with dropping a couple of dress sizes, Davey boy.' A few people in the waiting room sat up and grinned. Entertainment at last.

'Alright, Bones. Take this bleedin' cup off of me, will you, before I have to go and have a skin graft. I lost me fingerprints back there in the lift, but luckily some little nurse found 'em.' He stopped and gave the receptionist a big grin, and set both cups down on her desk. 'How do they make this stuff so hot, love? Is it made with radiation, or what?' She frowned at him over her glasses.

'Shut up, you big nancy boy,' said Mark. 'Come and sit down. We'll be in in five minutes. Give us a bite of your cake.' Jordan followed his brother, who had already reserved two seats with a newspaper spread over them. He sat down and pulled the squashed apple Danish out of his pocket. Immediately there was a high pitched beep and the words, 'Mr Jordan. Room 5. Dr Jarap' in bright red LED flashed up on a black screen set high on the wall above the TV.

Jordan stood back up. 'Oh bollocks! I didn't want the bloody cake anyway.' He took a big bite, scattering crumbs onto the floor, and followed his brother to Room Five.

* * *

Jock Hudson had had enough. He got up out of his seat, walked over to the window and snapped the blind shut. Strips of sunlight had been slanting their way through the blinds and hitting him in the eyes for the last five minutes and he wasn't going to sit through the whole meeting with it. Paterson jotted down the names of those present: DCI Carr, DS Jordan, Jock Hudson, senior pathologist, Kim Wall, senior CSI. He was waiting for one other.

'Has he turned up yet, guv?' Jordan plonked himself down next to Paterson, coffee in one hand, biscuits in the other. He looked tired and agitated.

There was a gentle tap on the door, and before anyone could answer, WDC Lena Andrews popped her head inside. She spoke with a soft West Country accent that belied her appearance. Andrews was in her late twenties, slightly built with a shock of pink, close cropped hair. 'Sorry to interrupt you, sir but I have a Mr Reichenbach for you. The BIA.'

'Cheers, Lena. Send him in, please,' said Paterson. Peter Reichenbach, carrying a large briefcase and an umbrella, barged through the doorway, managing to press his chest against Lena's as he came through.

Reichenbach was sixty years old, six feet tall and had a small grey moustache the same colour as his hair. He wore a gold rimmed monocle in his left eye and his suit was probably the height of fashion back in the eighteen hundreds. Paterson shuddered. Jordan rolled his eyes.

Peter Reichenbach threw out a big smile. 'So sorry, m'dear,' he said to Lena Andrews, still trying to extricate himself from the jam they were now in. 'Really sorry. Should have waited a moment longer. In a rush you see. Very embarrassed.' Lena gave him the benefit of the doubt and her best practiced smile, while half pushing him into the room. Paterson and Jordan shot each other a look and rose to shake his hand.

'Mr Reichenbach. Please, take a seat.' Paterson gestured towards the chair in front of his desk. He introduced everyone and opened the file in front of him.

'Thank you for coming in. I want you to know we appreciate your input on this.' Jordan rolled his eyes again. Paterson ignored him and carried on. 'I take it you've had a look at the paperwork relating to these two murders? I understand they were sent to you by email after we spoke.'

'Thank you, Mr Paterson. I did receive them, yes.'

'Good. Mr Hudson, Miss Wall, can you bring us up to speed, please?' Each ran through their findings, but neither brought anything new to the party. Hudson spent a few minutes pointing out the differences between the two murders.

'Similarities. Throttled one handed, throats cut, two strokes. One to kill, one to decapitate, both of which failed so perhaps he didn't want to take the heads completely off. Both had words carved into the skin. Vaginas cut out, not too skilfully. Times of death anywhere between two and two-thirty a.m.' He coughed. 'Dissimilarities. Stomach contents removed from first victim, not the second. Word carved on breastbone of first victim, word carved into breast of second vic. Repeated word painted on a shutter some distance from the first victim, not repeated on the second.

'Why the differences?' said Jordan. Hudson shrugged and looked at Reichenbach for an answer.

'I can't be certain at this stage but most likely designed purely to confuse. Let me tell you my findings based on what I have gleaned from the facts I have so far. I will of course write up a much more in-depth report for you but in the inter—'

A sharp rap on the door interrupted his flow. DC Walker stuck his head around the door, looked for and found Paterson.

'Sorry to butt in, sir, but I heard the BIA was in here and I thought it might be a good idea if I sat in. See if we tally up.' Without being asked, Walker strode in, introduced himself and pulled up a chair next to Reichenbach. He dropped a small, thin, manila file on Paterson's desk. Jordan glared at him but said nothing. Not the place. Walker flashed him a smile and made himself comfortable next to Reichenbach.

'If I may continue, Superintendent?' Reichenbach said. Paterson gave a small nod and gestured for him to carry on. 'This man is of likely reasonable intelligence, nothing special. He is white, no older than forty. He will have studied to degree level, but he won't be the brain of Britain. He will have a highly developed fantasy life and is an avid user of violent pornography in support of that fantasy. The removal of the sexual organs in such a manner indicates he will have been heavily sexually abused by his mother over a long period of time. His father, for as long as he stuck around, would likely have known and perhaps been party to the abuse. I believe our man would have had a sister who was also likely to have been abused in the same fashion.'

'Oh great,' said Jordan. 'So his sister could be off her trolley too?'

'Possible, but unlikely,' said Reichenbach. 'It is however likely that his father would have handed out severe beatings to both children. Our man is very, very angry about the abuse and this is his form of revenge acted out. Going back to his intelligence level, he will hold down a good job and for all intents and purposes there will be little to mark him out from his co-workers. I would suggest he is most likely in a long-term relationship with a woman or married, and is likely to have been so for a number of years.'

'And the words carved into the victims?' said Paterson. 'Why is he doing that?'

Walker jumped in. 'He's giving instructions, sir.' Reichenbach cocked his head, annoyed at being upstaged. Paterson and Jordan sat back in their chairs, looking puzzled.

'My sentiments exactly.' Reichenbach extended his hand to Walker. 'I'm sorry, officer. We were not properly introduced. Peter Reichenbach, behavioural intelligence analyst.'

Paterson leaned forward. 'I'm sorry, gentlemen. I should have—'

Reichenbach held up his hands. 'No need for apologies, Superintendent. You were focussed on other things.' He held out one hand.

Walker shook it vigorously. 'Walker. Detective Constable Adam Walker. I studied at Quantico for a while.'

Reichenbach looked at him with interest. 'Did you indeed? I hear they're very good.'

'DC Walker is one of the officers on my squad and has offered his own expertise in this case,' said Paterson. 'There's not going to be a problem, is there?'

'Not with me, sir,' Reichenbach said. 'I'm good. I do not anticipate any problems, Superintendent, but I would like it noted that I am the official BIA on this case and would expect to be the first to know of all developments, however small or irrelevant they may seem. They could well have a significant impact on my profile.' He gave Walker a slight grin. 'I'm sure you understand, Officer.'

Walker grinned right back at him. 'Of course I understand, sir,' he said, his tone belying his expression. 'And I would like it noted that I'm the official police officer here, and if we're working on the same team I expect to be informed of any changes in *your* profile, however small or insignificant they may seem. They may have a significant impact on *my* investigation.'

Jordan snorted so hard he blew a drop of snot. Cuffing it away, he smiled at Paterson. 'Have a good look, guv,' he said. 'Welcome to the psychological profilers' pissing contest.'

Paterson fought back his laugh. 'That's enough, please, gents. Mr Reichenbach, there is no question of your status on this case. As I said, DC Walker is here in his capacity as a detective but, given his background, I value his input and would like to run any ideas he has by you in the first instance.' He looked hard at Walker. 'DC Walker, so we're clear, this is not your investigation and you will not be the first to know anything unless either I, DCI Carr or DS Jordan deem it appropriate. Understood?'

Walker stared back. 'Sir.'

'Now, what's this about him giving instruction?' Paterson said. Walker looked to Reichenbach, eyebrows raised.

'It is quite apparent that something has affected him very deeply. The words he is carving are quite hard in tone, quite directive. For instance, the word 'Don't' is an instruction as opposed to a word like 'Happy,' which is descriptive. The two words we have so far indicate that this message is heading in the direction of an instruction, an order.'

Paterson pinched the bridge of his nose, and sighed deeply. 'Do either of you want to hazard a guess as to what the instruction will be?' Both men shook their head.

'Not at this stage, Mr Paterson,' said Reichenbach. 'It's too early, I'm afraid.' Walker shook his head.

Paterson stole a glance at his wristwatch. 'Do you have anything to update us with, Adam?'

'Yes, sir, I do.' Walker pulled the manila file toward him and opened it up. Everyone shifted in their seats.

'I've identified a possible link between the girls and a Donald Williams. Male, black, late thirties.' He pulled out a series of photographs. The first one showed a black man with a thick unkempt goatee and a small thin scar that ran down from his forehead to his cheek. His left eye was white, blind as a result of a Stanley knife attack he'd been on the wrong end of five years ago. The others were crime scene photographs of a young murdered girl and head and shoulder shots of three teenage girls. One had two black eyes. All three had cut lips and cuts on their faces. The murdered girl had had her throat cut and was lying naked on a floor in a pool of dark blood.

'Williams is a local pimp with a reputation for extreme violence. Goes by the street name of "Pussy" because of his trade, and his particular fondness for, well, pussy. He's a local boy with a cat house over in Devon Mansions. I've spoken to a couple of the local skanks and they've put him in the frame for working Lynn Farrow. I'm still working on a link with Donovan. Word is that he always carries and keeps guns, due to a number of attacks from rivals. He's been implicated in at least one murder of a prostitute, but walked owing to lack of evidence, and a few severe beatings of young girls. He's striped at least three girls, but they were all too scared to put him in the frame. Bastard's a walking, talking piece of shit and the best we have so far.' He handed the pictures to Reichenbach.

Jordan glanced at the images. 'Why would he slash them? That just lowers their value to him, surely?'

Walker shrugged. 'Perhaps he works on volume. Lots of girls. Some are cheaper because they're damaged but still usable. And let's face it, some people will shag anything.' Paterson winced. 'Or, maybe he's done with them. Perhaps they crossed him. Sending out a message to others who might step out of line.'

'Feasible I suppose,' said Jordan.

Paterson looked around the room, waiting to see if anyone had more to offer. 'Mr Reichenbach. Thank you for coming in. Work closely with DS Jordan on this.' His chair scraped the floor as he stood up. 'Adam, get surveillance on his HA. I'll let Kelly know and see if we can round up the cavalry for an early morning knock.'

* * *

At 04:45 the following morning, two armed response vehicles, one unmarked Astra, a marked police van and a van containing a search team drove silently out of the back yard of Tower Bridge police station. They turned left then made an illegal right, cutting across the sparse early morning traffic before driving through the no entry signs at the junction of Tooley Street. A hurriedly put together surveillance team had placed Donald Williams at home.

In less than four minutes all three cars, doors already open, began to pull into the kerbside. The vans held back slightly. Two middle-aged women office cleaners had a temporary heart stoppage when four men, dressed head to toe in black, with Kevlar helmets and full body armour, stepped out of the lead car with machine guns pressed to their chests. Behind them, another four officers from SCO19, the Met's specialist firearms command, simultaneously left their vehicle. Two peeled away from the group, and ran to take up position at the rear of the building. Any and all sprinters would be stopped. PC Nigel Morris sent the women on their way, holding a black gloved finger to his lips. He expected their silence, and got it. In the last car, Clocks and Walker stayed put, watching the scene unfold through the rain-spattered windscreen.

Inspector Billy Kingston and his team quickly made their way toward the entrance to the block of flats. He pulled on the door. To his surprise, it opened easily and the small team of heavily armed men quickly disappeared from view. Reaching the top floor, Kingston pulled on the large wrought-iron security gate protecting the drab, graffiti-laden street door. To his surprise, the gate swung open. That was the one good thing about junkies — thick as shit.

Kingston stood with his back to the wall and pushed on the door, testing it to see where it gave. It rattled quietly and he was soon satisfied that it was fastened with only a single mortice lock and Yale. Easy.

With a loud bang and a splintering of wood, Kingston kicked the door in.

'Armed police! Armed police!' he screamed into the darkness. The beam of the mini-mag on his MP9 pierced through the dark and he turned immediately left and took the stairs up to the bedrooms, back to the wall, eyes fixed on the dark cavity of the hall landing above him. He could hear the rest of his team thundering their way into the flat and barking commands at the empty air as they peeled off into different rooms. Two raced up the stairs to support him.

Every couple of seconds, Kingston heard 'Clear!' from below, making it ever more likely that somewhere in the blackness, his target was waiting for him. At the top of the stairs he stopped, listened, straining to hear above the noise of his adrenaline-fuelled Trojans clomping around downstairs. He stepped forward, swinging the gun from side to side, the torch beam cleaving through the darkness like a tiny searchlight. Three doors, all closed.

Kingston went to the first door on his left. He kicked the door hard and his foot met with cheap plywood. Crouching low, he moved in, pointing the searchlight around the room. Empty. He stepped back out into the hall, where two of his team now stood outside the remaining doors, guns levelled. With time now against him and the arrival of his team clearly and loudly announced, he ran to the opposite end of the hall and shouldered the door in. Definitely not text-book and patently not clever, this at least had speed of entry going for it. The door gave way more easily than expected, and Kingston struggled to keep his balance while his momentum propelled him in.

Crashing into a bedside cabinet, his torch flailing wildly around the room, he picked out a shape and dropped to the floor. Behind him the familiar voice of his backup officer, WPC Lyndsey Mullins, shouted, 'You! Stay still. Armed police!' Mullins's torch beam locked onto the face of a spaced out, naked, teenage girl sitting up in bed and staring at them blankly. Mullins snapped on the light switch, revealing another young girl, coffee-coloured, lying face down. And, between them, a large shape under the duvet.

Kingston approached the bed. Mullins's hand tightened on the barrel. The girl sitting up turned glazed eyes toward the shouting voice. Both her hands were visible, as were the sleeping girl's. Minimal threat. Kingston grabbed hold of the sleeping girl's arm and dragged her off the bed. She hit the floor face down with a thump. Mullins's eyes never left the shape under the duvet. Kingston poked at it with the barrel of his gun.

'You! Under the covers! We are armed pol—'

The shape exploded upwards, catapulting space cadet two out of bed and sending her tumbling to the floor. Both officers jumped back instinctively. Donald Williams sat bolt upright, waving a gun around, shouting, 'Don't shoot! Don't shoot!'

Kingston was on him immediately. He jammed the barrel of his MP9 against William's temple and screamed, 'Drop the fucking gun, boy! Drop it now!'

Mullins pointed her gun directly at Williams's head, finger curled firmly around the trigger. 'Do it!' she yelled.

Williams dropped the gun. Kingston swiped it off the bed, and sent it clattering onto the floor behind him.

'Shit, man,' slurred Williams, squinting into the light. 'I mean no harm. I not realise you is de po-lice.'

Mullins snorted. 'Well, you should have paid more fucking attention when we let ourselves in and shouted we were de po-lice, you dumb dick! Hands behind your head. Do it now.' She grabbed Williams by the hair, and pulled him face down from the bed and onto the carpet beside the space cadet. She kneeled on top of him, pulled out a set off plasticuffs, and secured his wrists.

* * *

Clocks and Walker strolled into the bedroom. 'Good morning, Mr Williams. Nice to meet you. As you may have realised, we're the police. Please don't bother getting up. I'm Detective Sergeant Clocks, and my colleague here is Detective Constable Walker.' Clocks took in the scene. 'Nice pants, Mr Williams. Calvin? Didn't know they were doing them with stain patterns on them these days. Must get myself a pair.'

Williams struggled to lift his head. Walker passed behind Clocks and went to the space cadet lying gracelessly on the floor. He hauled her to her feet and sat her on a chair. He wrapped his jacket around her shoulders and pulled it across her. Then he dragged a sheet off the bed and draped it over coffee girl.

'Mr Clocks, sir. Wha' happening, man? Why drag me from me bed? The bitches is old enough. Wha' you want wit' me, eh?'

'Need to talk to you, Mr Williams. Christmas is coming and I want to find out if you've been naughty or nice.'

'What you mean naughty? Me told you, bitches is old enough.'

'Debatable,' said Clocks. He rolled Williams over onto his back and pulled him into a sitting position in one quick, practiced movement. 'As for being naughty, let's have a look, shall we?' Clocks waved his arms around the room in a theatrical gesture. Drug-related paraphernalia lay scattered around the large, sparsely decorated, filthy room. The wallpaper was hanging off in places, and the carpet stuck to the soles of their shoes. It stank like a schoolboys' changing room in the height of summer. To call it a total shit-hole would be to undersell it.

Clocks wandered about the room, noting with a faint smile the set of electronic scales, five or six used hypodermic needles, a length of rubber tubing and several empty wraps of silver foil. On the dressing table were several bags of marijuana, a pile of fifty-pound notes, another set of electronic scales and a filthy, much used calculator. On the floor, three used condoms. Boy'd been busy.

He pulled open a drawer, mindful of needles, and took out a poorly hidden half-pound bag of cocaine.

Clocks held up the bag of cocaine and waved it at Williams. 'For starters, possession of drugs with intent to supply.'

'Personal use, Mr Clocks. I swear.'

Clocks held his hand up. 'Room tells me otherwise. Haven't finished yet. Possession of a firearm. Possession of a firearm with intent to resist arrest. Possession of a firearm with intent to frighten the shit out of these nice officers here by pointing said firearm at them. Possession and supply of drugs, already said that, unlawful sexual intercourse with a couple of schoolies. Suspected murder of your two toms. I'm going to have to report back to Santa that you've been a bit of a cunt, Mr Williams, and to take you off his Christmas list double quick.'

Williams glared up at him. 'Wha' you mean murder? I ain't murder no one. Get me a brief. I saying nuttin."

'Didn't expect you to.' Clocks tossed the bag of cocaine to Walker. He gestured to Mullins to remove Williams from the room. 'Put him in the car for me please, love. On your way out, send in the search team. I want this flat ripped to shreds. Get a plonk up here to wake up Beyonce and Britney here and we'll see if we can squeeze a rape allegation out of the pair of them.' Mullins didn't like taking orders from anyone, let alone some poxy Jack-the-lad DS. She glared, face set. Inspector Kingston said he'd do it.

Williams put up a token struggle as Kingston manhandled him to his feet and bundled him out of the door. Clocks knew that the bits and pieces lying around, especially the half of coke, were left as a distraction for any of the local crime squad officers who happened to execute the odd warrant. They'd piss their pants at finding a whole half pound and ride off into the sunset without turning the place over properly. Clocks, though, wanted something in particular. In less than five minutes he found what he was looking for, hidden in a small slit in the bottom of the mattress. Leverage.

'Adam, you might want to see this.' He held up a small black diary.

Walker smiled. 'Nice one.'

CHAPTER SEVEN

Sitting uncomfortably in the back of Clocks's unmarked Astra, his cuffed arms stiff and burning, Donald Williams peered out at the figures of Clocks and Walker heading toward him. He knew what would happen now. Good cop, bad cop. One would holler and hoot, the other would try his best to calm down his 'psycho' buddy. Williams had been riding in the backs of police cars since he was thirteen and knew all about this little act. They wrenched the car doors open, Clocks next to him, Walker behind the wheel.

'Donny, old son. We need to talk,' Clocks said, a smirk on his face.

'I say nothing, Mr Clocks.'

'Suit yourself. To be honest, I couldn't give a fuck one way or the other. You, on the other hand, should give a fuck.'

'How so?' Williams said indifferently. Clocks reached into his coat pocket and pulled out the small black diary. He let out a heavy sigh.

'See? All those nasty drugs you take do impair your judgement. This wasn't too well hidden, was it? I've had a quick look inside, and guess what I found?' He flipped through the pages. 'You guessed it, loads of names and numbers. Nothing unusual in that, but I reckon if we turn it over to the big boys at the Yard, they'll all get a rocket on because I'm betting that most of the names in here belong to your bad boy gangsta mates. Would I be right?' Williams turned his gaze away from the window and faced Johnny Clocks, who donked him on the head with the diary.

'I reckon my Yardie mates will have a right old tear up with your Yardie mates. Think how pleased they'll be when they find out it was you that dropped them all in the shit. It was you who deliberately grassed on them in return for a lighter sentence.'

Williams stared at his captor. 'You would do this to me?'

'I would happily do this to you, Donald.'

Williams's eyes narrowed. 'When I get out, I cut your white arse to pieces.'

Clocks snorted. 'Y'know, if you were anyone else, Donny boy, anyone else at all, there might be a very slim chance I'd be scared. But as it's you, and you're just a woman-beating piece of shit, I'll put it down to the drugs talking.'

Donny Williams exploded. 'Fuck you! Fuck you! I will cut your bones out, you piece of white shit!' Both officers were taken aback for a second. Walker spun around. Clocks slammed Williams's face hard against the car window. The gunman still keeping guard outside turned his back and resumed watching his colleagues getting into their van. Clocks threw his weight against Williams. His expression was calm, almost serene.

'Listen up, you black fucker. That's enough of the racist shit, ok?' He pushed Williams's face harder against the glass. Walker turned round to get a better look. There'd be no good cop, bad cop scenario today.

'Couple of things we need to get straight, *boy*. You're a scumbag, drug dealing paedophile cunt. Gottit?' Williams grimaced and gave a weak nod. Fair enough. Except for the paedophile bit. 'And second, it don't pay to show off and run your mouth when you're all cuffed up in the back of a police car with a couple of 'orrible fuckers like us. Got it, *boy*?' Williams nodded again.

Clocks released his grip and his temper, pulled Williams roughly back into his seat and set about straightening up his ruffled clothes. 'Donny, I want some answers and at the moment you're the man to give them. We're taking you back to the nick for questioning. Consider yourself cautioned, and if I was you I'd have a little think about the shit you're in and how much you suddenly want to help us.'

Williams remained silent. Walker started the engine, nodded to the SC019 officer and pulled away.

* * *

Interview room two at Tower Bridge police station was a dingy little corner with no room to swing anything, let alone the proverbial cat. In typical Victorian style, the ceiling was gratuitously high and thick walls hemmed in its unfortunate occupants. Four people made it snug, five made it uncomfortable. Complete with several layers of old, tired paintwork covering generous smatterings of blood from the times when justice used to be dispensed in a rather different manner, it no doubt breached every guideline for the treatment of prisoners ever to be incorporated into the Police and Criminal Evidence Act, but it was the only one available. It would have to do.

Donald Williams sat on one side of the worn table next to his solicitor, Winston Cooper, a sharply dressed, young, and highly educated black man with the smarts and ambition to get to the top. He'd long ago realised that the big money was in criminal defence and he was *the* go to guy for most of the local criminals, black and white alike. DS Clocks and DC Walker sat facing them.

Clocks fingered a buff folder and went through the rigmarole of informing Williams what was happening. This was done more as a pacifier for Cooper than anything else. Clocks wasn't about to give him the satisfaction of halting the interview, or getting Williams to walk, on a technicality. When he was ready, he pushed the button on the recorder and began. Reading from a crib sheet, he informed Williams of his rights and even managed to give a proper caution. Cooper seemed satisfied.

'Donald, I want to talk about Kerry Donovan. A local girl, known prostitute, who lived in the same block of flats as you, murdered on Friday the twentieth of November. I have good information that you are, among a lot of other things, a pimp, someone who controls prostitutes, finds them clients and takes a substantial cut from their earnings. I'm also told that Kerry was one of your girls.'

Williams kept his hands in his lap and stared at the desk. 'On the advice of me solicitor, I make no reply.'

'Ok. Let's try Lynn . . .' he checked his sheet, 'Farrow. Murdered on the twenty-seventh of November, one week later. She was also one of your girls I believe, albeit at the higher end of the market. What can you tell me about her?'

'On the advice of me solicitor, I make no reply.'

'Can you account for your movements on both of these nights?'

'On the advice of me solicitor, I make no reply.' Clocks was becoming impatient but kept himself in check. Cooper smirked, knowing that all the while the recorder was running, Clocks would have to behave himself. But Clocks had been interviewing prisoners for a lot longer than Cooper had been a solicitor, and he had his own way of putting doubt into a suspect's mind. His next question, sounding innocent enough, sowed doubt deep.

'Donald, we know they worked for you. Even Mr Cooper here, if you've been honest with him, knows they worked for you. We've spoken to other girls, so it's a bit pointless carrying on like this. I know you're only acting on the advice of your solicitor, but if you know nothing about these murders, nothing at all, and if you're an innocent man, why don't you just say so? Do yourself a favour and at least protest your innocence.' Cooper stared at him. 'This is your chance to put your side of the story. Row yourself out of it. It's up to you. I'm just trying to help.' Williams repeated his chant. Clocks tried another couple of questions. He'd done enough.

Feigning disappointment, Clocks said, 'Fair enough then, Donald. I tried to help you.' He glanced at his wristwatch, double checked it with the clock on the wall and reached for the stop button. 'As it is clear that Mr Williams has been advised by his solicitor to be as unhelpful as possible, I'm terminating this interview at ten forty-two.' He switched the recorder off.

The atmosphere changed. No need for games any more. Cooper's stare became a full-on glare. He wasn't happy at being wrong-footed, and even less happy that the jury would no doubt agree, at least in part, with Clocks's summation.

'Donny boy, you're a fuckin' half-wit, d'you know that?' Clocks scooped up his folder and straightened the sheets. 'You had the perfect opportunity to help us out, and now you're deeper in the shit than ever because you've been given bad advice.' He threw a grin Cooper's way.

'Mr Williams, do not answer this man. Mr Clocks, I suggest you either charge or release my client.' Cooper turned to face Walker. 'Mr Walker, you seem to be the sensible one here. Rest assured we'll be pressing charges for excessive force in the back of the police car.' He dropped his bundle of papers into his briefcase and snapped it shut.

Walker grinned. 'Between you and me, Mr Cooper, I couldn't give a fuck what you do, but,' he pointed at Williams, 'he's going nowhere. Far as I'm concerned, by the time we get through with him he should go down for fifteen to twenty.'

Williams leapt to his feet. 'Wha' you mean, fifteen to twenty?'

'Not complicated is it, Donny?' said Walker. 'We haven't even started on you yet for the murders, *and* those two girls we found you in bed with are just kids. Fifteen years old, both of them. Fifteen, you dirty old bastard. Good news for us but bad news for you is they've both put you in the frame for drugging them up. The blood samples we've taken from them will no doubt tie in with all the shit we found lying around your bedroom. The drugs have been sent for analysis,' he tutted and shook his head, 'plus they reckon you buggered 'em as well. So, that's two counts of rape on minors, front and back. Drugs, a loaded gun, resisting arrest, you do the maths. I think the expression is "bolloxed."' Walker moved toward the door. 'We'll confiscate your assets, freeze your bank accounts and when you eventually get out of prison, we'll put you on a big white bird back home to Jamaica. Of course, that's assuming you make it out of prison. Kiddy fiddlers aren't too popular in the nick.' Walker nodded to himself. 'Yep, bolloxed with a capital B.' And he opened the door.

Williams looked suddenly thoughtful. He might just have a chance if he started cooperating. Twenty years inside could play havoc with a man's business interests and more importantly, his health.

'All we wanted was a bit of help here, Donny. A name perhaps. Maybe we could've helped you out a bit. Still, your choice.' Walker stepped outside.

'Wait!'

'Mr Williams,' interrupted Cooper, 'I really—'

Williams waved his hand at him. 'Shut your mouth. I is talking now.'

'They're just trying to frighten you.'

Williams glared at Cooper. 'Then they've done a good job of it, mistah Cooper. I ain't go to no prison for twenty years.'

Cooper muttered angrily.

'I help you, Mr Clocks, and you help me?' Williams looked into Clocks's impassive face, then over to Walker, waiting at the door. Clocks shrugged and glanced at Walker. 'We don't need to help you, Donny. Seems to me you're the one sucking the shit end of the shitty stick, so you need to tell me what I want to know. If I decide what you're telling me is genuine, then I'll think about helping you. Clear?'

'Mr Cooper, I is finished wit' you. You can go.' Williams waved him away. Walker stepped aside and held the door open. Cooper snatched his bag up from the floor and stormed out of the office. Walker gave him a friendly wave.

Clocks gestured for Williams to sit back down.

'Fucking briefs. Do more harm than good sometimes. Now, Donny, what'd you want to tell us?' Walker said.

'I don't know who killed them, Mr Walker. That is the truth of it.' He gazed at Walker. 'But I tell you, if I find him, I kill him myself. They was good workers.'

'I don't doubt you will,' said Walker. 'But right now we need a list of their clients. Gonna give it to me?' Williams would give them his mother right now if it got him a lesser sentence.

'Kerry tell me she see a strange man once or twice. In the clubs. Tell me him freak her out.'

'Why's that?'

'Says him like to hurt girls. 'Tis his thing. Say he carries knives and threatens girls. She say gun too.'

Walker drew his chair forward. 'Name? Let's have it.'

Williams looked awkward for a moment or two. He exhaled deeply, and his shoulders sagged. 'Mistah Tony Pullman. Well known. Maybe it help you, maybe it won't but I not kill those girls.' He rubbed his hands together as if he were washing them.

Walker stood up and looked at Johnny Clocks. 'Timex? Ever heard of him?'

Johnny Clocks raised his eyes to the ceiling. 'Fuck yeah. We'll need the cavalry back out for this one.'

* * *

Travelling the nine odd miles to Kew Gardens during the morning rush hour was going to take the best part of an hour, maybe an hour and a half if the traffic was backed up. Dave Jordan couldn't have cared less. Behind the wheel of Paterson's Aston, he was in seventh heaven, quite happy to stay there for as long as possible. Temporary traffic lights seemed to have sprung up all over the place, choking key arterial routes and causing major problems for the weary commuter. Pretty much the norm these days. Jordan settled back into the leather and hit the play button on the sound system, wondering what Paterson liked to listen to. The mournful voice of Dido flooded the interior. Jordan decided he was depressed enough without her help and switched it off, preferring instead to listen to the comforting snick-snick of the windscreen wipers as they washed away yet another day's rain.

Tapping his fingers on the steering wheel in time with the wipers, his mind wandered back over the events of the last few days. Something had been nagging at the back of his mind from quite early into the investigation. His parent PC once told him that feelings will get you so far, but don't mean shit unless you can back them up with hard evidence. Jordan had learned the hard way that his PC dad was right. He felt a bit bad about deceiving Paterson as to where he was going, but if his hunch was proved correct it would work out well for everyone. Sure, he'd get a bollocking, but he'd take that if he could put a bit of meat on some very dry bones.

Pulling into the car park of Eaton's Investigations, he was conscious of the envious eyes that followed him all the way to a parking spot, and even more conscious of the need to exit the car with a modicum of style. To his own surprise he managed it fairly well, albeit slightly more Gene Hunt than James Bond. A couple of young girls sitting on a bench managed to hide their disappointment at seeing this lumbering sack of a man instead of the rich hunk they had hoped for. They threw him a casual wave and a fixed smile. It's the car, he thought.

'Oi!' a whiney voice called to him. 'Where's your blue badge then?' Jordan saw a thin man with a thin moustache and a dark suit. He wasn't sure if he was a car park attendant or just a busybody with a case of the green eye. He considered arguing with his challenger but decided that discretion was the sensible option. He grudgingly apologised and slunk back in to the car, all credibility now completely dissolved. The girls gave him a different smile this time.

* * *

The reception area of Eaton's reminded Jordan of those new-fangled modern libraries he disliked so much. All plate glass windows and brightly coloured plastic seats. He'd last gone to a library two years ago to look up some old newspaper clippings for a case he was working on, but before that he couldn't remember the last time he'd set foot in one. What he did remember was that they were usually dank old council buildings with a musty smell, corridors that echoed loudly and ominously and were staffed by an old biddy in a cardigan and bottle-bottom glasses who threatened anyone who dared speak above a whisper with the wrath of the Lord God Almighty. Libraries, he reflected, used to be sanctuaries, one of the few places outside of a church where peace and quiet was mandatory. A place you could go to escape the hustle of life. Nowadays, it was all banks of PC terminals connected to the internet, manned from opening to closing time by people talking to their 'friends' on Facebook and watching YouTube videos of cute cats. No librarian would dare ask them to keep it down.

The young lady who greeted him from behind the reception desk at Eaton's was definitely nothing like the librarians of old. Tall, slim, long blonde hair pulled back into a swinging ponytail and immaculately dressed in a crisp white blouse and navy blue pencil skirt, her smile made his old heart jump a beat. She smelled every bit as good as she looked. He knew it was pointless, but he couldn't help but try to impress. He pulled out his warrant card from his back pocket and flicked it open to reveal the cheap nickel-plated badge.

'DS Jordan, Southwark Homicide,' he said, hoping it made him sound sexy. 'I have an appointment with Mr Eaton.' The receptionist flicked her ponytail and peered over the desk at his badge, smiled politely and invited him to take a seat while she punched buttons on her phone.

Jordan took his seat and wondered when it was that women stopped finding him attractive. His last wife had obviously decided that about fifteen years ago when she took off with a younger man. Jordan accepted he was getting on a bit, wasn't quite as slim as he used to be and definitely wasn't the best dressed man about town, but he didn't think he was too bad a catch. He had most of his teeth if not his hair, owned his own flat and had a few quid in the bank. Shouldn't that give him some points on the dating scoreboard? His profile on www.wheresmylove.com had received a fair few hits and he'd had a few email conversations as the result of it. He'd even had a few dates with some of the women he'd spoken to online but ultimately, nothing had come of it. Doesn't really matter anymore he thought to himself as he watched Kimberley go about her business.

To the left of her desk a glass panelled door swung open and a smiling, smartly dressed man appeared. Jordan guessed he was late forties, fifty at a push, but no more. Kimberley, ever smiling, pointed toward Jordan and the smiling man, without missing a step, turned toward him, hand extended. Everyone around here is always smiling, Jordan thought, and rose to greet him.

He shook Jordan's hand warmly. 'DS Jordan? Christopher Eaton. Thank you for calling us. How can I be of assistance?'

'Thank you for meeting with me. I'm investigating a murder, two actually, and I wondered if you might be able to help me with an idea I have. I need some information and I want to do it off grid. To be honest, I don't know if you can help me. I don't even know if I'm in the right place.'

Eaton listened carefully and asked Kimberly to arrange for tea and coffee to be brought to his office. Jordan hoped Kimberley herself would bring the drinks.

They took the lift to a corridor made up, it seemed to Jordan, of nothing but glass offices. They reminded him of a rat lab he once had to visit for a case. He had an idea of what Eaton's office would look like. Modern and soulless.

Inside, Jordan immediately clocked the three abstract prints hanging on the stark white wall facing him. Hideous. The wall to his right was made entirely of glass and gave a stunning view over Kew Gardens, spectacular even in the rain. Placed to take full advantage of the view, two deep leather chairs were set out either side of a white coffee table. To the left of the doorway, Eaton's desk was a large plastic affair, somewhat too large for its contents — a telephone, a two tier in-out tray with just a few sheets of paper in each, a charging dock for an iPhone and oddly, Jordan thought, a blotting jotter. Jordan stared at the abstract prints for a moment before heading toward the view.

'Interested in art, Mr Jordan?' said Eaton.

'Not much, sir. I'm an old-fashioned kind of a guy to tell you the truth. I like a bit of that Dutch fellah, what's his name — Vermeer. And that Turner chap. I'm not a lover of this modern stuff,' he gestured toward the prints on the wall.

'Take a seat,' said Eaton with a glance at them. 'They're Pollocks.'

'They are, aren't they? Total load of bollocks.' Jordan nodded sagely and sat down. 'Why don't you just change them then?'

Eaton gave a slight smile. 'No, no! Jackson Pollock. He was an artist, a major figure in the abstract expressionist movement. These are his famous "drip" paintings.'

Jordan flushed. Good start. 'Course they are, sir. Only joking.' Before he could do any more damage, his mobile phone rang. A quick glance at the screen showed Paterson's name. He grimaced and stabbed at the 'end call' icon.

'Sorry,' he said to Eaton, grateful for the respite from his embarrassment. Yet another attractive young girl entered the office carrying a tray with tea, coffee and biscuits. She was no Kimberley, but she definitely wouldn't get herself kicked out of his bed.

She poured the drinks and left. Eaton pushed a cup toward Jordan. 'To business then, Mr Jordan. Tell me, why does a detective need the services of a detective agency?'

Jordan, realising he was unlikely to get his finger into the tiny handle, picked up his cup by the rim and reached for the chocolate digestives. 'Because I have trust issues,' he said.

* * *

News at Ten was playing quietly on the portable TV in Dave Jordan's kitchen as he sat in front of his newly acquired MacBook Air. He was trying his best to come to terms with the thing and, overall, not doing too badly. His old Dell had recently suffered a complete hard drive failure and he'd decided to bite the bullet and buy himself an Apple, purely because everyone he knew owned one. The price nearly gave him a heart attack in the middle of the store but after a bit of thought, he decided to get it on credit. He threw in a small wireless printer while he was at it.

To his surprise, it had been a lot easier to set up than he thought it would be. Perhaps he was getting the hang of this tech lark after all. The world was always moving a bit too fast for Jordan's liking. Back in the late eighties, he had railed against the Met's widespread introduction of computers and the need to enter everything into 'fields.' He held out for a year with his clunky old typewriter.

Now, he tapped away with two fingers at the report he was putting together. On the counter, a few sheets of paper were scattered around and a number of ten by eight photographs lay face up. He was on to the third page now and was puzzling over what to do about a paragraph he had somehow managed to select. Wherever he clicked, the block of text remained bathed in light blue. A sudden pinging noise from the laptop resolved the issue for him, making him jump and accidently tap the delete key. 'Oh, fuckin' shitballs!' he muttered to himself, and banged his fist on the counter. His first instinct had been to scoot the bloody thing onto the floor, but common sense had prevailed. He needed his computer tonight. In a sulk, he went to get another coffee.

He scooped three big heaps of coffee into a large mug, splashed in some milk and poured in the boiling water, narrowly avoiding scalding his hand. Hidden behind a few bottles of juices and cokes, he found his quarter empty half bottle of scotch and poured a generous helping into his coffee. He wandered back over to the laptop. A little icon had unfolded itself on top of his document, informing him that he had an email from Christopher Eaton. The man worked quickly. He skimmed through the message and clicked on the attachments that Eaton had provided.

He spent the next fifteen minutes reading these, before printing out both the email and the attachments. Gathering up the sheets of paper from the printer and the bits and pieces scattered around his counter top, he wandered into the living room where he pulled a stapler from a messy drawer in his DVD cabinet, clipped the pages together and rummaged about for a big paper clip. Then he went back into the kitchen and placed everything into an A4 envelope marked "Private and Confidential. Det Supt Paterson." When he'd finished, he topped and tailed the report he'd been working on, printed it out, signed and dated it and slid it under the staple holding everything together. From his back pocket he pulled out a set of handwritten instructions from the salesman and opened up the video recording function on his laptop. After a couple of test runs, he centred himself up in the little 'selfie' window and stared directly into the tiny camera.

‘My name is Detective Sergeant David Jordan. If you’re watching this, it’s most likely because I’m dead.’

CHAPTER EIGHT

At exactly 8:50 p.m., Inspector Billy Kingston strode into the canteen of Southwark police station. He was not a man to be late. The jibber-jabber of the assembled officers suddenly dropped in volume and heads turned towards the new arrivals. Some looked on in awe. He was used to it. Baseball caps and guns had that effect on people.

His venerable old instructor at the firearms unit training sessions had told him and his classmates about the 'John Wayne effect.' Most male coppers wanted to be him, one or two imagined they were him, the one with a gun fetish would likely get a semi hard-on, and he'd get to shag pretty much any of the plonks he wanted. No one in the class had believed the old guy, but it turned out he was right on the money.

From force of habit, Kingston scanned the room and within a matter of seconds had noted the exit door, the counter, counted the exact number of windows, including which ones were open and which were closed, and had mapped where everybody was placed within the room. No threats. Behind him, his team of attack dogs piled in and began dropping bags, two-way radios and coats all over the chairs and tables, making more noise than was really necessary. That's the thing about SCO19. They do love to make an entrance.

Kingston removed his baseball cap and dropped it onto the nearest table, swung the heavy black bag from his shoulder and let it fall to the floor. He lowered his muscular frame into one of the padded chairs, and thought briefly of his impending retirement. Part of him couldn't wait to call it a day, pack it all in and bugger off to his little cottage on the Welsh coast. Another, bigger part wondered desperately how he would cope with the monotony of life on civvy street. Retirement was the only thing that truly scared him. Running a hand through his greying crew cut, he rubbed the back of his head, closed his eyes and sighed.

At the other end of the canteen, Carrie Gedmine was busily raking in a pile of five and ten pound notes that a few minutes ago had belonged to PC Mark 'Taff the Tosser' Jones. The other four players, including Adam Walker, were just glad they threw their hands in early on.

'Bloody hell, woman. How can you be so bloody lucky?' Jones said in his thick, rise and fall Valley accent. 'That's not bloody possible that is.'

She had him now. With just the gentlest of pushes she could send him over the edge, causing him to play even worse, and likely squeeze another big pot out of him. There was another ten minutes to go before the briefing started, and she knew there was no way Taff would ever let a 'bloody girl' beat him. Easy meat.

'Luck, boyo! There's no luck there, isn't it, wasn't it.' The mock accent was based on once having heard Tom Jones on the radio.

'Don't you take the bloody piss out of me, woman,' Taffy retaliated. He spoke just loudly enough to catch Kingston's attention. He took in the fat, sweaty, angry little man jabbing his finger at Gedmine. Less than zero threat to anyone. Besides, Kingston knew she could take him.

'Calm down, Blodwyn,' she said. 'It's not my fault you can't play the game, is it?'

Taffy pulled himself up to his full indignant five foot nine inches, and started to come around the table at her. Gedmine smiled at him, completely unfazed by his aggressive display. He made a move for her, and her chair scraped back. Kingston's eyes snapped open and he tensed, ready to launch himself out of his chair. His dogs turned sharply toward the commotion and a couple more chairs scraped.

'Can't play the fucking game, woman? D'you mean can't play?'

'Sit the fuck down, Taff.' Walker was up on his feet. He put his hand on Taffy's chest with just enough force to stop him dead without pushing him. 'Don't even think about it.'

'She's got no right to say I can't fucking play,' he mumbled. 'No fucking right.'

'You had bad luck, Taff. She's just tilting you,' said Walker. Kingston sat back and closed his eyes. His dogs went back to their business slightly miffed that the Welshman had bottled out. 'And she's done a bloody good job. I wouldn't waste your money on another hand.'

Gedmine smiled. She'd had a good night.

* * *

Ray Paterson walked into the room at the stroke of nine. He indicated that DCI Carr should take a seat next to Dave Jordan, and began to address the rapidly quietening room.

'Ladies and gents. You've all been pre-briefed by your respective team leaders so you all know why you're here tonight. Hopefully we get to take down the man responsible for the murders of Kerry Donovan and Lynn Farrow. As I'm sure you'll have read in the papers or picked up on the news, the press have now given our unsub a title: "Unsub-Unidentified Subject."' Jordan sneered. The term was straight out of *Criminal Minds*. 'It seems the *Daily Mirror* liked "Jack the Gripper" best of all because he strangled his victims first. I don't want to hear anyone here using it. Understood?' At the back of the room, Johnny Clocks had a little grin to himself. He'd given them that one, and was chuffed they'd run with it.

'Moving on. Thanks to sterling work by DS Clocks and DC Walker, we have received solid information from this man,' said Paterson, as Donald Williams's face lit up the screen. 'This is Donald Williams, local boy. Some of you likely already know him. Among other things, he's a known drug dealer with priors for violence and, in particular, extreme violence against women. He has admitted to running the two girls that were killed. During a raid on his premises we found him in the sack with two drugged up schoolgirls and a loaded firearm which he thought would be a good idea to point at Mr Kingston and Miss Mullins.' He gestured toward Kingston who gave a slight nod to the turning heads. The mention of a gun got everyone's attention, and the energy in the room shifted up a notch.

'During his interview, it was pointed out to Williams that he was royally fucked. He gave us a name. Ladies and gents, meet Anthony Thomas Pullman.' Pullman's mug shot filled the screen, and Paterson followed it up with a few more images taken by the local CID on a stakeout a couple of years ago. The stubbled face glaring back at them could, in the right light, be Jason Statham at his moody best. Pullman, though, had dark, baleful eyes, topped by thick eyebrows. In the middle of what was a strangely handsome face was a badly broken nose, and down the left side of his face an angry jagged scar ran from the bottom of his eye to just above his jawline. It was believed, but never proven, that the person who gave Pullman his scar ended up in a shallow grave in Joyden's Wood in Kent minus his own face. Just a picture, yet the face staring out at them radiated menace.

'He's thirty-nine years old, nearly six foot five, weighs about twenty stone, all of it muscle, and is a well-known violent bastard with an intense dislike of the police. He does contract work for some of the bigger faces on the ground and has previous for GBH with intent, ABH, drugs, thieving and handling. He is suspected of a number of violent assaults on women, including sexual. None of the girls would give statements for fear he would come after them.'

With perfect, almost rehearsed timing, Detective Chief Inspector Carr cut in, talking even as he stood up. 'This is a dangerous man who carries knives and guns and, at the moment at least, he is the best, and only, suspect we have.' His voice was big and filled the room. It carried a hint of Geordie underneath the Oxford-educated diction. Not a particularly personable man, he often came across as a bit gruff, likely the result of being the butt of numerous racing car jokes throughout his life. Always immaculately dressed in a suit, collar and tie, Roy Carr was comfortable addressing groups of people, big or small. He loved his job, and was pretty good at it, but his one failing was his slavish belief in the hierarchy. He wanted and expected people to respect his rank every bit as much as he respected those senior to him. Ray Paterson, senior to him, looked a bit miffed that he'd been interrupted when he was on a roll, but let it go and introduced him.

'Apologies all. Most of you know DCI Carr. He's here tonight to act as Silver Command and will be with me for the evening. Together, we will decide what action, if any, is to be taken on any sightings of Pullman.' Carr sat back down, satisfied that his presence was now acknowledged.

'We have a problem in that we have been unable to identify Pullman's place of residence and we are currently unaware of his location. However, our information indicates that he likes the nightclubs, and it is hoped that he will show up at one of these tonight. We have set up eight observation points around our three main night clubs, each containing two officers. We also have a four-man team in plain clothes on motorbikes and one helicopter call sign, India 99.

'As I said earlier, Pullman is known to carry weapons so the SCO19 boys over there will carry out any arrest. I want to make it crystal clear that it is SCO19 officers and *only* SCO19 officers who will make the arrest. Nobody else is to even think about tackling this vicious bastard. If it turns out he is our killer, I doubt very much he'd hesitate for a second before he sliced your throat open. Are we all clear?' Heads nodded and voices murmured around the room, all quietly pleased to be relieved of any sort of heroics.

'The sheets that DC Gedmine will be handing out have everything you need to know. Telephone numbers, call signs, who's what and where,' added Carr. Taff the Tosser glared hard at Carrie as she picked up the small pile of papers and began handing them out.

'Any sightings, any suspicious activity, anything at all is to come through us first. Understood?' There was a collective nodding of heads as everybody rose from their seats and began heading for the door.

* * *

Save for the very rare visits from old Jim Dawson, the night security guard, the old textile warehouse overlooking Zones nightclub hadn't seen a human face in a good ten years or so. Jordan gave the rotting wooden door a gentle push and took a few tentative steps into the darkness. Walker, carrying a large black holdall slung over his shoulder, followed him inside.

Bathed in the half-light that filtered in from the street behind them, Jordan and Walker clicked on their Maglites and flashed them around. They found themselves standing in what Jordan supposed had been some sort of reception area in its day. The desk still had an old bell type telephone sitting on it. It was off the hook. Poking his head forward a little bit and peering through the gap, he picked out a filing cabinet with the bottom and top drawers open and a few hanging files sitting at odd angles. Probably been burgled at some point. Over in the corner was an old-fashioned coat stand with a couple of dusty overcoats hanging from it, and next to that was a wooden desk that held the remains of an old smashed up fax machine. Everything was covered in a thick layer of dust and gloom.

'This place smells lovely,' he muttered.

'Pissdamp,' said Walker, moving to stand beside Jordan. 'Place has been shut a long time. Time and tramps take their toll.' A sudden scratching sound made them jump and they caught the bright red eyes of a large rat that darted behind an old busted up wooden palette.

'Oh fuck!' shouted Jordan, his voice rising. 'Did you see that? I fucking hate rats. Fucking hate 'em. Bastard things have got the plague.'

'Don't you like them then?' Walker asked, unfazed.

'No I bloody don't, son. And don't you go telling anyone. Understand?' Walker nodded. They both knew he would. They moved forward a few feet until their torches picked out an old service elevator. Neither felt the slightest inclination to try it. With Jordan in the lead, they began the hazardous climb up the old rusted metal stairs to the fourth floor, the climb made even more unsafe because of his insistence on looking back and down for rats.

By the time they reached the fourth floor, Walker had overtaken Jordan. In front of them a heavy wooden door rose up before the beam of the Mags. 'Shit, the bloody padlock's still on,' Walker said. 'I thought the night watchman had been told to get it off?'

'Yep. He was supposed to,' Jordan took a handkerchief from his jeans pocket and wiped his sweaty face. 'But I can't blame him for not doing it. This place is a death trap.'

Walker pressed his shoulder against it. 'I reckon a few good kicks should see it off.'

'Well good luck with that, son. I can't help you for a minute or two. My old legs are wobblier than a plate of jelly on big Nell's big old nellies.' Breathing heavily, he put his torch face down on the ground leaving him in virtual darkness before lowering his big carcass heavily onto the top step. 'Gimme a minute. We're not in a rush.'

'I am,' Walker said. The sudden crash of his foot against the wood reverberated loudly around the empty stairwell, causing Jordan to jump.

'Fuck me blind!' he shouted, turning and knocking over his torch. The light went out. 'What the fuck's wrong with you? I nearly shit meself, for Chrissakes.' He scrabbled around in the dark for his fallen Maglite.

Ignoring him, Walker kicked the door again and again until it cracked and flew inwards. 'We're in. Thanks for the help.'

They found themselves in a vast empty space that years ago had housed fifty staff, including three management, two tea-ladies and a ragged old street mongrel that wandered in one day and never departed. In the shadows off to their left they made out a couple of large, rusty, old textile machines and a few tipped-over chairs. Running alongside the textile machines was a big old-fashioned conveyor belt that, if it were in use today, would give any modern day health and safety inspector chest pains. Ahead of them they could just make out a large set of windows hidden behind a couple of decades' worth of dust and dirt. Picking their way carefully over the scattered bits and pieces, they pitched up by one of the windows.

Walker pressed himself sideways-on against the wall and peered out into the street below, checking that the view was clear and unobstructed. Satisfied, he dropped the heavy kit bag with a grunt. He then pulled out two radios, a mobile phone, a pair of binoculars, two tin cups and a flask containing not tea but Irish whiskey. He set everything out neatly on the floor in front of him and began carrying out signal checks on the radios. Satisfied that the two-ways were sending and receiving clearly, he poured two cups and handed one to Jordan.

Jordan sniffed. 'Cheers, son. This, I'm gonna need.' He necked it straight down.

* * *

'Will! Come here quick!' With the binoculars pressed firmly to his face, Johnny Clocks beckoned urgently to DC Will Rodgers. With a slight stagger, the young detective shot up out of the chair that had been his resting place for the last two hours and moved to the window. Clocks handed the binoculars over and pulled him in tight to where he was standing. 'There,' he said, and pointed over Rodgers's shoulder down toward the front door of Hedonism.

'What am I looking for?' Rodgers slurred.

'The fucking tits on that little Doris down there, son!'

'Oh for Chrissakes, Timex. I thought it was something important.' Rodgers had been in the middle of a pleasant dream involving horse racing and Ascot women in big hats. He clamped the binoculars to his face and swung them in the direction of the nightclub doorway.

'How is that not important?' Clocks stared at his younger colleague.

'Good God!' said Rodgers. He stared down both barrels of the binoculars and let out a small whistle.

Alone and slightly inebriated, Chrissie Brown tottered in the general direction of the kerb, half bending, half hopping, trying to recover one of her white stilettos. Two heavyset doormen watched her with a mixture of slight concern and a lot of disdain. They had seen too many girls like Chrissie to be overly distracted by her, big tits or not. The two detectives ogling her from a third-floor window of an office opposite had not had that luxury, and weren't going to waste the opportunity. Clocks grabbed for the binoculars but Rodgers elbowed him off.

After a short scuffle, Rodgers pushed the binoculars back into his eyes and swung them wildly around, searching for Chrissie again. 'Wait! Get off a minute!' His voice took on a sudden urgent tone. 'Grab the radio. We've got ourselves a visitor.'

* * *

Dave Jordan stared out into the street below. He'd lost count of the number of windows he'd looked out of since joining the Met. Must run in the hundreds easily. The glossy recruitment leaflets and re-runs of *The Sweeney* on TV portrayed life in the police, and in particular the CID, as glamorous and exciting. As a young man, fresh out of Hendon police training school, Jordan had set his sights firmly on joining the CID, where the action was, the real policing. He could see it mapped out in front of him. After the mandatory two years in uniform it was the fast lane for him. Flash suits, fast cars, fast women and big villains. When he finally got to join the CID, it was somewhat of a disappointment to find it was T shirts and jeans, Vauxhall Cavaliers and the odd police groupie. However, it was a good solid grounding and Jordan learned fast. He had blossomed into a very savvy detective with an instinct that was second to none. In his time, he had put away some of the biggest villains in London. He figured one out of four wasn't bad.

Johnny Clocks's tinny voice came over the radio. It sounded urgent. 'All units stand by. We have a possible. Male, IC1, mid-twenties, early thirties. Could be our man, although the hair's different. He's just picked up a very drunk girl from outside our venue and he's half-pulling half-helping her along the pavement. She's dressed like a tom.' Every police officer on the operation bucked up, hoping that this was what they were waiting for. Johnny Clocks was a lot of things, but a time waster wasn't one of them.

Paterson broke in. 'OP4 from Gold, why do you suspect?'

'Nothing concrete, guv,' Clocks came back. 'It looks like our suspect. She's a tom, there's an alley. Who knows?'

Paterson looked across at Roy Carr, beside him in the driver's seat. He shrugged.

'How do you know she's a prostitute?' Carr said into his radio.

'I don't. But then, how do we know she's not?' Clocks shot back. The two senior officers nodded. It was a fair point.

'Can you see him clearly? Can you positively identify him as our target?' Paterson said.

'No, sir. Not from here. I'm looking from up above him and I can't see clearly. Light's pretty shitty too.'

'Could be a chancer,' said Paterson, and clicked the transmit button. 'Seen a half dressed, pissed-up girl in the street and figures he's in for a quick knee trembler. In and out, home she goes and nobody knows.'

'Charming, sir. Thank you for that.' WDC Jean Winter, tucked away in her observation point, wasn't impressed.

'Sorry, Jean,' said Paterson, shamed by his own words. He recovered quickly. 'I need a positive ID before we move on this. DS Clocks, can you or can you not give me a positive ID?'

The radio went silent for a moment as it dawned on Johnny Clocks that Paterson was passing the buck to him. If he called a positive ID and it turned out to be wrong, it was his arse on the line. 'No, sir, I can't confirm from here,' he said after a few seconds. Paterson shifted uncomfortably in his seat and rubbed his face and eyes with both hands.

'Standby,' said Clocks with a renewed urgency. 'A cab's just pulled up in front of the two of 'em.' He paused. 'He's putting her inside and getting in with her. Standby.' Several seconds ticked by. 'They're off!' said Clocks. 'Cab's pulling off towards Tower Bridge. Your call now, guv,' he said, passing the buck right back where it belonged.

DCI Carr turned on the ignition, and the Rover's V8 engine growled into life. He hoisted the radio to his face ready to give the order to move in, when Paterson pulled it away. 'Wait,' said Paterson. 'We're not going anywhere.' His voice was flat, emotionless.

Carr stared at him. 'What? Sir, we have to move in.'

'Turn the car off.' Paterson lifted the radio and spoke. 'All units. We do not, I repeat, do not have positive confirmation on DS Clocks's suspect. Without positive confirmation we hold our position.'

'Sir, for Chrissakes, at least send a bike to follow him, see what he gets up to. You can't just let it go.'

Paterson, his stomach churning, stared straight ahead and took a deep breath. He turned slowly to face the expectant DCI Carr. 'We can't confirm that this man is Anthony Pullman, and I can't afford to send officers on the off-chance. We hold.' Carr shook his head in disgust, got out of the car and slammed the door. Paterson said a silent prayer.

* * *

Johnny Clocks, stuck in the OP point, lost the plot. 'What a fucking idiot! The fucking dopey prick!' he shouted, stamping like a petulant little boy who's had his toys taken away.

Clocks took an almighty kick at a metal waste bin, launching it across the room where it landed with a clatter a bit too close for comfort to the glass fronted door of his OP.

'What's the matter with this man? How the fuck did he become a copper? The useless no good tosser.'

Will Rodgers had seen him like this before and knew better than to contradict him. 'I'm with you. I don't agree with it, but he's made his call.'

'Yeah, yeah, you're right, Will, you're right. He's made his call. He's made his fuckin' call.' Clocks turned toward him, his face contorted and red. 'Tell you what. If it turns out this guy does kill her and cuts her to fuckin' pieces like the last two,' he jabbed the air a few times, emphasising his point, '*you* can pop round to her mum and dad in the morning and tell 'em to nip down the morgue to identify what's left of their daughter, if they wouldn't mind.'

Rodgers tensed himself up, half expecting Clocks to lash out. He'd done it before when he was pissed off, and he was *seriously* pissed off now.

'Tell 'em we had a fucking good suspect but our idiot of a senior officer couldn't make a decision, so we all sat on our fuckin' arses and did fuck all. That ought to impress them.' The steam suddenly went out of him. He stomped toward the door and opened it, looked back at his ashen colleague. He breathed deeply.

Calmly, with more than a hint of derision in his voice, Clocks said, 'And if it turns out he cuts her cunt out like he did the other two, tell 'em we've got a spare one sitting in a car and pretending to be a fuckin' policeman. They can bury her with that useless one of ours.' Clocks's fist slammed through the glass panel and he stormed off, leaving Rodgers wondering if his sergeant wouldn't perhaps benefit from some sort of counselling.

* * *

'Should've gone after them,' said Walker. He turned away and peered down into the street below. The bouncers were milling around under the neon sign above the entrance, waiting for the waifs and strays to arrive from other, smaller clubs.

'Nah,' said Jordan. 'I reckon the guv's right about this one.' He joined Walker at the window.

'What makes you say that? It was the only thing worth looking at all night.'

Jordan looked at him. 'So far.'

'What's the problem, skip?' Walker said. 'Is there something you're not telling me? Something I need to know about?' Walker stared at Jordan's profile, waiting for an answer. Saying nothing, Jordan watched a small crowd of happy drunks heading toward the nightclub. He wondered if they'd be let in.

'Time to go?' Jordan said.

Walker peered at his watch in the half light. 'Do what?'

Jordan sighed and rubbed his face. 'I said, "Time to go." Is it time? For you to go now?'

For a moment or two, Walker was unsure how to react. 'Fuck are you talking about now? I was checking my watch. I'm bored. I wanted to know the time. What's wrong with that, for fuckssake?'

'Nothing, Adam. I just got the feeling you need to be somewhere else, that's all.'

'Well, I don't. I'm bored. This is all for nothing apparently.'

'I'm sure it is,' said Jordan, wearily. He turned his gaze back to the window. He spoke indifferently, sounding almost bored. 'I'm close to cracking it, son. Little bit of the puzzle missing still, but I'm nearly there. I know you're keen to be getting off but give me a couple of minutes. I want to tell you a story.'

Walker said nothing.

'Need to bounce this off of someone. You're a clever lad, and I figure you'll be likely to tell me where I'm going wrong with it. Would you do that for me?' No answer. Jordan gave a shrug. 'So, I got talking to Reichenbach. He's a bit of an odd bod but it turns out he knows his onions. I gave him a bit of a theory I was working up, and he actually said he was thinking along the same lines but needed a lot more to substantiate his idea. Showed me his notes too. We were definitely along the same lines. Anyway, I needed to do a bit of off the grid thinking, so I went to a private detective and gave him my thoughts and notes and asked him to do some digging for me on the hurry up . . .'

'A private detective?' Walker sounded perplexed. 'Why do you need a private detective? I don't understand.'

Jordan shifted his body slightly. The brickwork digging into his arm was beginning to make him uncomfortable. 'I didn't want *anybody* knowing what I was up to until I could firm things up a bit. You know me. I likes me evidence.' He gave Walker a broad smile, then turned back to the window.

Walker began to feel annoyed and slightly nervous. 'What you got then?'

'Well, as it turns out I think I've got it figured. Just something else I need to do to ensure I'm right.' Jordan never moved, never turned to face him. Didn't see much point.

Walker stiffened slightly, checked himself, shrugged. 'What are you fucking talking about? You're seriously pissing me off, skip. Seriously.' He began moving about, unsure of what to do.

'I'll tell you, cause you're gonna do me a favour,' said Jordan.

* * *

Walker finished up and stepped back to admire his handiwork. Not his best of course, but it had gone quite well considering he was under pressure for time. He knew he'd have to run now. Knew it as soon as that fat bastard started yapping at him. He wiped the sweat from his forehead with the back of his hand, mindful of the scalpel he still held onto, and peered out through the window in case police were coming. Bouncers, punters, but no police.

Adam Walker didn't believe in luck or God. Both of them had fucked off the day he was born, but tonight they both showed up like a couple of repentant runaway dads, and brought him the mother of all presents to make up for treating him like shit. Anthony Pullman was standing right in front of his observation point with a girl and a much-needed gift — time.

CHAPTER NINE

Paterson sat quietly in the dark of his car, humming tunelessly to himself as he watched the rain roll in rivulets down his windscreen. In the amber light of the street lamps they looked like tiny golden streams. A quick glance in the rear-view mirror showed him DCI Carr leaning on the back of the car, looking up at the sky and pulling a smoke out of its packet. He'd pissed him off big-time. Until two minutes ago, Paterson had never experienced the head-splitting, gut-wrenching on-the-spot pressure of making a life or death decision. This must be what it's like for soldiers on the battlefield, he thought. Christ, no wonder they went crackers after a while. But he had made his choice. Pullman was the target, Pullman it would be. No deviation and no loss of manpower. But supposing he was wrong? He shook his head and tried to think of something else, anything — football, the upcoming commanders board he was due to sit, Lisa. His mind settled on Lisa.

Their wedding day. That had been a good day. Good turnout. Packed with old friends, celebrities, family, press. Teetering on the brink of a divorce after just seven years of marriage came as a bit of a shocker. It certainly hadn't figured in his life plan. He wondered who'd been the first to go over the side with another partner. In his heart, he knew it was him. In his ignorance and arrogance, he never imagined that Lisa would cheat on him but, in the heat of one of their many rows, she gave it to him with both barrels. Her ferocious confession stopped him dead in his tracks. She just smiled at him, a tight smile loaded with contempt, anger and hurt. Of the three men she'd slept with since they married, she was about to leave him for the last one, the dickhead lawyer. He never found out who the other two were, she wouldn't tell, and in truth, it didn't really matter. It was all over now bar the screaming and they both knew it. She'd moved on, so all that was left was to divvy up the assets and get on with his own life.

* * *

The sudden urgent squawk of Walker's voice over the radio broke into Paterson's trance. 'Gold One, Gold One. Suspect has arrived on scene. I have eyes on suspect. He's in company with a white female, late teens, early twenties.'

'Can you confirm it's our man?' Paterson said.

'Affirmative. DS Jordan also has full eyes on and confirms.'

Paterson barked into the radio. 'Are they static?'

'Negative. They're just on the move, on foot toward Bethel Street. He's just patted his breast pocket. Believe he's tooled up. Trojans will need deployment. Silent approach. No two-tones.'

Carr jumped back in the car, radio in hand. 'DC Walker. Where's DS Jordan?'

Walker looked over at Jordan, flat out, face up, cut up, and grinned to himself. 'I'm relaying, sir. DS Jordan's changed his position.'

* * *

Inspector Kingston gunned the first of the two V8 BMWs through the traffic on Tooley Street, weaving in and out of the traffic toward Bethel Street, the shops and office blocks a multi-coloured blur. Rain battered his windscreen and he scanned the road ahead. The last thing he needed was some pissed-up pedestrian dancing in the street and spoiling his night. His radio operator and the two in the back were silent, busy pulling on the checked baseball caps that branded them as police marksmen.

Kingston peered into the maelstrom of brilliant spots of light, smeared in arced blocks by the periodic sweep of the greasy windscreen wipers. Tap dancing between gas and brake, he raced the BMW through the streams of traffic, dodging in and out, narrowly missing passed and oncoming cars and terrifying the life out of the wide-eyed unfortunates who fleetingly found themselves facing a head-on with an enormous, fast moving machine. In the slipstream behind him, car number two stayed tight on his tail, mirroring Kingston's twists and turns move for move.

They pulled silently to a halt one street away from their target, and all eight decamped their vehicles and hit the ground running. Moving in a dark blur, their Heckler machine guns pushed against their shoulders, barrels raised, they responded instantly to Kingston's sharp hand signals. Four broke away and crossed the road, moving in the shadows of the building line.

High above, the rhythmic thump of India 99, the police helicopter's rotors, grew louder as it drew closer. Ahead, Kingston recognised DC Ronnie Baker, flattened against the corner of a building and peeking into Bethel Street every couple of seconds. He made a break toward Kingston. 'They're about two hundred yards in,' he whispered, high with excitement. 'On the right, stairwell entrance to a block of flats. The lights are out.' Kingston nodded and with snapped hand commands to his team, he stepped forward into Bethel Street. Crouching now, they pushed forward on their haunches, their weapons pulled tight to their faces.

'Fucking bitch! Do as you're fucking told!' Out of the darkness, his voice rang out, echoing slightly off of the glazed brickwork in the stairwell.

The sudden loud crack of a slap caused Kingston to thrust his hand forward. 'GO, GO, GO!' The street suddenly lit up in a nuclear flash as India 99 snapped on its dragon light. Instantly, night became day. They saw him now. He stood with his back to them, big and powerful. White shirt, black trousers, short dark hair. Screams of 'Armed police!' broke the silence of the street as two of the team rushed the stairwell. Kingston moved dead centre to give himself a clear shot if needed.

'You! Hands out to the side. Do it! Do it now!' he barked. With his back still toward them, the man very slowly and deliberately raised his hands. Kingston saw the girl lying on the floor, struggling to get up. Her skirt was up high around her hips. *No blood,* he thought. *Good sign.* Within seconds the man was dragged unceremoniously out of the stairwell by the scruff of his neck and slung face down. His head hit the pavement hard and bounced a couple of times before settling into a puddle like a discarded paper cup. His hands were pulled roughly across his back, plasticuffs applied and pulled tight. He never made a sound. A quick body search came up empty.

* * *

Paterson pushed past the two armed officers at the entrance to the street and ran toward Kingston and his prisoner. 'Turn him over,' he said. Kingston gestured to his boys and they flipped him over into the merciless glare of 99's dragon light. Paterson took a first good look at his fugitive. His face was set, expressionless and unmoving but his eyes locked on hard to Paterson. Blood bubbled around his mouth and mingled with the rainfall.

'Has he been searched yet?' he said.

‘Only for weapons, sir. None found,’ said the officer who’d thrown him to the floor.

Paterson crouched down and began to pat the man down. ‘Calm down, mate,’ he said. ‘It’s over now. Don’t even think about resisting. It really won’t go your way.’ He put his hand into the man’s coat pocket and pulled out a wallet. He stood and began checking the contents — roughly six hundred in notes, a half used book of stamps, a couple of petrol receipts, two sealed condoms and a driving licence. Paterson angled the licence to read the details. ‘Anthony Robert Pullman,’ he said. ‘You’re fucking nicked.’

* * *

Interview room two was bad, but number three was a karzi. The room hadn’t seen a painter and decorator for at least ten years. The harsh overhead strip lights picked out the stains on the grimy beige walls and highlighted the upturned corners of the shabby, greenish carpet tiles. A small window framed in metal looked directly at the opposite building, which reflected back a depressing flat light. The scent of stale tobacco and desperation hung in the air and added to the atmosphere of claustrophobia.

Protocol dictates that two experienced DCs should carry out an interview, the theory being that interviewing prisoners was their bread and butter work so they were more proficient than a deskbound detective superintendent. But, heavily under the gun and feeling it, Paterson wanted to be a part of this, to be the one who stopped this crazy bastard.

He was busy re-acquainting himself with Anthony Pullman’s previous. The docket contained a number of photographs, mostly mug shots of Pullman and a few shaky black and whites taken covertly through someone’s grimy lace curtains, plus a computer printout of his previous convictions and a typed A4 sheet.

An enforcer for some of the local 'faces,' Pullman had shown an English football fan's propensity for mindless violence, until he was finally arrested after a longstanding girlfriend committed the cardinal sin of burning one of his Sunday roast Yorkshire puddings. Normally, she would have received a backhander but on that day he treated her to a feel of his Stanley knife across the back of her neck as she ran for cover when his rage erupted. Once was bad enough, but after she went down he kept on slashing her until her back looked like it had been through an egg slicer. Five years for that. Out in eighteen months for good behaviour. The good behaviour bit surprised Paterson.

He stopped reading when Roy Carr ripped open the cellophane around a blank DVD and popped it into the PaceNet recorder bolted to the scarred Formica topped desk. Once he was ready, he hit the REC button.

Pullman, still handcuffed behind his back, sat quietly as Paterson and Carr formally introduced themselves to the duty solicitor, a small Asian man by the name of Ashok Patel. He was a thin, slightly built man with a few nervous tics going on. It didn't take a Freud to work out that Patel was the kid who got bullied at school for being too clever for his own good.

He'd done well, though. A sharply tailored grey suit — Gieves & Hawkes, Paterson noted — fitted beautifully but the offensively bright yellow tie that matched his cotton socks, told him that Patel hadn't made it good enough. Patel tapped at the nose piece of his thick black-rimmed glasses and ran his hand over his thinning hair. He took out a notepad and gold-nibbed Parker fountain pen from his attaché case and lined them up neatly on the table. The attaché case went behind his chair.

Introductions and formalities out of the way, Paterson went straight into the offensive. 'Anthony Pullman. You were arrested tonight because we have reason to believe that you have been involved in the murders of two girls, prostitutes. What can you tell me about them?'

Pullman cocked his head like an inquisitive dog. 'Nothing,' he deadpanned. His voice was deep and gravelly.

'I have evidence to suggest that you—'

'No, you don't.'

'Er . . . yes we do, Mr Pullma—'

'You have fuck all evidence and we both know that. My solicitor here has advised me to make no reply at this moment but having thought about it, fuck that.' Ashok Patel nearly fell off of his rickety wooden chair. Paterson gave a lop-sided grin. This could be interesting.

'I didn't do those girls, and you two fuckers ain't puttin' me in the frame for it.' He shook his head. 'I have my moments, as I'm sure you know. You know I use a knife, but this ain't down to me. Way out of my league. This fucker though, that one's up there with the gods.' Carr frowned.

'I want to talk to you about your whereabouts on the nights of—'

'What's your name again?'

'Paterson. Detective Superintendent Paterson.'

Pullman grinned. 'Fuck me! A superintendent. And you just out of shorts.' He looked across at Carr, nodded back at Paterson. 'The Old Bill running out of grown-ups these days, is it, mate?'

'Mr Pullman.' Paterson was growing agitated. 'I want to ask you abo—'

Pullman stared directly at him. 'Listen to me, son. You can fucking drag me up to dance with you, but don't think for one minute you're gonna get to fuck me on the way home. Now, I'm tired of all this bollocks. Good luck trying to load it on me but I'll have a dozen witnesses that will say I was upstairs collecting fares for both of those girls. Now, I ain't saying no more, so either charge me or let me go. We're done.'

Paterson blinked a few times, and half balled one of his fists. Pullman saw it, and pushed his chin forward, daring him to take a pop. A few quid in compensation would come in handy. A sharp knock on the door cracked the tension and all four heads swivelled toward it.

Carr scraped his chair backward, snicking a leg on one of the upturned carpet tiles which caused him to struggle to lift himself up. As he wrenched the door half open and thrust his head into the gap, Paterson explained the interruption for the benefit of the recorder and any potential future barristers who would jump on an unexplained happening. Might even use it as a technicality for their boy.

Ready to fire off an angry 'What the fuck?' DCI Carr stopped short at the sight of Johnny Clocks's ashen face staring back at him. 'Guv'nor. We've got another girl. It's not him. It's not him.' Johnny Clocks was never the diplomat and his news, just loud enough, squeezed its way past Carr and into the interview room, where it landed happily on two sets of ears. Paterson closed his eyes.

'Fucking told you, didn't I?' said Pullman.

'I believe that concludes the interview, Mr Paterson,' said Ashok Patel. He reached behind for his case, stood up and smoothed out his suit. 'I expect my client to be released immediately.'

'If you would, sonny.' Pullman turned his chair round, offering his handcuffed wrists. 'Quick as you like, there's a good lad. I've got a busy night planned.'

Paterson looked at Roy Carr's back and prayed to a god he didn't believe in that it had all been a bit of a mix-up. Even he knew life wasn't *that* good to him. Anger, frustration, fear and helplessness all exploded in his brain. The feeling lasted just long enough to block out common sense and cause him to suddenly backhand Pullman.

The blow sent the big man flying sideways and drew blood from the side of his mouth. Paterson began to scramble frantically over the desk to get to him. If Pullman was walking, then he'd make sure the cocky bastard, now wriggling furiously to get up and get his hands free, was walking with a limp at the very least. Patel dropped his briefcase and scuttled as far away as he could get.

Enraged, Pullman began banging his body onto the floor, trying to smash the chair. Roy Carr spun back from the door and slapped the alarm strip. Johnny Clocks pushed past him, launched himself into the room, and dragged the screaming and kicking Paterson off of the downed man. Clocks pulled at his collar, spun him around hard and smashed his face into the wall. Paterson's nose exploded, smearing the grimy walls with a fresh trail of blood. He fell to the floor, dazed. Pullman kept kicking and screaming obscenities until Billy Kingston showed up and punched him off to sleep. Mr Patel, cowering in the corner, looked up at the CCTV camera where the little red light blinked away Paterson's career.

* * *

Roy Carr sat on a bright orange plastic chair in an unusually quiet A&E department at Guy's Hospital, and looked across at Paterson. He shook his head. Paterson, jacket ripped, shirt untucked, pressed a blood-soaked handkerchief against his tender nose. His head was thumping, and he squinted to keep out the harsh glare of the overhead lights. He fumbled in his pockets for his Ray-Bans but remembered they were in the Aston. He tapped his foot impatiently and made a show of looking at his watch. 'Roy,' he said, 'what's your opinion of Pullman?'

Carr sniffed. 'He's a first class piece of shit.'

'Yeah, he is,' said Paterson.

'He's one wicked woman-hating, low-life scum-bucket.' Carr nodded. Paterson nodded too. 'But he had nothing to do with those two girls, Ray. Nothing.'

They sat in silence for a moment. Paterson pulled the bloodied handkerchief away from his nose and wriggled it a bit to see if any more blood dribbled out. It didn't. 'Listen, I'm sorry for what happened back there, I really am. I just fucking lost it. I'm so stressed it's untrue.'

Carr snorted. 'We're all bloody stressed. You should know better, sir. The bastard wound you up and you bit down like a like a fat man in a chip shop.' He shook his head. 'Bloody amateurish. We'll all get dragged through the shit now because you had a temper tantrum and clumped an innocent handcuffed man and, not only that, you were stupid enough to do it in front of his brief and in full view of the CCTV. Internals are going to have a field day with this, and there's nothing we can say or do to protect you. Consequences, sir.'

Paterson turned the handkerchief looking for a dry bit. Finding none, he put it back to his nose. 'Anyone heard from Dave? Is he back at the nick yet?' He spoke like he had a cold.

Carr shook his head. 'No idea. We were all too busy dragging you off of a handcuffed prisoner lying on the floor to notice.' Paterson pulled out his iPhone. No signal. No point asking Carr.

He looked towards the reception desk and spotted Rosie Brennan. She was in her late fifties, an extremely stout woman by anyone's standards, and she knew he was coming over before he did. Fifteen years working the graveyard shift on reception gives you a sixth sense. She could spot them a mile away, the ones with the 'agitates.'

Paterson got up and made his way groggily across the polished floor towards Rosie. She'd known he was police the moment he stepped through the sliding doors. Her two boys had had more than their fair share of police involvement over the years and she'd lived through the Troubles back home in Ireland. She had no love for his kind.

Paterson steadied himself with one hand on her desk. Her eyes went to the hand and then to his face. 'How can I help you, sorr,' she said, laying on the thick Irish accent.

'I'm Detective Superintendent Paterson,' he said and flashed his warrant card at her. She threw it a cursory glance. He dabbed at his nose, inspected the hankie. 'As you can see, we've had a bit of a rough night and I was wondering if I could use your phone for a moment to check on a colleague, please. I don't have a signal on the mobile. It's urgent.'

She eyed him up and down and issued a sharp, 'No.'

'Excuse me?' he said, unsure if the blockage in his nose had travelled to his ears. 'Did you say no?'

'This phone is for emergencies only. You don't look as though you're an emergency.'

'I'm sure I said that it was urgent.' He clocked her name badge hanging sideways-on her blouse. 'And in police speak, that means emergency, Rosie.'

'Well, in hospital speak, Officer, it does not. This phone is for emergency calls coming in to me, not going out. I need to keep the line clear.'

Feeling his anger rise again, Paterson checked himself, took a deep breath and decided that there was nothing to be gained by losing his temper. 'I appreciate that, I really do, but I won't be more than about thirty seconds, I promise.'

'Uh, uh,' she said, and wagged a finger at him. 'Could be that someone calls, and if I miss it that someone could die.'

'Rosie, old girl,' he said as he reached over the top of the desk to take the phone, 'that ship's already sailed tonight, take my word for it. Now I'm going to use your phone whether you like it or not. If you have a problem with that, I don't give a fuck.' He picked up the phone.

Carr was on his feet and making his way over. 'Sir!' he shouted. 'Pack it in. You're in enough trouble as it is.'

Rosie, pleased to see trouble in the ranks, took advantage of her opportunity. 'You're a very rude man. You can't swear at me. I'm going to report you to your seniors.'

Paterson had the phone between his ear and shoulder and was busy dialling the station. 'It's alright, Roy,' he waved his free hand at him. 'I've got it.' He threw Rosie a wink. 'Sorry, love. I didn't mean to be rude but honestly, you're being a stroppy bitch right now and I really don't have time to play around with you. If you want to complain, feel free.'

Roy Carr closed his eyes and shook his head in despair.

As Carr tried his best to placate the irate Rosie, he half heard Paterson's side of the conversation. He sounded concerned.

Paterson put the phone back on the cradle and turned to his DCI. 'No one's heard from Dave. He's not shown up at the nick. Neither has Adam. Not answering their radios either.' He looked worried.

'Anyone gone to the OP, to see if they're there?' said Carr.

Squaring her phone up on her desk, Rosie chimed in, 'I'm still going to report him, he can't ta—'

'Oh will you shut the fuck up, woman!' Carr rounded on her. 'Just shut up!' He spun back to Paterson, who was already running out of the door and into the rain.

CHAPTER TEN

Billy Kingston karate chopped the air in a sign for his team to enter the warehouse. Checking the main doorway, they stepped inside, moving fast and precise. Up the stairs, one to the left, one to the right, alternating and covering each other's ascent. Text-book entry. The night vision goggles they wore bathed their world in an eerie electronic green light as they worked their way through the abandoned warehouse, floor by floor.

Picking their way over bits of old debris, abandoned office furniture and holes in the floor they made their way up to the last known position of Jordan and Walker. Paterson had sounded distressed when he called Kingston and ordered them into the warehouse to find the two men. It had been over three hours since Anthony Pullman was taken into custody, and no one had seen or heard from either officer since then. Something was definitely wrong. Johnny Clocks reckoned there was nothing to worry about. They'd probably gone for a beer in the Tap, a local pub that did many an after-hours lock-in for the boys in blue. Paterson wasn't having it. Dave Jordan was a bit of a wide boy and liked a beer, but for him not to report in one way or another wasn't right. Not his game. Neither of the two was that neglectful. Paterson wanted it checked out.

Two uniforms were sent to the Tap and spoke to Liam, the landlord. Liam was a short, stout Irishman with the pallor of a hardened drinker, and the breath and the eyes to go with it. Paterson's concern turned to panic when O'Toole told them that the pub really had closed at eleven o'clock as it should, and that he hadn't seen either officer.

When the call came in, Inspector Kingston and his boys were back in the canteen having a well-earned rest and just about to stand down for the night. Tired as they all were, they moved themselves, pulling on body armour and weapons on the fly. The cars screamed out of the yard of Tower Bridge police station, blues and twos on full, racing toward the abandoned warehouse they were now searching.

Ahead of them, the glow from the faint street lights caused a slight flaring in their goggles. All of them looked toward the windows at the far end of the room. For a second Kingston considered removing his goggles and allowing his eyes to adjust to the gloom before advancing further. He abandoned the idea.

Kingston could see in the distance a small corner office. He signalled for two of his team to advance on it, and for the remaining five officers to fan out and move in a line toward the windows. Kingston silently cursed at the noise of their boots on the debris scattered on the floor. Any hope of a silent approach was long gone.

Kingston now made out a shape underneath the middle window. He brought his arm up sharply and his team stopped dead in their tracks. Breathing heavily, he squinted, trying to make out the shape through the flares obstructing his view. The goggles couldn't handle the contrast between the half-light and shadows and he failed to make out any detail. He signalled again and they moved forward, still in line. About fifteen feet away from it,

Kingston finally made out the shape. It was a man. Lying on his back, stomach sticking up in the air. He didn't need to see the face. It was Jordan. He ripped off his goggles and shouted, 'Flare!'

His team snatched their glasses off as Kingston pulled out a magnesium flare. A jet of brilliant blue white light shot out as the flare roared into life. He rolled it toward Jordan and watched the little sparks bounce and jump off the concrete floor until it came to a halt, some three feet away from him. One of the team let out an involuntary, 'Oh, fuck me!'

In the harsh flickering light of the flare, Jordan lay staring up at the ceiling, his face locked into a wide rictus grin. It took a few seconds for Kingston to realise his eyelids had been sliced clean off and that his mouth had been carved from the corners all the way up to his ears. His nose and teeth were broken and his face was bathed in blood. Carved into his chest was a single word: 'What.'

Billy Kingston had seen serious violence before, he'd been responsible for a fair bit of it too, but this was just too far. Rage and fear rose up inside him, and he made himself a promise there and then that if he was ever lucky enough to come up against the fucker that did this, he would shoot him straight in the face and dump his body in the Thames.

Kingston forced himself to kneel by Jordan, and he looked at his gut for any sign of movement. In the dying, spitting light of the flare, he thought he saw a slight twitch and barked, 'Ambulance now!' SCO19 officers were trained in battlefield first aid but this was way outside his competence.

The sound of running feet made him look up, and he saw the two officers he'd sent to check on the office. He'd completely forgotten about them. *Dangerous.* As the flare coughed and died, someone took up the baton and re-lit the scene. Kingston saw one of the two carrying what looked like a coat and the other was holding out a small evidence bag. Kingston stood up and as he did so both men caught sight of Jordan.

'Ohjesusgodalmighty, what the fucking hell is that?'

His jaw tight, Kingston spat out, 'That,' he pointed to Jordan, 'is a man. A policeman. One of us. Don't ever say "that" again, you understand?'

'Sorry, guv. Caught me off guard. I'm sorry.'

Kingston gave a nod. 'What have you got there?'

'It's a coat, a jacket. Looks new. In good condition, no dust or damp on it so I'm guessing it belongs to the other one. Didn't find him but,' he looked over at his colleague, 'this was in one of the pockets.'

Kingston peered into the bag and let out a half whispered, 'Shit.' He was looking at a cleanly sliced off little finger.

In the distance an ambulance siren wailed its way toward them.

* * *

Girl number three. They'd got the call to attend the scene on their way to the warehouse and diverted across. DCI Carr was making himself busy outside, gleaning what few facts were known from the uniforms on scene.

Paterson stared at the saturated body of the girl. Twenty years of age, couldn't be much more. Her hair looked to be blonde but it was difficult to be sure caked in all that blood. A small pearl earring still attached to her severed lobe floated in the pool of congealing blood by her head. Her eyes were wide open, staring blankly up at the canvas of the white tent that had been hastily thrown up around her. Evidence needed to be preserved as much as her dignity. A rictus grin of horror and those glass eyes told him that she had been awake when her throat suddenly opened up. He knew that, for a few seconds at least, she would have witnessed her blood spew out of her. He wondered what that must be like, to see your own blood pump rhythmically out of your body. To know that you were about to die and there wasn't a damn thing you could do to stop it. He ran his eyes over her body. He hoped that death had done the decent thing and had been quick in coming for her. Please God she was long gone before work began.

Teresa Bailey's arms were by her side, palms up, her left leg bent at the knee while the right one, minus the expensive red stiletto lying nearby, was perfectly straight. Vagina cut out. Par for the course. But this looked different. Not so precise. Hurried. He bent down, read the word cut in to her breastbone: 'Touch.' Unable to think properly, he pulled out his notebook and flicked a few pages over. 'Isn't,' 'Don't,' and now 'Touch.' Whatever this man was saying, he couldn't make head or tail of it.

Paterson stepped outside into the driving rain. The cold night air burned his lungs and for a second he forgot about the dull ache in his nose, across his eyes. Looking up into the starless night sky, he managed to take some small comfort from the rain pounding on his face before he lurched forward and threw up. He half sat, half fell into the gutter as his legs gave up the ghost and he threw up again, more violently.

When he'd finished, he dragged himself onto the kerb and sat, feet in a deep puddle. Wiping away the thread of sticky spittle hanging from his lip, he began to sob, grateful that the rain would partly disguise his pain from the uniformed officers looking at him with curiosity and concern.

* * *

Paterson and Carr left girl number three to the forensic team, and were now outside the warehouse, pushing past the uniforms. The lights from the ambulances and police cars lit up the streets like a strange azure discotheque. Amid the swarm of emergency services people, Paterson spotted Johnny Clocks talking to Billy Kingston, and shouldered his way through the crowd to where they stood. 'How is he?' he asked.

It took Clocks a second to recognise Paterson. Nose looked broken and the eyes were beginning to swell. Did a better job than I hoped. He looked at Kingston. He can tell him.

'It's not good, sir,' said Kingston, unable to hold Paterson's gaze.

Paterson searched the man's face, and watched his mouth move, unable to fully comprehend. Billy Kingston took him through the events as best he could, and gave him the full details of the savagery inflicted on Jordan, including the word carved in his chest. He held back about Walker's coat and finger though, he'd get around to that. Something had gone badly wrong up there, but he couldn't figure it out. Roy Carr kept his eye on his boss, watched the colour drain from his cheeks and wondered just how much more the man could take. He'd seen people go under for far less.

'Will he make it?' said Paterson, his voice tired and weak. Clocks shrugged. He wished he knew.

'So where is he now?' Before either officer could answer, the sound of a loud metallic clattering behind them announced the arrival of two paramedics running out of the doorway with a metal trolley bearing Jordan's lifeless body bouncing around underneath a red blanket. A third paramedic ran alongside, holding up a bottle with a tube going somewhere into his body.

Time slowed down. *Face not covered with a sheet — good sign. He's alive.* At the back of the waiting ambulance, work continued on Jordan. Frantic work. Needles, pipes, drips.

'Where's he going to?' shouted Paterson to the paramedics. They ignored him, busy, but Clocks answered, 'Guy's. They'll take him to Guy's.' A paramedic nodded, not missing a beat.

'I'm going with him. Roy, meet me there.'

Almost as an afterthought, he said, 'Where's Adam? Who's with him?'

Kingston said, 'Before we were interrupted, guv, I was going to say there was no trace of him. We searched all over. No idea where he is, but . . .'

Paterson knew he wasn't going to be happy with where this was going. 'But what?'

'We found a little finger. Sliced right off. Left on top of a coat that we believe to be Walker's. We're guessing it's his. It's been sent for fingerprinting.'

Paterson shook his head in disbelief, turned away and seeing the paramedics were ready to leave, hauled himself into the ambulance. Looking back, he shouted, 'Find him, Timex! Whatever it takes, find him. Fast.' Paterson slid into a little seat opposite the trolley, keeping out of the way of the lone paramedic who was wiring Jordan up to various machines. Someone slammed the doors shut and the blood box, two-tones blaring, tore off towards Guy's Hospital.

'The fuck we gonna do that then?' said Clocks to no one and pulled his collar up against the rain.

* * *

Bouncing around in the ambulance, Paterson watched intently as the paramedic hurriedly peeled off the blood-soaked gauze in order to change it. He sat, transfixed, unable to pull his gaze away from Jordan's face. Mixed in with his sheer disbelief and anger was an unbidden feeling of revulsion.

Two vicious streaks of red either side of his mouth, running up his cheeks until they met his ears. It looked to Paterson like someone had sliced through a rare steak at a Harvester's and then baulked at the sight of blood. The eyes, watery and bloody and deprived of their lids, looked like two half sunk golf balls. In a moment of that dark humour that comes to all police officers, he thought that at least his friend looked happy that he wouldn't have to pay the bill. He hated himself for that thought.

Above the noise of the two-tones and the activity in the back, Paterson could just make out snippets of broken frantic radio conversation coming from the front of the ambulance. 'Crash team . . . severe lacerations . . . massive bleed . . . policeman . . . very bad way . . . not good . . .' He wondered if Jordan would live, and then he wondered if he would really want to go through life in this state. He wouldn't if it was him lying there. *Fucker's destroyed his life one way or the other.*

The paramedic worked frantically, relentlessly. Paterson winced as he pushed needles into Jordan's chest and face, guessing at both adrenaline and localised morphine to keep him going until they got to the hospital.

His thoughts turned to Walker and his mind raced with questions. *How did this mad fucker get the drop on both of these boys? Both of them are built like brick shit-houses and both of them are more than capable of holding their hands up in a fight. So how come this happens? Why did he do this to Dave? Did he know something that he hasn't shared? If he did, how would this mad bastard know about it? How did he manage to take Adam away, let alone cut off his finger? Was he dead or dying? Where the hell is he?*

And then a dark thought ran through his mind.

* * *

A crash team was waiting outside the A&E drop-off at Guy's. They ran toward the ambulance as it screeched to a halt at a right angle, and before it had settled, the back doors were wrenched open and hands grabbed frantically at the trolley. They pulled it out and dropped it down hard, where it bounced about on its little grey wheels before being twisted around and pushed at a run toward the sliding doors. A pack of agitated doctors herded alongside the trolley, all shouting instructions to each other. A night porter, seeing the commotion heading his way, stood in front of the security sensor to ensure that they didn't get delayed waiting for the doors to hiss open. Every second was precious.

Paterson ran with the pack, determined to stay with his colleague until, at the end of a long corridor, he was forcibly barred from entering the operating theatre. Flattening his head against the porthole windows, he saw three people — doctors, surgeons — same thing, dressed in scrubs and wearing masks. He watched Jordan's butchered carcass being unceremoniously hoisted from the trolley to the table to begin his next fight, and then the blind snapped shut. He thumped his head against the glass.

A small hand pulled him gently away from the window and he turned to see a young nurse, thirty years old maybe, looking directly at him, her mouth moving. Dazed and confused, he couldn't make out the words and he stared at her blankly. Among those words, he picked out, 'Coffee . . . Look after him . . . Sit down.'

Paterson allowed the nurse to lead him back along the corridor, where she sat him down, bent forwards and looked into his face. He suddenly stepped out of the fog. 'What are you doing?' he said, recoiling slightly. Out of the corner of his eye, he saw another nurse heading his way. This one looked about fifty, chunky and crammed into a uniform so tight it showed every roll of fat she possessed. She held a mug. He caught the scent of strong coffee as she closed in on him.

'You drink this,' said the first nurse. 'Then we make face batter.' He looked up at her. It is battered, he thought, then cottoned on to her accent. Polish perhaps? Didn't matter. She handed him the coffee, and for the first time in a while, he let himself breathe.

Paterson took the coffee in both hands and brought the cup to his face, breathing in the aroma. He nodded in thanks. Then, from nowhere, he began to shiver, the shock finally catching up with him. Coffee rained over the top of the mug, burning his fingers. He yelped and it was quickly taken from him. The Polish nurse laid him down on the bench and placed both her hands over his mouth, telling him to 'breed slowly, deeply.' Nurse fifty-odd hurried off to find a doctor.

Ten minutes or so later, Paterson found himself lying on a trolley behind a green, flower-patterned curtain, wrapped like a cocoon in a sliver foil blanket that crinkled like a bag of crisps every time he made a move. He wasn't at all sure what was going on. He'd been given an injection by a tall, elegant doctor with a greying beard and a classy accent. He was beginning to feel a bit better, though his head, eyes and cheekbones throbbed mercilessly. He figured there was some sort of painkiller in the injection and wished it would hurry up and kick in.

Roy Carr and Johnny Clocks had arrived just as they were putting him on the trolley and were now standing beside him. Carr had been told by nurse fifty-odd not to expect too much coherence from him, to the amusement of Clocks, who said, 'No fucking change there then, love.' He gave her a cheeky wink and a grin. She blushed and hurried off, beaming. Life in the old girl yet.

Paterson looked around and tried to focus on the voices, fighting the effects of what was a *very* powerful painkiller now beginning its march through his bloodstream.

'Boys,' he said, his voice thick. 'Listen to me.' He beckoned them in closer. 'Whoever did this to Dave,' Carr leaned in, Clocks followed, 'he's probably got Adam somewhere. Probably gonna kill him if he hasn't already.' Nobody disagreed. Paterson's head lolled and he fought the sleep creeping up on him. His voice thickened. He mumbled, 'Adam's wife. Check on her. I . . . have a . . . a feeling. Danger . . . Get a team over there now. Tonight. Now.'

'It's okay, sir,' said Carr. 'We have the FLOs on the way over to her now. They'll keep her informed of what's happening, stay with her until we find Adam.'

Paterson mumbled, through dry, heavy lips. Shook his head. 'No . . . not what I mea . . .' He drifted off. His head lolled back, then snapped forward, and he blinked his eyes open. 'Get me back to Dave. Take me back.'

Clocks, in a rare moment of humanity, patted his arm gently. 'Just rest, boss. Take it eas—'

Paterson snatched his arm away. 'I'm not fucking asking, Clocks! I'm telling! Get me up to Dave. Now!'

Startled by his tone and his sudden burst of lucidity both officers stood undecided, until Clocks seized a nearby wheelchair, hauled Paterson up by his lapels and dragged him off the table. Paterson landed heavily in the chair.

'C'mon, guv,' he said. He grinned to Carr. 'You heard what the big guv said. Fuck hanging round here like a bunch of lemons. We need to be with the skipper.' He extricated himself from the flowery curtain, tangled around his head, and shoved the chair forwards.

To a chorus of protests from nurses Polish and Fifty-odd, Johnny Clocks took off at speed with Paterson hanging half out of the wheelchair. Left to play catch up, Carr was sure Paterson was going to come flying out of the wheelchair at any moment. He figured that if he did, Clocks would probably run over him just for the fun of it. Weaving frantically from side to side, the wheelchair and its cargo of semi-conscious copper made its way precariously along the silent corridors, and pulled up noisily outside the operating theatre. The doors were still shut and the blinds still down.

A team of half scrubbed surgeons standing by the check-in desks looked up in surprise. Through his stupor, Paterson thought he recognised one of them from somewhere, but the memory wafted in and out as he tried to focus on the figure coming blurrily towards him. He saw the dark stains all over the front of the approaching green scrubs. Blood. That's what it was. He knew it was Jordan's. Just knew it. He began to breathe heavily again, struggling to rise against the tide of powerful meds. *Ah, no. Don't you dare. Don't you fucking dare . . .*

The doctor stopped in front of this pitiful sample of the Met's finest and delivered his message. Paterson struggled to hear. Everything was muzzy. Spinning. Then black.

* * *

Paterson was awake now. Sort of. Groggy but coming round rapidly, flat on his back on a rickety trolley and looking up at a badly painted, grubby ceiling. The harsh overhead lights hurt his eyes but his headache was easing off. He took that as a good sign. Lifting his head, he looked around until he found Roy Carr sitting in one of the hard plastic chairs, his head down and showing off a slight bald spot that Paterson hadn't noticed before. He ran a quick check of his own body, moving various parts to ensure that they still worked. Seemed to be. He gingerly touched his face. Everything was swollen and tender. All around the eyes his cheeks were swollen and he could feel the soft puffy bags that must now be a nice shade of sunset red and purple. His nose felt about a foot wide.

An image of Jordan flashed into his mind — his eyes. That face. The flashbacks came thick and fast then, the ambulance ride, the urgent rush to get him to the operating theatre, the two nurses, the doctor, the mad wheelchair trip and then the blackness that came for him. His own smacked up face was nothing in comparison, and he was engulfed in guilt for thinking about himself.

'Roy,' he called weakly. 'What's happened? Where's Dave?' Roy Carr lifted his head, his eyes watery and red, and looked over at his senior officer, tired, dishevelled, battered. Timex did a right number on him, threw him against that wall a lot harder than was necessary. Carr didn't much care. He lowered his gaze.

Paterson struggled to pull himself into a sitting position. Swinging his legs over the side of the trolley, he wondered for a moment what the doctor had given him. Whatever it was, it was damned good stuff.

'Roy,' he said again, and planted both feet on the floor. He leaned back against the trolley frame, testing his legs for stability. A bit wobbly, but not desperate. 'Where's Dave? What's going on? How long have I been out?' He started to totter toward the chairs.

Carr looked up and Paterson noticed the watery eyes. They were tired for sure but he also saw despair, desperation and hopelessness. These were tears.

Roy Carr sniffed loudly and swallowed hard. 'Sit back down, guv.'

Paterson stopped dead, as a cold rush of dread surged through his body. In the corner of his eye he saw a white coated doctor heading quickly toward him. He knew it was the doctor who had drugged him up earlier.

'Mr Paterson!' he called. 'Please lie back dow—'

Paterson wheeled around and pointed a threatening finger at him. 'Fuck off, Doc!' The venom in his voice stopped the doctor dead in his tracks. Paterson turned back to Carr. 'Talk to me, Roy. What's happened to Dave? Fucking tell me now!'

Carr looked at his battered, emotionally wrecked colleague and said softly, 'He died, sir. About an hour ago. You passed out.'

Paterson's legs gave way under him, and he clattered to the floor, knocking chairs over as he fell. The doctor was running towards him again. DCI Carr didn't move. Paterson pulled himself up just as the doctor reached him and he felt the strong hands on him. He waved him away. 'Leave me! I'm ok, I'm ok!' The doctor took a step back and hovered nearby, just in case. Awkwardly, Paterson pulled himself upright. He closed his eyes and breathed deeply, trying to centre himself before he dropped down heavily next to Carr. The doctor kept a watchful eye.

Paterson gathered his thoughts before speaking. 'Any news on Adam?'

Carr shook his head, seemingly unable to speak.

Paterson looked at him, looked away. Looked back again. 'Listen. We have to find him. Has the message gone Metwide? Has anybody informed his wife? Did you send anybody over there?'

'Yes,' Carr said. 'Walker's description and photograph has gone up to the yard for dissemination to every nick in the Met and also to surrounding forces. All CCTV units are being notified — police, traffic, council, everyone. The Yard has deployed officers to every hospital within fifty miles on the off-chance that he turns up there. We're putting heavy pressure on our snouts to give us any sightings or leads. We're sending the family liaisons over to his HA shortly to tell his missus. Poor little cow'll be devastated.'

Paterson struggled to his feet. 'We need to get back to the office. Now!' Carr just looked at him, tired, finished. 'Listen, Roy. We both know I'm not much of a policeman. I'm a flyer, on my way up the pencil-pushing ladder. Well I was, but that's gone south. Dave was the closest thing I had to a friend in this miserable bastard of a job. He looked after me and straightened me up. He had my back. I have to find out why and how this happened to him, and where the hell Adam is. We have to stop this . . . *creature* from killing again. The only thing I can do for Dave and Adam is get back, round up the troops, find out where we are and what's happening. Then we'll hunt this bastard down like the animal he is, and when he's cornered, when we've finally got him, kick the living daylights out of him until his head comes off.'

He turned to the doctor and glared at him. It was a 'you just try and stop me' look. The doctor held his hands up in surrender, and turned and walked away. He had plenty of other stuff to do.

DCI Carr shrugged. As plans went, it wasn't the best he'd ever heard, nor one he particularly wanted to hear either, but he could see the reasoning behind it.

CHAPTER ELEVEN

DCI Carr drove them through the deserted streets. Paterson got on the radio, and called the team back to the station for a briefing. He knew that by now word would have seeped through that Dave Jordan hadn't made it out of the operating room and Walker was on the missing list. Paterson gazed unseeing out of the car window as the bright lights of the shopfronts flashed past in a blur, mulling over the thought that his reputation, such as it was, now lay in tatters. What little credibility remained, had died on the table with Dave Jordan. He would carry the can for this. He was the officer in charge and a colleague, possibly two of them, died on his watch. It would follow him for the rest of his career.

The only hope was if he could somehow pull it out of the bag and capture whoever was responsible, and fast. He let out a small grunt. More chance of kissing the queen. The more he mulled over what he could piece together of the events in that warehouse, the more something niggled at him. But he couldn't voice it just yet.

* * *

The incident room was packed to capacity and buzzing as he and Carr walked in. More than a few winced at the sight of his battered face.

As they moved to take their seats, a forensics officer handed Carr a sheet of paper. He glanced at it quickly before pushing it across to Paterson. A glance. A scowl. Through painful, swollen eyes, Paterson looked around the packed room at his audience. CID, crime squads, uniforms, dog handlers, uniforms from other districts, traffic cops and even the home beats had crept out of their little hidey holes. It looked like every copper south of the water had turned up to help. Most of them had no idea who Dave Jordan was. All of them knew he was one of them. That was enough. At the back of the room, Billy Kingston sat with his team. They looked tired, dishevelled and furious. Dangerous.

To his left, in full dress uniform, Commander Kelly glared at him. It wouldn't be long before news of the night's events leaked out to the rags, and then a press conference would be the order of the day. Kelly wanted something to give them, and he didn't want to go with his arse in his hands. 'At the end of this briefing, my office, Paterson,' he hissed.

Paterson glowered back at him. 'Sir.'

'Listen in everyone!' Paterson waited a second or two for the talking to die down. 'For those of you who don't know me, I'm Detective Superintendent Paterson. This is Detective Chief Inspector Carr. I'm the officer in charge of this operation.' He paused, looking for the right words. There weren't any. 'It is my very sad duty to inform you that Detective Sergeant Dave Jordan was killed this evening in the line of duty.' A few sharp intakes of breath, lots of head shaking, fist balling.

'Dave was a good friend to me and one of the finest coppers I ever had the privilege to know. Those of you who knew him will know exactly what I'm talking about. Those of you who never knew him, you missed out. I've let him down. Badly. His death will be with me forever and I'll have to live with that. The man responsible had already butchered two young girls and sadly, a third was also found in the early hours of this morning. This girl was, we think, murdered not long before he killed DS Jordan. We await confirmation. However, the most pressing issue for us all right now is the abduction of Dave's partner, Detective Constable Adam Walker. Walker was in the OP with DS Jordan. After they failed to report in, I sent officers from SCO19 to search the OP. Unfortunately, they found DS Jordan in a critical condition and DC Walker was missing. The only trace of him was his jacket.' He paused. 'And his entire little finger. Cut off near the knuckle joint.' More gasps, more head shaking, fist balling.

DCI Carr spoke. 'The finger has been confirmed as Adam Walker's. We are working on the assumption that he is still alive and we must concentrate all of our efforts on finding him. We find him, we find our sicko.'

DS Clocks put his hand up, halfway, like a hesitant schoolboy. 'Just a thought, guv'nor,' he said, and held Paterson's gaze.

Paterson breathed deeply. This had better not be a silly game. 'Go on.'

'Well, this might sound a bit far-fetched and probably no one wants to hear it, but I've got a theory.' Heads turned expectantly. 'What if Walker hasn't been kidnapped? What if he's our boy?' That got the whole room's attention. 'What if he killed Dave and did a runner?'

Paterson stared at him. This was it. This was what was nagging in the back of his mind, but with a combination of a broken nose, a headache the size of Hong Kong and a more than healthy dose of morphine in his system he couldn't follow his own line of thought clearly.

'Why would you say that?'

'Well, he's fucking odd for starters, and Dave never trusted him. Never liked him. Felt he was a wrong un.'

'Lot of odd bods and wrong uns in this job. Doesn't make them killers. Do you have any evidence to back this up?'

Clocks shrugged. 'Not a scrap, guv, but maybe Dave did, and maybe that's why he got himself killed. Perhaps he found out something about Walker and perhaps he confronted him with it.'

'Like what? Was he looking at Walker for something? Do you know anything?'

'Nope. Nothing. But looking back, Dave always stayed a lot later than most of us and don't forget, he took off on his own a couple of times. Anybody know where he went? What he was up to?' Clocks looked around the room, at a lot of blank faces including Paterson's.

'Spent a bit of time with that Reichenbach geezer too, so maybe the pair of 'em came up with something but couldn't confirm it. You know Dave. If he couldn't back it up a hundred per cent, he wouldn't bring it to the table. He used to say to me that a hunch without proof was a waste of fucking time.'

DCI Carr scowled at him. 'This is a murder enquiry, for fuck's sake!' Commander Kelly shot him a look, not happy with this language from a senior officer in front of subordinates. Carr pressed on, undeterred. 'Surely he would have mentioned it? Told someone, wrote it down somewhere? He knows the score.'

'Anyone spun his locker or drawer yet?' said Clocks.

'Anyone?' said Paterson, looking around. Nothing. 'Clearly, it never entered anyone's head. Fuck knows we've all been a bit busy tonight. We'll do it after this.'

'If it was Walker,' said Commander Kelly, shifting around in his seat, 'why would he cut off his own finger and leave it at the scene? I don't follow.'

Clocks didn't even look at him. 'Look. If you've just killed someone and you want to get away, what's your most pressing need?' Kelly's expression was blank. So were the others.' 'Oh, come on. Someone? Anyone?'

'This isn't a damn quiz show, officer. Spit it out!' Kelly barked.

The penny finally dropped. Paterson spoke quietly, thinking as he went. 'Time. He needs time. He cut his finger off so we would think he was a victim, and he knew we'd throw everything into looking for a kidnapped copper. Misdirection.'

'There you go, guv. And where's the last place you'd go looking for a kidnap victim?' Clocks waited. Another penny had to drop somewhere in that room.

'His HA,' said Paterson. He scraped his chair back, rose out of it, moving fast.

Johnny Clocks clapped his hands together, 'Boom! There you go, guv'nor. His home. He bought himself some time to go home.'

Commander Kelly still looked confused. 'What? I don't get it. Why would he want to go home? What's there for him . . ? Oh shit!'

Good day for Johnny Clocks. He'd out-thought two people at least three pay grades above him.

'It's his wife,' said Paterson. 'He's going for her.' He began barking orders, already on the move.

'Kingston. Get your troops to Walker's house now! Rapid entry. Full assault, on my authority. Roy! Timex! With me. We're going there too. Mr Kelly, get someone to search Jordan's drawers and lockers. Get into his computer and get someone over to Peter Reichenbach's house right now. If he worked something up with Dave, he's in the shit too.'

The room emptied. Rapidly.

* * *

Peter Reichenbach woke up at three fifteen in the morning. His first thought was to wonder how Detective Sergeant Jordan was doing. Jordan's plan to accuse Walker had worried him from the moment he first listened to it. It went against not only the rules but all common sense. It was dangerous and ridiculous, he said to Jordan, that anyone should want to confront a sociopathic butcher single-handedly. They had argued the merits of his plan back and forth. Yes, he could understand the man's need to obtain solid evidence but no, he couldn't agree with his proposed method of obtaining it. He withdrew his initial threat to inform Paterson when Jordan eventually swore to him on a stack of bibles that he would do so himself at the evening's briefing. Reichenbach was a religious man, and he considered that sufficient. He just hoped to God Jordan would be true to his word.

Wide awake now, Reichenbach sat at his desk staring at the computer screen that glowed quietly in the corner. It was his only concession to the modern world, and looked out of place in his Victorian home office with its dark red flock wallpaper and the variously sized bell jars containing his collection of dead bats, exotic spiders and snakes. Heavy dark velveteen drapes kept out the sodium glow of the street outside. Facsimiles of nineteenth century newspapers littered his desk. An enormous tatty stuffed bear, with angry yellowing fangs and glass eyes, dominated the room and lent authenticity to the era he had recreated in such minute detail.

Hanging in the hallway was his most cherished possession, the self-commissioned twenty by sixteen inch oil painting of himself dressed as the most famous man who never lived — Sherlock Holmes. Complete with deer stalker, horned pipe and an oversize magnifying glass, Peter Reichenbach looked every inch the clichéd consulting detective he considered himself to be but hid from everyone outside of his bi-monthly murder mystery weekends. He sipped quietly at a glass of gin.

The sudden tinkling of the antiquated front door bell startled him. Stealing a glance at the mantelpiece clock, he knew that only the police would come calling at four-thirty in the morning. Dave Jordan had promised him he would contact him once Walker was in custody, to appraise him of the night's events. He assumed that Jordan intended to phone him, but a visit in person was much better.

Adam Walker stood outside in the porch, soaked through from the incessant rain. His hair stuck to his face and tiny rivulets of water ran down his cheeks. He wiped them away with a hand wrapped in a blood-soaked handkerchief tied in a crude knot over the stump of his missing finger. It had come off easier than he thought. Good quality precision tools were worth their weight in gold. Nevertheless, it throbbed like a bitch. Cutting off his finger bought him time, and he needed time. Killing the girl was necessary. Part of the plan, part of the message, and easily done on his way back home. Going home, punching out his wife Trish, tying her up and putting her in the boot was also necessary. Reichenbach was necessary. He had to keep him quiet, buy more time. He dropped the scalpel out of his sleeve and caught it in his hand, the blade still red from working Jordan.

As the door opened a crack, Walker slammed his shoulder against it and forced his way in, sending Peter Reichenbach crashing back against a heavy oak sideboard in the hallway. He dropped heavily to the floor with a grunt.

Walker was on him. He straddled his chest. His injured hand, pain forgotten, grabbed the lapels of Reichenbach's dressing gown and pulled the terrified man's head and shoulders off the floor. Walker pressed the blade against his cheek. Reichenbach's eyes were wide with fear, his mouth open, too frightened to make a sound.

Walker kicked the door closed behind him. 'Good evening to you, Mr Reichenbach. A pleasure to see you again. I suspect that you're not so happy to see me. Correct?' Reichenbach trembled, couldn't answer. 'Listen up. I don't have a lot of time. I'm sure you've guessed that. So, it would seem that you and fat boy worked it out, found that the dead girls are down to me. Good work. But, I need to know whether you or he told anybody else about it. Have you written it down, made a report, sent an email? Before you answer, you should know that I'm really not in the mood to be fucked around. If you lie to me, you will suffer. Do you understand? You should also know that I'm extremely good at spotting lies. Again, do you understand?'

Reichenbach's trembling had reached almost epic proportions and his eyes ran with tears. Walker pulled his face closer to his, staring, scrutinising him, enjoying his terror, smelling the fear. He ran the knife gently down the man's cheek toward his neck and rested it lightly against the carotid artery. It pumped against the tip of the blade. Walker could feel it. He fought the urge. 'Answer me.'

'No. No, sir, no one knows. I swear it, I swear, I swear . . . Jordan . . . ordered me to tell no one . . . He wasn't sure. No one knows . . . Please . . .'

Walker stared into the frightened eyes of his prey. He held him close, watched the snot dribble from his nose, filled with nothing but contempt for this cowardly man. 'I believe you,' he said, and loosened his grip. 'And for that, I thank you. Just so you know, you will not be part of the message.' He jerked Reichenbach forward and pushed the knife, up to the hilt, into his throat and twisted it like a ratchet screwdriver. He yanked it downward and opened up the throat like a side of beef. Before the blood began to spurt, Walker hopped neatly to one side and in a single movement flipped him over, face down, and dropped his full weight onto him, forcing the blood down into the carpet.

Reichenbach twitched and jumped frantically under his weight. Walker pressed him down, surprised at the effort required, at how strong he was, until less than two minutes later, Reichenbach finally gave it up. Walker wiped his blade on the back of the dead man's dressing gown, stood up and looked around the hallway. The Sherlock painting stared back at him accusingly. A grin spread across his face. Reichenbach falls. Johnny Clocks would be proud of him.

* * *

Adam Walker's house was set back off of the main road, tucked away behind a thin line of trees at the top of a small flight of steps. There was nothing to mark it out from the other thirty or so Goldstein terraced houses that lined the road, apart from being end of terrace. The quiet residential street was dead at five in the morning as Paterson dumped his car two wheels up on the pavement a couple of feet from a junction, giving him a partial view of the house.

From where he sat, craning his neck for a better view, he could just make out the top of a metal shed running along a side wall and what looked to be the top of a conservatory, both partially hidden by a small weather-worn wooden gate. It looked pretty flimsy. Squinting to get a better view, he counted five steps leading up to the street door. The house was in darkness. The blinds were down top and bottom. A sudden movement caught his eye. He started. In front of him a small urban fox jumped over a neighbouring garden wall and ran across his path carrying someone's training shoe. For a split second he had the urge to hit the horn and frighten the shit out of the little ginger rat-bastard but resisted. The fox ignored him and trotted into a garden, darted between a couple of green and brown Dalek bins, defied gravity and scaled a fence vertically before disappearing with its booty.

To the right of the house, Inspector Kingston and his team were edging their way along a large garden wall belonging to an immediate neighbour that backed on to Walker's narrow driveway at a right angle. A second team were quietly plotting up at the back and to the sides of the property, ready to catch any backdoor Johnnies. Kingston waited for them to confirm their position. He would then start the assault on the house. It troubled him that there'd been no real prep time for this, no time to look at the blueprints and get the layout of the house imprinted on his mind, and no surveillance to see if Walker had actually gone home.

He recalled a similar night shortly after he joined PT17, the old name for SCO19. Still relatively young in service, he was already showing signs of the leader instinct. They approached the door of an urban semi, where the occupants' regular Friday night domestic argument had deteriorated to the point where Kingston and his teammates were called in. The screams of the wife had brought the neighbours out just in time to see her pissed-up husband smacking her around the front lawn before dragging her by the hair, back into the house. Witnesses claimed he was waving a large kitchen knife around, threatening to 'Do the bitch.' They said he seemed 'upset.' Uniforms never had a hope of talking him out or down. Armed bastards were the order of the day.

In hindsight, he would have done things differently, but it wasn't his team, he wasn't in charge and he was still new to the job. He should have insisted. With no time for preparation, his team leader had ordered a rapid entry back and front, relying on shock and awe to 'freeze' the suspect while they brought him down.

A couple of things the assault team didn't realise was that, stressed, agitated and with a limited view in the darkness, the single witness had made a slip-up. A gun was mistaken for a knife. Nor did they know that the husband was a PTSD squaddie gone AWOL. So, no prep time. Poor witness. Gun, not knife. Head fucked soldier, not civilian. Lights were out. All in darkness. No idea what, if any, barricade was in place. Woman screaming, man shouting. Extreme sense of urgency. A bit of panic, if truth be told. All in all, a massive clusterfuck waiting to happen.

They crashed through the front door and moved along the hall into the living room, where squaddieboy was waiting for them, quite calmly. He fired twice. Double tapping they call it. Bullet one hit the assault leader in the chest, his Kevlar saving his life. Bullet two blew out the man's right hip, dropping him hard and heavy and pensioning him off right there and then. As he fell, the backup officer came into squaddieboy's sights. Dropping low, backup man returned fire with a panicked burst, hitting squaddieboy full in the upper body with seven shots from his Heckler. Dead before he hit the ground.

In the ensuing pandemonium to secure the room, they found the wife lying on her back on the floor. Severe facial lacerations and heavy bruising. Dead in a pool of rapidly spreading blood from the single stray bullet that had caught her in the throat and exited out the back of her neck. Backup man's shot.

From that day on, Kingston made sure he voiced his opinions and made damn sure they had as much solid intel as they could muster before they went knocking. This morning though, intel was a luxury no one could afford. All Billy Kingston had was a deep sense of urgency to be squared with the fear that Trish Walker just might be a hostage, trussed up somewhere in the middle of the house with her seriously fucked up husband holding a scalpel to her throat. That was the better of the two scenarios.

He gave the hand signal to move forward and take up breach positions by the front door. Lyndsey Mullins, crouching low, waddled up to the street door and pressed it gently, testing it for solidity. Behind her, PC Nigel Slater carried a 'universal key,' a ten pound short length hand-held battering ram, pitted with scars from contact with countless doors. Held by a single Yale and puny little mortice lock, Mullins knew this door wouldn't be a match for the key. Two good hits should send it in, hopefully just the one. She stood, readying herself, MP9 tucked in tight to her shoulder. Billy Kingston and the rest of his team crept up the stone stairs and took up position.

Kingston made a chopping motion with his hand, while at the same time shouting, 'Go!' into his radio. Two rapid heavy thumps sent the door crashing inward, bouncing back off the wall and into Mullins as she stormed into the house, Kingston seconds behind her.

From somewhere in the back, she heard glass breaking and the sound of a door being kicked in by the back garden team. They swept through the house like a heavily armed virus, going from room to room before declaring the place clear.

* * *

Paterson got out of his car and walked towards the house he knew so well and wished to God he didn't. Clocks followed him. In the surrounding houses, heads began to peep out from behind curtains and one or two brave souls opened their front doors a crack so as to watch the show. He and Clocks swept past the SCO19 officer who had taken up a guard position, and wandered through to find Kingston.

The house was tastefully decorated, dotted with pricey ornaments and candles. Expensive carpet, showing early signs of wear, ran up the stairs to the bedrooms and bathroom. Beautifully polished parquet flooring was laid throughout the lower part of the house, extending through to the conservatory. They met up with a relieved Sergeant Kingston in the kitchen.

'Primary search of the house shows clear,' he said. 'I have my team searching it thoroughly though. Could be rooms we don't know about.' Paterson nodded. Lyndsey Mullins stepped into the kitchen from the back door and said, 'Sir. You need to see this.' All four turned to her.

'What is it?' Paterson walked toward her. She stepped out of the kitchen and into the small, neatly kept garden. 'We just forced open the steel shed. There's a chest freezer in there and some things you'll have to look at.' A look of mingled distaste and sorrow etched her face.

The shed wasn't particularly large. The freezer took up most of the space available, but there was enough room for one person to stand inside and open it once one of the doors had been fully opened. A couple of LED strip lights were attached by magnets over the top of the freezer and lit up the interior of the shed. Johnny Clocks pushed in front of the senior men and took a look inside.

He thrust his hand in and pulled out a small frosted plastic bag which he held up to the harsh light. Having wiped a hand across it to create a smeary, wet window, he found himself looking at a frozen vagina. Written on the bag in indelible ink was a single name — Kerry. Still with his back to them, he let out a slow breath of air.

'What you got, Clocks?'

'A chest full of frozen fannyburgers if anyone wants one? There's a lot of 'em in here.' Clocks turned, grinning, and held up the bag for them to see.

'You're a funny fucker, ain't ya?' Kingston said, shaking his head in disgust.

'I reckon that'll warm up nicely in the microwave.'

Clocks never saw the punch. Lyndsey Mullins hit him in the side of the head, and he bounced off the metal doors and dropped to the floor. Paterson and Kingston turned in surprise.

'Show some fucking respect for the dead, you low-life piece of shit,' Mullins growled at him. Paterson thought perhaps he should restrain her and decided against it. Kingston nodded at her in approval. She'd beaten him to it. Good punch. Good girl.

'Sorry,' she said, turning to them. 'But that foul-mouthed fucker is long overdue for a right-hander.' They looked at her, then at Clocks, now struggling to pull himself up, his eyes wide and glazed, and nodded. Paterson bent and helped Clocks to his feet, where he swayed for a second or two.

Finally Clocks stopped swaying and held out his hand to her. 'Fuckin' good punch, love. I deserved that. I can be a bit of a prick sometimes. Sorry.' Mullins eyed him. At least he took his lumps and wasn't snivelling about it. She walked away.

'Right,' said Paterson. 'Now you two ladies have kissed and made up, we've got to get the forensics team down to sweep this place. This is a crime scene now and we still don't have Trish or Adam. I'm just hoping she's not in among this lot.'

'Mr Paterson!'

Paterson and Kingston moved back inside and found the shouter standing in the dining room. One of the SCO19 boys was looking at the floor, a small rug kicked to one side. 'We've got a cellar.'

* * *

Kingston snapped on his Glock's torch and tested the integrity of the old wooden stairs leading into the darkness. These kinds of entries were difficult. Single man entry, limited vision and plenty of time for a suspect to take you first. No light switch at the top of the stairs. There was usually a reason for that.

Taking a deep breath, he cautiously began his descent, crouched low and peering into the dark. The air felt cold on his face and the place smelled faintly of damp. Kingston would later tell everyone that the place had a 'bad vibe,' and from a man not given to fancies, this was a first. His torch beam picked out a number of old paint cans, some rusty garden tools, a workbench that appeared to run the length of the basement, a large metal rack against the far wall with a tattered tarpaulin hanging off the back and cobwebs everywhere. Lyndsey Mullins followed close behind, her torch beam adding to his. Reaching the bottom step, Kingston found the cord for an overhead light and clicked it on. They moved forward, sweeping the room in a practiced arc until they were satisfied it was clear. Then they snapped off the torchlights.

Kingston holstered his gun and walked toward the workbench. Edgy, Mullins kept her weapon half-pointed to the ground, ready to raise it. The workbench was old, made of heavy solid wood, and bore the marks of years of use. A few old tools were scattered all across its pitted, saw scarred surface. Kingston clocked an old wooden hammer, a couple of chisels, three or four different sized screwdrivers but what caught his attention was the nylon tool wrap lying next to a surgical bone saw. He unwrapped it carefully and winced at the collection of scalpels, scissors, picks and saws inside.

'Lyndsey. See this?'

She took a quick glance over his shoulder. 'Uh, uh.'

'These stains are old,' he said, running his gloved fingers over the largest, darkest stain that ran across the bench. 'Ingrained. Pound to a pinch of shit that they didn't come out of a tin of Ronseal. I've got a bad feeling that our boy has been a lot busier than we thought.' Mullins was walking around slowly, moving toward the tool rack leaning against the back wall. 'I'm guessing that this is a fucking killing room.' She didn't answer. 'You listening?' he said.

'Yes, guv. Heard every word. Ronseal, killing room, blah, blah.'

She looked toward the back wall. 'You notice anything odd about this big ol' tool rack?'

Kingston looked at it carefully. 'Nope. Looks like the sort of thing you'd pick up out of B and Q. Couple of old paint tins and what looks to be a tool box.'

'Yep. Lot of wasted space. Nothing heavy on it. Why wouldn't you use it, and why is there a tarp *behind* it?' Kingston nodded. 'It's hiding something,' she said. They walked toward it slowly.

'There you go. Scrape marks on the floor,' she said. 'Wanna bet there's a door back there?' Kingston grabbed the heavy steel frame and pulled at it. It moved with ease and swung outwards thanks to the hinges they hadn't noticed.

'Bingo!' he said. They dropped at once into room entry mode on either side of the door. 'Standard lock. No light under the crack. Weapons up. Flashbang. I'll hold.

Go tell 'em upstairs.' Kingston raised his gun as Mullins backed away. She took the first four steps two at a time and quietly informed Paterson standing at the entrance of what they had found and what they were going to do. He looked anxious.

Back with Kingston, she carefully tried the door handle while he kept his eyes on the jamb, watching for any sudden movement. Locked. She backed off, kicked it in, rolled a flashbang, and they turned their heads away for protection. The sudden crack of light lit the room up. Both moved swiftly into the room, covering each other's entrance. Text-book. 'Clear!'

Kingston found and snapped on the light.

'What the fuck?' Mullins stood with her mouth open, staring at the walls and ceiling of the room, every inch wallpapered with pictures of Detective Superintendent Ray Paterson in flagrante delicto with a very attractive blonde.

'Who the bloody hell is she?' asked Kingston.

'No idea, guv, but I'll bet a tenner it's not his missus. We'd better get Clocks down here first. Maybe he knows who she is.'

'I'll go get him.' Kingston turned to leave the room. 'Don't touch anything.' She frowned. As if.

Like an angry whack-a-mole, Kingston popped his head up through the trapdoor and looked up at Paterson and Clocks. He gave a brief description of the main basement area, told them of the stains, surgical instruments, the bone saw and the fact they'd found a hidden room. 'Need you down here and take a look around. Found some other interesting stuff in the hidey room.' Both men started to move. Clocks, keen to make up, moved first.

'Stay put for a minute, Mr Paterson. It's a bit tight down there,' Kingston lied. Paterson gave a little shrug and continued to look around the room he was in.

As they descended the staircase, Kingston, keeping his voice to a whisper said, 'We've found something in this back room. Best you see it first. Maybe you can put a name to a face.' Johnny Clocks looked perplexed but said nothing. Kingston led him into the room, where Mullins was eyeing a small laptop sitting open on a desk. The power was on.

Clocks's eyes turned to saucers as he struggled to take in the room and its decor. 'What the . . ? Oh no, no, no. You stupid bastard, Paterson. What have you done? What *have* you done?' He turned to Kingston and Mullins. 'Do you know who this is?' He pointed at a picture of Paterson, naked and on top of the blonde woman. Her face was clearly visible. Both could hazard a pretty good guess by now.

'That. That woman there,' Clocks stabbed his finger angrily on the woman's face. 'Is Adam Walker's wife. Paterson's been fucking our killer's old woman! Oh Jeez . . . us!' He ran his hand through his hair.

* * *

'One of you go and get the silly twat down here now. No, wait, I'll get him.' DS Clocks stormed out of the room. 'Paterson!' he shouted up the stairs. 'Get the fuck down here. Now!'

'Who the hell do you think—?' said Paterson angrily. Before his toe touched the last step, Clocks tore into him.

'You're an idiot, Paterson. No, no. You're beyond a fucking idiot. Way beyond. What the hell is wrong with you?' Flecks of spit jumped out of his mouth.

'What are you talking about?' Paterson caught sight of the metal rack ahead, saw the room behind it with Kingston wandering about, saw that the walls looked darkish, disjointed somehow, and though he couldn't quite make out what was actually on those walls, his stomach knotted up. He moved inside, impelled forward like a zombie. Then he saw clearly. The room began to whirl as he fought off yet another wave of nausea.

Billy Kingston shook his head. Mullins snorted and walked out.

Clocks went for him again. 'Why the fuck didn't you tell us you were shagging Walker's wife?'

Paterson, sandbagged, looked at him bewildered and then his hackles rose. 'Why the fuck should I tell you or anyone else who I'm seeing? It's nobody's business.' He squared off to his DS. Kingston pulled himself up straight.

'What'd you say? Nobody's business? Nobody's fucking business? I'd say it's everyone's business, wouldn't you, Ray, eh? Do you not see what's on the walls? On the ceiling. Have another look. Maybe you missed it first time around.'

Paterson deflated. 'Look, I never told anyone because it wasn't an issue. In all fairness, no one even considered Walker a suspect before tonight. None of us did, John. Alright, I'm out of order for doing his missus, I accept that, but it's got nothing to do with him killing the girls.' Clocks looked at him in disbelief. Kingston gave a half grin and shook his head.

'What? Fuck me. How dumb are you? How can you be so . . ? It's got everything to do with you. Everything. What do you think this room is about? Most people who think their wife's over the side will get a few snaps and bung 'em in a paper folder for their solicitor but look around you, guv, these ain't in a folder, are they? More than just a few snapshots here. No. This is a man who's clearly off his fucking nut! Off his nut, Ray! And he's pissed off. At you, you fuckwit.'

Paterson's hackles rose again. 'You saying this is my fault?' He stepped just too close for Johnny Clocks's liking and he lost control. Clocks lunged forward and slammed Paterson up against the wall, with his forearm tight against his senior officer's throat, his fist cocked at his face. Paterson's head bounced off the wall. Kingston didn't move.

'Of course it's your fault. All your fucking fault. The dead girls. All of them. Dave too. All on you. Every one of 'em. And all because you had to go and stick your pencil in someone else's pocket. He's taking revenge. Can't you see? Those carvings on the bodies, the messages. They're for you. He's telling you something.' Clocks suddenly let go, and Paterson slumped.

'Go home, Paterson. I'm calling in DCI Carr to figure out what we do with all this shit. In the meantime, do us all a favour. Put your papers in and call it a day. Fuck off on one of your boats and go shag yourself to death. You make me fucking sick.'

* * *

The laptop suddenly beeped, breaking the tension.

'Hello, Mr Paterson.' Adam Walker's face filled the small screen. 'Nice to see you again.' A small blue light flashed underneath the tiny webcam. 'I trust you're well?' He cocked his head to one side. 'Perhaps not. You're looking a bit rough. Been a bit of a stressful night, hasn't it?' Paterson wiped the back of his hand across his mouth, and said nothing. 'I take it by now you've found my trophies I bagged up and left for you.'

'You sick fuck!' Paterson spat.

'Hey, hey! No need for name calling, Raymond. I thought you were better than that.'

'Where is she?'

'You mean my whore of a wife? Oh I wouldn't worry about her.'

'Adam, for Christ's sake.' Clocks pushed in front of the camera. 'Don't do this. Don't punish her because of him. Tell us where she is.'

'Hello, Timex. Good to see you too. Figured you'd be here, given that Paterson's care worker is now, er, deceased.' Paterson lurched forward. Kingston grasped his shoulder and held a finger to his lips.

'I'm punishing them both. She chose to screw him. Free will, conscious choice and all that. No one made her. She knows now that actions have consequences.'

'Adam, please tell me she's alive!'

'I could tell you that but then it wouldn't be any fun, would it? And I've been having a lot of fun lately. Besides, things aren't always what they seem.'

'I don't understand,' said Clocks. 'Surely you can tell me if she's alive?'

'Ever heard of Schrodinger's cat?' said Walker. Puzzled, Clocks shook his head.

'He's fucking about with us,' said Kingston. 'Saying she's both dead and alive but we won't know until we find her. Schrodinger's cat is a thought experiment. A live cat in a sealed box. Radiation sample, bottle of poison. If the radiation decays, the bottle of poison breaks and kills the cat. Point is, nobody knows if the poison bottle broke or not and until the box is opened the cat is considered to be both dead and alive at the same time. Used to point out the flaws in the Copenhagen interpretation of quantum mechanics. I'm a bit rusty, but that's close enough.' The others stared at him. He shrugged. 'What? So I read.'

'Good Lord.' Walker broke the silence. 'Where did that come from? And here was I thinking you were just a fuckwit with a tommy gun.'

Kingston stepped closer to the screen, and looked Walker in the eyes. 'That's a bad mistake to make, prick.'

Walker beamed. 'Well, that's scared the crap out of me, mister brainy bollocks. Now, move out the way and let me see Timex.' Kingston, glowering, stepped aside.

'I don't believe you've done all this because of him and your missus. No one, no matter how pissed off they are, does this kind of thing,' Clocks said.

Walker cocked his head to one side, paused. 'You're absolutely right. You should be a detective.' He smiled.

'My guess is that you've been at this for a long while, haven't you? This room has seen some action. Right under our noses.'

'Right again, Timex. You're on fire.' Walker hesitated a second. 'What's that old saying? "Never trust a copper. They'd shop their own mother." In my case it was kill my own mother — and my father.' Walker left that out there for a second. 'Haven't you read my file yet, the one Dead Dave put together?' Walker was goading them now.

'What file?'

'Apparently Dead Dave said he'd figured it all out, and from that little chat we had, it seems he did. I was quite impressed actually. He wasn't as dumb as I had him down for. I'd imagine he had a file on me somewhere, wouldn't you? Anyway, if you don't have it I guess you'll have to nip down to the nearest spiritualist church and ask him where it is.'

Paterson suddenly wriggled out of Kingston's grip and moved into view of the camera. 'Listen to me, you mad—'

Kingston's hand shot out, grabbed him by the hair and wrenched him back, forcing him down onto one knee. He pulled his gun and pointed it at Paterson's head, finger off the trigger. 'Shut the fuck up, arsehole,' he snapped. 'Let the policeman talk. You've done enough fucking damage for one night.'

'Thank you, Inspector Kingston, I appreciate that. Feel free to pull the trigger. I won't tell.' Walker giggled. 'We'll say he went mad with stress and attacked everyone.'

'Why did you kill Jordan, Adam?' said Clocks. 'You never had to do that.'

Walker lowered his eyes for a second then looked up, a faint smile on his face. 'That was . . . unfortunate. I never meant to kill him.' He suddenly brightened. 'I meant to fucking hurt him though! I actually wanted him to live. Can you imagine going through life looking that happy? They say that if you're sad and you fake a smile, pretty soon you'll feel happy, and I thought the clever bastard deserved to be the happiest man on earth. But the stupid fucker upped and died on the table.'

'How do you know that?' said Clocks, 'That's not out yet.'

'Not difficult. I phoned and asked the hospital. I'm a copper, don't forget. Told her he was my guv'nor and she broke the news. Very sad. I shed a little tear.'

'So what now?' Clocks asked.

'Well, the first thing you need to do is pop over to Peter Reichenbach's house. He was a strange little man, wasn't he? Do you know he was the president of some puerile Sherlock Holmes society? Silly little man thought he *was* Sherlock, I'm sure of it. Off his fucking head, or what?'

Clocks breathed in deep. 'You said "was." Does that mean . . ?'

'Oh yeah. He's gone too. Busy old night in mad town tonight, eh? Still, what's a man to do? It's down to him really that Dead Dave ended up dead. From what I gather, it was him that initially figured me out and went running to Dead Dave with his ideas. If he'd shut his mouth up in the first place, none of you would have been any the wiser, and Dead Dave wouldn't be, well, dead. Though in hindsight, he might have been. He was *such* an annoying bastard.'

'Adam,' said Clocks, keeping his anger in check, his voice calm and reasonable. 'Why are you carving words into them? What's the point of that?'

'I'm sending him a message. Paterson, that is. It's a moral message, and it'll teach him a very valuable life lesson.' Paterson closed his eyes and breathed out heavily.

'Just tell him, Adam. He's listening. We're all listening. Tell us now and stop fucking killing people.'

Walker stared, unblinking. 'I could I suppose, but the message has to be driven home. He mustn't forget it. Ever.'

'You must know this isn't going to end well for you. Why not just call it a day now and nobody else gets hurt. I'll see to it you get the best care, I swear.'

Walker rolled his eyes. 'Oh, fuck off, Clocks! Just when I thought you were the half sensible one, you come out with bollocks like that. Let's think that through, shall we? I give myself up and what do you know? I get banged up in Broadmoor. End up wearing a canvas cuddle coat for the rest of my life sucking soup through a straw and sitting in my own shit. Hmmm? Let me think a minute.' He paused. 'Fuck that! Of course somebody else is getting hurt. I'm nowhere near finished. Surely that's obvious? I'm so far ahead of you lot it's ridiculous. Even Stevie Wonder can see that.' He waved Clocks away. 'Mr Kingston. Hold Paterson up for me, I want to talk to him.' Clocks stepped aside and Kingston hauled Paterson to his feet. Paterson stared at him, seething with rage.

'Hi again, Ray. You must be feeling like the prick of the century.' Walker's tone was harder now, less jovial. 'Since they put you on the case, three girls, a fat copper and Sherlock Holmes are dead. Not going to enhance your career prospects too much, I imagine. This'll stop your ascent to the stars, I should think. Still, no use crying over spilt milk. Talking of spilt milk, my next kill is especially for you.' Walker's face suddenly contorted with rage. He spat his venom directly at the camera.

'I have her, Paterson, and I will take her life. I am going to rend the fucking whore limb from limb. I am going to cut her to ribbons. I am going to fucking destroy her. I will keep her alive while I do her, and she will beg me, beg me for death. She will grovel and cry and call your name, and when I've finished carving her up, I will slice her heart right out of her body and show it to her just before she dies! Do you understand me? Do you see what you've done?'

Sick, helpless, Paterson looked at the twisted, contorted face on the screen. 'Please, Adam, don't . . . I'll do whatever you want. I'll step down, I'll go away, just please, please don't hurt her . . .'

The screen went blank. Paterson closed his eyes and bowed his head.

* * *

On the drive home, Paterson had given serious thought to smashing his way through a bottle of Jack Daniels. Christ knows he needed it, but he sensibly figured he was in enough shit without getting his collar felt for drinking and driving.

His first stop after crashing in through his front door was the fridge. He grabbed a bar of chocolate, chugged a quick tin of Coke, burped loudly and wandered off to bed, chomping on his quick meal. His head hit the pillow and he went out like a light. Fully clothed, unwashed. Couldn't be bothered.

He woke with a start. The doorbell was ringing and someone was thumping the door in time with his almighty headache.

'Boss! Boss! Open the fuckin' door. It's me, Timex.' Johnny Clocks banged on the door again. Paterson glanced at the clock and staggered sleepily along the hall to let him in.

Clocks pushed his way in, taking a second to examine Paterson's battered face. 'Too late for steak on that, guv. Fuck me, can you even *see* out of those eyes? They look like two piss holes in the snow, except they're purple.' He looked a bit closer. 'There's some yellow in there though, so . . .'

'What d'you want?' Paterson moved aside, saw Clocks's face. 'Seems our gun girl gave you a bit of a lump too. Normally I'd be worried if someone had a head injury but in your case, won't make much difference.' Clocks grinned at him. That was Clocks all over. He'd said his piece, told Paterson what he thought of him, and moved on.

Paterson shuffled off towards the kitchen, shook the kettle, filled it up. Forgot to switch it on. 'Why are you here?'

'Where'd you keep your cups?'

Paterson sighed. 'Behind you. Cupboard over the sink. I'll have a black coffee no sugar if you're making it. What do you want, John?'

Clocks took out two mugs and flicked the switch on the kettle. 'They got into Dave's drawer. Turns out there was a file in there after all.' He sniffed the milk before pouring some into both mugs. 'Don't know the ins and outs of it. Wouldn't tell me shit. For your ears only, I guess.'

Paterson sat himself on a shiny metal stool, swinging his feet under the counter. 'They're waiting for me?'

'Yep. Commander Kelly sent me to come get you. I have to run you up to the Yard. You have an eleven o'clock with Kelly and Assistant Commissioner Young. He's a bit of a hard arse, I've heard.' He spooned three sugars into Paterson's white coffee and pushed it to him. 'Take that in the shower with you and get yourself sorted a bit lively. It's half eight and we've got to get across London in the rush hour.'

Paterson sipped the coffee, grimaced and headed back to the bedroom and its *en suite*.

Clocks looked around the living room. 'Fuck me!' he said spotting the television occupying most of the wall. 'How big is that telly?'

'Hundred and five inches. Brand new. Samsung. Bit pricey,' Paterson called from the bedroom.

'Flash bastard,' Clocks muttered under his breath. 'Put it on before you go, guv. That Susanna Reid bird's on. She's a right sort.'

Paterson shouted, 'TV. On. ITV1.'

'Double flash bastard,' Clocks said, as Susanna Reid's smiling face appeared in 5K HD.

CHAPTER TWELVE

Commander Kelly was used to taking centre stage, but this morning he found himself sitting to the right of the Assistant Crime Commissioner, Wallace Young. Now in his sixties, Young was a legend in the force. Still in fine physical shape, he kept himself fit with a strenuous running, boxing and yoga regime. His neatly pressed, immaculately tailored navy blue suit fitted him to perfection. Today he wore it buttoned up to signify the formality of the occasion. In his day, Young had been a hugely successful detective, his file bulging with commendations for detective ability and bravery. Some of the country's biggest criminals were now languishing away at Her Majesty's pleasure due to his razor-sharp mind, dogged determination and complete lack of fear.

An only child, he had chosen early on to live his life alone. No wife, no kids, parents dead, no known next of kin. After he joined up he kept it that way. No weak spots for anyone to exploit. With nothing to leverage, the bad boys had to go for him directly. Two attempts had been made on his life. The first, back in the late eighties when he was a detective sergeant in the now defunct Flying Squad at Limehouse police station, came as he walked across Tower Bridge late one evening. Michael Norton, head of one of the most notorious crime families in South East London, had decided he'd had enough of Young fucking about with the empire he'd built. It was time to deal with him. Unfortunately, the gunman they sent was inexperienced, sent as a try-out.

Everybody has to start somewhere. So, dressed entirely in black and riding a motorbike, Danny Rofe thought he looked the business. Wallace Young however, *was* the business. Pumped up with adrenaline and first time nerves, Rofe made a few mistakes that night. First, he didn't know that Wallace Young was returning from an armed operation and was still carrying a side arm as he walked along a row of parked cars in Tower Bridge Road. Things were different back in the eighties, not so strict about firearm management. Second, and this was the big one, Danny Rofe revved the bike just a bit too loudly on his approach. Still on high alert from his earlier activities, the sudden noise made Young instinctively drop to a crouch and the first two bullets whizzed over his head. The third shot, aimed lower, caught him square in the shoulder, spun him off his feet and sent him crashing down onto the pavement behind a parked car.

Full of himself now and keen to finish the job, Rofe dropped the bike on its side and ran toward his target. One in the face was his orders. Finish him off. Be sure. Big mistake number three. He rounded the back of the parked car and found himself staring down the barrel of a Smith and Wesson .38 and the expressionless face of Detective Sergeant Young behind it. The man in black stopped dead, eyes wide with surprise behind the reflective visor. Young calmly put two shots into his chest, punching him off of his feet and onto the boot of a Ford Sierra, from where he dropped down into the road. The coroner's report said that Mr Rofe *might* have survived the shots but not the passing number forty-seven bus that trundled over his head. That was Young's ninth commendation.

The second time he wasn't so fortunate. The bad guys had wised up a bit and sent the boys out on pedal cycles. Clever. Leaving the gym after his daily workout session, Young didn't hear the pedal cyclist speed up behind him until the last second. As he turned, the full force of a baseball bat caught him on the side of the head and sent him down. Before he could collect his thoughts and pull himself to his feet, three more men rode up on cycles, threw them to the ground and laid into him with bats and feet. By the time the ambulance got to him, he was unrecognisable but, crucially, alive. Three months of hospital time later he was back on the streets and vindictive. One of the gang had panicked upon hearing the arriving police sirens, and had left his bike behind. Forensics found enough prints to convict the rider. That still left three, and Young wasted no time in seeking revenge on the rider's known associates, figuring that he'd eventually get to the right ones.

Within the space of a year, the Nortons lost three of their low level enforcers to acts of extreme violence. No arrests were ever made, and it seemed that it was a case of the bad boys putting the hurt on each other. In truth, the police never took too much of an interest. Whenever police attend an incident they call in a result to the control room, often using an acronym for brevity. Some were official. ASNT meaning Area Searched, No Trace. Some were unofficial, such as SOS, for Scum On Scum. That was Norton's boys.

* * *

Facing the desk, Paterson sat nervously, picking at his trousers. Young locked his steel grey eyes onto Paterson and began to speak. 'Mr Paterson, it would seem we have ourselves an unholy mess.' Paterson nodded. 'We have a couple of things to discuss and I expect straight, honest answers. Understood?' Again, Paterson nodded. 'Explain to me the relationship between yourself and Walker's wife. No bullshit now. Straight to it.'

'Sir,' Paterson said. 'We began seeing each other about three or four months ago. We'd known each other for a few years, mostly through work functions, parties and the like. My marriage had collapsed a few months before that and we started seeing each other. Just a fling really. She was bored and apparently unhappy with DC Walker, and we kind of fell into it. We never saw any real harm in it.'

'No harm in it?' Young said, rubbing his chin. 'Sleeping with another man's wife. No harm in it? I would say that there is considerable harm in it, Mr Paterson, even if the husband didn't happen to be a homicidal maniac with a tendency to kill people at the drop of a hat.' He opened up a manila folder and flicked through the contents. 'Did you know Dave Jordan had cancer?'

Paterson sat bolt upright, stunned. 'Sorry? Cancer? No, no I didn't. He'd shaved his head recently but he said it was his brother who had cancer. Said he was dying from it. I offered him the chance to stand down to be with him, but Dave said he wouldn't. He said work kept his mind off of it.' Kelly and Young both watched him closely. 'Sir, I swear I had no idea.' He searched their faces. 'How did *you* know about it?'

ACC Young glanced down at the paperwork in front of him. 'A search was carried out of DS Jordan's locker and we found a file. In it he has included a copy of his medical reports and letters from the hospital. We've called them and they confirmed that he had inoperable, incurable brain cancer. Six months at most.' Paterson cupped his face with both hands and rubbed it a few times, shaking his head, trying to block it out. 'He also left us a video explaining his actions.' Paterson let his hands drop. 'It would seem that Jordan had Walker down as a suspect for a while but lacked sufficient evidence to bring him in. As you know, there is no useful forensic evidence to substantiate his suspicions and no witnesses, so DS Jordan set out to put that right.' Commander Kelly picked up a remote control on his desk and pointed it over Paterson's shoulder. 'Turn around and watch.'

* * *

'My name is Detective Sergeant David Jordan. If you're watching this, it's most likely because I'm dead.' Jordan's face appeared on the screen, the camera tilted upward, showing the flaps of loose skin under his jawline. 'To accompany this video, I have left a file of documents. In it are my suspicions that Detective Constable Adam Walker is the individual responsible for the murder of at least two women, the focus of Operation Stammer.' Paterson's jaw dropped.

'In my paper report, exhibit DJ 07, I give a full outline of my reasons for reaching this conclusion, but regretfully, at the time of putting it together, I still have no hard evidence to support my allegations, only suspicion. Strong suspicion, mind, but not strong enough for an arrest. Bear with me and I'll explain everything.

'I got suspicious when Walker and Reichenbach were having a dick fight in the office. Walker said that he went to Quantico. That got me thinking. To go to Quantico, I figured he'd have to have been in the FBI, but not once did he ever mention that, not once. Not something you'd want to hide, I would think. Now, it's possible, but it's extremely unlikely, that the Met would have sent him to the US on a course with the FBI. But certainly not at his rank. Just to be sure though, I put in a call. Seems they'd never heard of him. But they did a bit of digging into his name and date of birth, and guess what they found? They came up with an Adam Walker who turned his toes up when his Harley Davidson came to a sudden halt after a tree jumped out in front of him and snapped his neck.

'Okay, I've got him for lying, false identity and all that, but it's not enough to prove murder. So I did a bit more digging. I remembered him telling me on the night of

Kerry's murder that he stopped to help out in a pub fight in the Old Kent Road. Seems he didn't. I pulled up the CAD report for the disturbance. No mention of him responding, and no one who attended saw him there.

'I also had a look at the custody suite CCTV for the morning that Clocks and him pulled in Williams. From the time he arrived until the time he was taken for interview, the CCTV shows Walker going into his cell at least twice. Nothing wrong with that in and of itself, but it wasn't logged on the custody sheet. Bad boy.

'I don't know, but I'm guessing that he was in there either threatening Williams or doing some sort of deal. I guess he got Williams to put Pullman in the frame so we'd end up nicking the wrong man and he could go off and kill another one while everyone was tucked up and back at the nick. I could have squeezed Williams for an answer but I couldn't take the chance that he wouldn't somehow warn Walker I was on to him.'

Commander Kelly stopped the video, stared at Paterson, and said, 'Were you aware of any of this, Paterson?'

'What? No. For God's sake, no. I had no idea. He never said a word to me.' Bewildered by it all, Paterson looked back and forth between the senior officers. Kelly started the video again.

'Anyway, so now I'm seriously curious. I decided to poke around a bit more and sent the FBI a set of his prints. They came back to a Timothy Deeming. A fourteen-year-old kid who went missing, and nobody tried too hard to find him. Fair enough.' On screen, Jordan shrugged. 'So, with that info in my back pocket I thought it prudent to go off grid and hire a PI. My reasoning for doing so is that Walker had access to pretty much all of the systems we use. If I went snooping into them, he may have seen what I was up to and legged it. Again, I didn't want to spook him because I still had no evidence that he murdered anyone. Anyway, my PI came back with some interesting stuff. He got in touch with the child protection services in the States and got the whole sorry tale.

'From what I can make of it, his long-term unemployable dad had a problem with the old Jack Daniels and most nights got a bit too punchy with Mum, Adam and his sister too. When he wasn't smacking the shit out of him he was behaving in a very ungentlemanly manner towards Adam's sister. She was six. The reports said that he used to spend most nights cowering under the blankets while Dad visited the sister. He was forced to listen to him, all the while praying that he wouldn't get hurt too. But the kicker here is that Mum was a midnight visitor herself. To him. Doctor's report said he had an unhealthy obsession with vaginas. He used to draw them. A lot. They always had things sticking out of them, like knives, or sticks, and one or two even had them on fire. Explains why he cut them out of the girls, I guess. Lot of anger there.

'Anyway, one night, Mum and Dad wind up dead. Dad was stabbed in the throat, Mum had hers sliced open and her bits were cut out. They found the sister upstairs. Terrified. Went into some sort of shock. Lost her voice, never spoke again and killed herself about five years back. Adam, sorry, Timothy went missing. He was suspected of course, but there was no direct evidence. He somehow stayed under the radar and surfaced here in dear old Blighty as Adam Walker. I suppose I should have nicked him for those murders but he could, just could, have got off with them if he stood trial back home and I still had no evidence this side of the pond. If I'd nicked him, he'd have clammed up. He knows the score, how we work an' I'm betting that a search of his address would have turned up zilch. I needed more.

'With his fancy degree he applied for, and got, a job with the Met police recruitment branch. He worked there for about a year, figured out the system and then whacked in an application to become a copper. Now, this is the bit I *really* like.' Jordan had a big grin on his face. 'He only went and processed his own application! Fuckin' genius! Back then, nobody checked too much, probably grateful that anybody still bothered applying if we're honest, and so off he went to Hendon. A couple of years after that he made detective and got himself onto a few murder squads. Always seemed to be first, if not *the* first on the scene when a young girl was killed. He even called one in when he "found" a body in Wandsworth while off duty. All along, he was hiding in plain sight. Of course, they weren't killed with the same savagery as the recent ones, but then, as we know, these fuckers have to work their way up the maniac tree.

'So . . . more lying. But not enough for a murder charge.' Jordan shifted, settling himself in his chair.

'As you now know, I have terminal cancer. There is no question about it, no mistake. I have been undergoing treatment for a while but it has proved to be ineffective. My doctor has told me that towards the end they can make me comfortable, give me something to ease the pain. I'll go into a coma and . . . die.' Jordan's tone suddenly brightened. He sat up straight and rubbed his meaty hands together.

'Well, fuck that for a game of soldiers!' He winked at his unseen audience. Paterson grinned. 'For the benefit of any and all senior officers and legal bods watching this, I wish to make it perfectly clear to you that I am doing this of my own volition. This is my idea and mine alone. I am of sound mind. I have not discussed my thoughts, suspicions or findings with Detective Superintendent Paterson or any other officer connected to Operation Stammer. Later this evening, I will enter an observation point along with DC Walker, ostensibly in order to arrest Anthony Pullman. I do not believe Pullman is guilty of the crime of murder — well, not these particular girls anyway — but I am allowing the operation to go ahead as I believe it will be of benefit to the case. We need strong, direct, hard evidence to nick and convict this bastard, and I'm going to provide it.

'Tonight, I intend to confront Adam Walker with my findings and, as far as I can see, it will end one of two ways. Either he will deny everything, and I will then have no alternative but to bring him in for questioning, or, and this is my strong belief and hope, he will go on the offensive. He will take the latter course for two reasons. One, if he does, it won't go well for me in the short term but it will provide you with solid, concrete evidence that he is a murderer . . .' Paterson stared at the screen, blinked and rubbed his forehead. 'Two, he puts me out of my misery and I go out my way.

'Way I see it is, it's a win double. You get enough evidence to nick him and lock him up for the rest of his natural, and I don't have to go out in a hospital bed with wires and shit hanging out of my head and lying in a bedpan. Basically, I myself will constitute the evidence we need.'

Paterson felt himself crumble. He wiped his tears.

Jordan moved closer to the camera. 'Seriously now. Don't fuck this up, boys. Find him and bring him down. Mr Kelly, I know you'll be watching this. Make sure it's done right. Ray, sorry I didn't let on about the cancer thing, but you'd have only kicked me off the squad. Good luck, son. You're a good man.'

The screen went blank. Silence draped the room like a heavy, black, curtain.

'Any thoughts, DSI Paterson?' ACC Young's tone was flat. Paterson said nothing. Young shuffled his papers into a neat pile and slipped them back inside the cover. 'That's a brave man. We'll sort out the legal ramifications of his actions later, but for now, he's outed Walker and given us definitive proof. What he did is in many ways very stupid, but it's also very clever. He knew that Walker wouldn't be able to bluff his way out of it and would have to attack him. He knew it would force Walker to run and hide, seeing as how the whole country would be on the lookout for him once it hit the wire. I suspect he also thought that by forcing him to go into hiding, he wouldn't be able to go out and about killing at will.'

Paterson nodded. He wanted to speak but the words couldn't get past the lump in his throat.

'What guts me is that he clearly had no idea you were screwing Walker's wife, or that he would take her hostage, or that he would kill another girl on the way. If he had, maybe he'd have done things differently.' Paterson bowed his head. 'But then again, most likely not. Clearly he wanted to go out on his own two feet.' Paterson brightened slightly, looked up at the two men. Both had faces of stone.

Young opened a second file. 'Moving on. I've been looking through your file and for a while there, it looked as though you had a very promising career. Says you were tipped to be the youngest ever commissioner.' Young closed the file and directed his gaze back to Paterson. 'Let me nip that little fantasy in the bud this minute. As of now, any hope you had of climbing the ladder is gone. Let's recap what we have here. Three dead girls, one dead policeman, a deranged killer, who unfortunately happens to be a policeman under your command. The wife of said deranged killer, whom you were screwing, has gone on the missing list probably due to be killed herself, if she hasn't been already. Oh, and amid all of this mayhem, I nearly forgot to mention your specialist advisor. He was found dead in his flat this morning. I think we can safely say it was our boy's handiwork.'

The room started spinning again. This was becoming a habit.

'The thin layer of brass above me is satisfied that you have successfully shit in your own bed, and as far as they're concerned, you can lie in it.' Commander Kelly compressed his lips, suppressing a faint smile.

All Paterson could manage was, 'Sir,' before he turned away from ACC Young's ice-cold stare.

'As of now, you are no longer working this case. While it is accepted that you couldn't know your affair with Walker's wife would trigger his killing spree, your involvement with her has rendered you a liability. DCI Carr will be in charge pending the arrival of an outside investigator from Greater Manchester later this evening. You will instruct your officers to provide DCI Carr with every piece of information they possess on paper or stored in their heads. When you leave here, you will tell him everything you know, big or small. Do I make myself clear?'

Paterson looked down at his feet, his Gucci shoes. He scratched his head.

'As of now, you're also suspended from duty while a full investigation is carried out into your handling of this case and to determine your competency to remain as a police officer.' Paterson stiffened. 'We'll call it gardening leave for now. Give your warrant card and mobile phone to Commander Kelly before you leave the building. Dismissed.'

* * *

The sun had finally broken through and given the good citizens of Bermondsey a rest from the rain that had been falling virtually non-stop for a week. To make up for it, the rain had given way to sleet. Paterson drove absently, left hand on the steering wheel, right elbow on the door frame, resting his head on two fingers and a thumb.

Racked with guilt and self-loathing, he tried to figure out the exact moment his world had fallen to pieces. The only thing he could come up with was the day he was promoted to chief superintendent and took up a post as SIO with the murder squad. He'd jumped a rank and even the brass felt he should do something, on paper at least, to justify it. The plan was to keep his head down, pass over any run-of-the-mill domestic murders to Dave Jordan and in six months' time, carry his accelerated promotion straight into a luxury padded leather chair in a big office overlooking the Thames.

The car pushed its way through the heavy traffic, past the big houses in leafy Beckenham and on towards his flat in Bromley. Beautiful as it was, it wasn't a home. At this moment he wanted nothing more than to be with his Lisa, to have his life back. Too much damage had been done.

As he pulled into his street, it dawned on him that he would be the Paterson family's first failure. His father, not a particularly nice man, was born into vast wealth. Despite this, or perhaps because of it, he had determined to make his own mark in the world and as a boy of thirteen had gone to work in the local street market. At seventeen he had his own stall, and over the years, through sheer hard work and underhand behaviour, he built up an import–export empire that extended into Europe and the States. By the age of thirty he was rich in his own right, and then by dint of selling off tracts of family land to developers and subsequently starting his own property development companies, he moved rapidly up to join the super-rich. His wealth was matched only by his indifference to his children, whom he saw mostly as an accessory, something required of a person mixing in polite company.

After twenty-six years of being trapped in a marriage to a man who constantly humiliated her with his less than discreet affairs, his wife overdosed, survived, and finally left him for an impoverished fisherman she had met while recuperating at one of the family homes in Cornwall. They say the apple never falls far from the tree, and as much as Ray Paterson tried to be a better person than his father, it was always the ladies that knocked him off of his perch. He guessed they always would.

At the flats, he clicked the remote and slowed to allow the garage doors to open. Parking up, he took a deep breath, switched the engine off and sat in the dark. His thoughts went back to the meeting with ACC Young and he replayed the short conversation over in his head a few times. He sighed, got out of the car and turned to close the garage door.

He just caught a dark shape out of the corner of his eye. It was moving fast. Paterson raised his hands and something hit him square on the back of his head, dropping him like a brick.

* * *

'Hello, Superintendent,' Walker said. 'Bet you never expected to see me so soon, eh?' Paterson peeled his eyes open and fought for focus in the gloom. After a second he made out the voice, already knowing who it belonged to. It took him another second to realise that he was still in his garage and that Walker had shut the door.

He seemed to be lying with his back pressed up against the cold metal of his car. Cable ties bit deeply into his wrists and ankles. Walker was crouched on one knee directly in front of him.

'I just thought I'd drop by and see how you're getting on. I'm guessing things didn't go too well at the Yard today if you're home at this hour. They don't usually send SIOs home in the middle of a murder case, do they? So what's happened, Ray?' Walker smiled and showed him the scalpel in his hand. Paterson pushed himself against the car door in a vain attempt to get away. His face was a mask of fear.

'Don't worry, Ray. Believe it or not, I'm not here to hurt you.' He paused. 'Unless, of course, I have to. You won't do anything silly now, will you? Like shouting. That will go *so* badly.' He tapped Paterson on the head with the flat of the blade.

Paterson shook his head vigorously. Sweat was beading rapidly on his forehead and top lip. He could feel himself start to shake, tried to bring it under control but failed miserably.

'There's a good boy. So, tell me. Where is the case now? What's happened? I want to know how close you are to catching me. Tell me everything, and if I think you're missing out stuff or lying to me, we both know how that will go for you, don't we?' Walker tapped him again on the head with the edge of the handle, harder this time. It made a hollow 'donk' sound. Paterson blinked.

'Nothing to tell,' he said shakily and recounted his meeting with ACC Young. 'I'm suspended. Greater Manchester's taking it over. The investigation hasn't advanced very far, but they know all about your background, Adam. Your picture's gone everywhere. Your passport's blocked. You won't get out of the country and it's just a matter of time before they get you.'

Walker moved his face closer to his prisoner. He grinned. 'It's possible, Ray, but they won't get me yet. I haven't quite finished. It won't be long though. This afternoon, in fact. As soon as I leave here. After that, if they do manage to nick me, so be it. I've had a good run over the years and let's face it, nothing lasts forever, does it?' Paterson could only agree with this. He doubted he'd be leaving the garage alive, despite what Walker had said. Hopefully he would get an answer to take with him to the grave.

'This isn't just about me and Trish, is it?'

Walker cocked his head. 'Complicated, Ray. When I first found out about the two of you I was, to say the least, pissed off. You have to understand that Trish was my everything. Not in a soppy love kind of way, I couldn't give a fuck about that, but she was my respectability, my cover. She made me look normal. The likes of you would see a married man with a decent house, holidays abroad, all the shit you so-called normal fuckers like to have. When you started screwing around with her, you threatened me, threatened the life I'd concocted. I couldn't let you get away with that, could I?' He grinned. Paterson looked away. 'I decided to kill you but after a bit of thought, I changed my mind. It might get a bit uncomfortable when it came out you'd been seeing my wife. The boys might have stumbled on something, dug a bit too deep. You know how it goes, they might have got lucky. So, if I couldn't take your life, the next best thing was to destroy it. You're a career man, Ray, a golden boy. I thought it would be interesting to see how you coped with a real murder investigation.' He shrugged. 'I figured you'd struggle a bit. Figured you'd drop the ball big-time and end up disgraced. Clearly, I was right. But it's not enough, Ray. I haven't finished with you yet.' A smile spread across his face. Paterson frowned.

'Before I go,' Walker said, 'you might as well know. I've been doing this for years. Being a murder squad detective comes in real handy. Think about it. Kill a girl, get seconded to the squad, find out what they know, and conceal any evidence. It's so fucking easy, Ray, I'm surprised more people like me don't join up.'

Paterson swallowed hard, pulled at his wrist ties. Pointless. 'How many more?'

'Oh, I dunno, Ray. Seven, eight, eleven? Who's counting? See, the thing is, the girls I kill are nobodies. They're just toms or runaways that no one gives a fuck about. Nobody tries too hard to find out who did them because they're the unwanted, Ray. I generally kill them in different ways, and in different places to make it difficult to link the kills together. But this time I wanted some fun. Fun with you, Ray. I thought it would be amusing to take your precious hoity-toity life and fuck it sideways to Christmas.'

Paterson nodded. 'Where's Trish? Is she alive?'

Walker stood, awkwardly, his knee unlocking from the crouch. 'You don't want to worry yourself over her, Ray. Not her.' Paterson looked at him, puzzled. 'God, you're a dumb bastard, aren't you?' Paterson's mind raced. He had a sudden flash of realisation, terror. Then the lights went back out.

CHAPTER THIRTEEN

Tower Bridge police station is always busy at eleven o'clock on a Friday morning. Someone always wants something. Today, the person on the receiving end of the public's wants was PC Ben Cunningham. Not a man to suffer fools gladly, he'd been reprimanded more than a few times for his complete lack of interest in people's complaints — moans, as he called them. Twenty years of policing makes you like that. He'd heard it all before and was bored with it. Why was it that everybody always seemed to choose this particular time to come in and make a nuisance of themselves, and piss on his day. There seemed to be an unwritten rule that whenever he had a cup of tea in his hand, someone came in to annoy him. He swore, as he had a thousand times before, that he'd take his tea break half an hour earlier in future.

He put his cup down on the counter, slid it out of grabbing distance and rested his arms on the Formica topped counter. He tried to pretend an interest in the soaking wet elderly lady before him who was sounding off about her next door neighbour's 'bloody dog barking its head off all night long. It's not right. Something should be done so decent people like meself can get some rest. I have to go to work, y'know, not like all these bloody soap dodgers out there scrounging off the welfare . . .'

He'd more or less tuned her out the second she opened her mouth. Anyone too stupid to walk about in torrential rain without an umbrella wasn't going to have the intelligence to say anything of value.

Sighing, he took out his pen and began to write down her details on a scrap of loose paper that would be filed in the shredder as soon as she left the station. From long practice, he nodded every so often, giving the impression to anyone nearby that he was listening and really did give a flying fuck about her piddly little problem. He stared transfixed at the mesmeric clump of thick black hairs that sprouted from her chin. He reckoned they must be at least an inch long and he couldn't understand for the life of him why she left them there. Surely she could see them in a mirror? What's the deal? Proud of them? Family heirloom, perhaps?

After a few minutes of nodding and scribbling he shook his head to help break the spell and, looking away, said, 'Yes, madam. I'll make sure something's done about it right away. It's a terrible problem. It's rife up and down the country at the moment. It's so bad the commissioner has made funds available for a specialist dog barking squad to deal with it. I'll get them to pop round later and sort it out for you.' He flapped his hands at her. 'Go on, love, you don't want to miss them.'

The lady with the chin turned to go, and he pressed the buzzer to let her out. Halfway through the door, she turned back and glared at him. 'Dog barking squad, my fanny. I pay your wages, you useless cock!' Then she was gone, shouting her head off as she walked out into the street. Only then did PC Cunningham notice the barefoot woman being led up the stairs by a cabbie. Her dark hair was matted to her face with the rain and her nightie clung to her like a wrinkled pink skin. He could see her shivering from where he was. He jumped the counter and swiped himself out of the locked door into the foyer. The top of her nightie gaped open, and he could see blood.

'Found her wandering the street, Officer,' said the cabbie, clearly distressed. 'We weren't far from here. Figured you'd give her first aid while she waits for an ambulance. I've called for one.'

Cunningham reached out to touch her, and she suddenly screamed, kicking out and flailing her arms wildly. Cunningham took a kick to the knee and lost his balance. The woman kept screaming, frenzied. More police came running to help and after a few minutes of struggle, two female officers had her secured, on the floor and wrapped in a blanket. They lifted her up and carried her, struggling and screaming, into the surgeon's room, where they deposited her as carefully as they could onto the green plastic couch.

Luckily, the divisional surgeon happened to be in the charge room, taking blood from a drink driver. He whacked a powerful sedative into her arm which calmed her down almost immediately. One of the policewomen held onto her head while the other took her feet and they swung her into the recovery position. Satisfied she was now no danger to herself or others, one of them gently covered her with a woollen blanket and walked off to wash the blood from her nose. A shaken PC Cunningham pushed his way past several officers and ran out into the corridor, past a blur of enquiry posters and upstairs to the CID offices.

As he pushed open the doors he nearly bowled over Johnny Clocks, who was barrelling out the other way.

'Fuck!' Clocks shouted. 'Nearly knocked me out! What you after?'

'Timex! There's a woman downstairs in a right state. Half dressed, soaking wet and screaming the house down. Cabbie brought her in. Dunno what the story is, but she might have been raped or something. Ambulance has been called, but can you or one of the other suits get down and have a look at her before she goes?'

Clocks rolled his eyes. 'Unless she's dead, no, I can't. I'm on the fuckin' murder squad. I'll get DC Chartwell down. She's doing sod all, as usual.'

From across the room, DC Kate Chartwell, with all of seven years' service behind her, flipped him the finger and mouthed, 'Tosser,' as she headed toward the door.

'You're coming with me, big-shot,' she said to Clocks. 'Might as well make out you're a CID officer for a change. Don't worry though, Skip. I'll do the writing. I know how you struggle to keep your crayons between the lines.' Cunningham smiled. Clocks didn't. They both followed her downstairs.

In the surgeon's room, the woman was still lying on her side, breathing deeply, and twitching every so often. Fighting someone or something in her dreams. Johnny Clocks took one look at her and stood stock still.

'Fuck me blind!' He moved forward, and leaned in for a closer look.

'Who is she?' asked DC Chartwell. 'I'd ask if she was one of your exes, but she looks like a real girl.'

'That's Trish Walker. Adam's wife,' he said, scrabbling to fish his mobile phone out of his back pocket. 'We thought she'd turn up dead. Roll her over and show me her chest.' Chartwell frowned, but did as he said. She peeled the collar open, saw the blood there, and grimaced.

'Christ!'

Clocks pushed her aside and pulled the collar wider, and stared at the word etched deep into her skin: 'Ray.' Punching his speed dialler, he headed outside. 'Stay with her, Kate. Where she goes, you go. If she wakes or speaks, belches or farts, you tell me, understand?' Chartwell nodded and watched him run.

Clocks threw open the back doors and ran to the car park, phone in one hand and car remote in the other. As he wrenched open the door to his car, a tinny voice answered, 'Hello?'

'Roy, listen to me,' Clocks shouted.

'Clocks?'

'We've got Trish Walker.' He threw himself into the driver's seat and started the car. 'She's at the nick. Now. Going to hospital.' He revved the engine and spun out into the yard in second gear, flicking the two-tone switch. The tyres screamed on the wet tarmac and he was gone, leaving behind a smell of burning rubber.

'Calm down, Clocks. Listen to me. Is she hurt?'

'She's in one piece as far as I could see, but she's in deep shock. Woodentops said she was staring at the wall and then just started screaming. Div surgeon gave her a sedative, and they're waiting for an ambulance. She's half naked and looks like something the cat dragged in. Got Paterson's name — Ray — carved into her chest.' He screamed straight through the first red light in Tower Bridge Road, causing oncoming drivers to flash their lights furiously. 'Listen to me, Roy, I'm going over to Paterson's home address, his mansion. Get me some backup. As much as you can get, the works. Guns. Lots of fuckin' guns.'

'Why? What for?' said Carr, his tinny voice sounding concerned. The two nearside wheels left the road as Clocks threw the car around the Bricklayers Arms roundabout, heading toward the Elephant and Castle.

'We all thought he was gonna do his own missus in cause she fucked Paterson and he had the hump, yes? Nah, nah, nah! He's thrown us a right crippler. The message, Roy, I've put it together.' He slammed on the brakes, pulled a hard right into the oncoming traffic, accelerated past the little Ford Ka that was crawling along in front of him. 'We're getting to the end now!' he shouted, the adrenaline pumping him up and on. 'We've got "Don't. Touch. What. Isn't. Ray," and the only other word that fits is "Yours." Don't touch what isn't yours, Ray. If I'm right, then I'm betting "Yours" is a reference to Lisa. He's gonna kill Lisa!'

'Fuck me,' said Carr.

'Listen, guv. Get some people over to Paterson's flat in Bromley as well. He could be in trouble too.' He threw the phone onto the passenger seat and burned another red light.

* * *

Lisa Paterson walked into her bedroom. She had just finished her second workout of the day and a quick shower and change was in order before she set off to meet up with her girlfriends in a nearby Costa. A few of them were, like her, ex-models and one or two were rising stars of the high fashion world and on the books of her newly formed modelling agency, Perfection. They would meet whenever their commitments allowed and catch up on the old days, while at the same time sharing their experiences and preparing the new kids for the challenges ahead. It was also a chance for Lisa to watch her protégés in an informal setting. They were ambassadors for her agency, her brand, and she wanted to see at close quarters how they behaved, how they carried themselves, how they spoke. She also wanted to see what they ate and drank, and woe betide any girl who ate more than a quarter of their skinny muffin. Eight stone was heavy enough for any girl, and anything over that required a change of attitude. Or job.

She caught sight of herself in one of the many full-length mirrors dotted around the bedroom and, despite being sweaty and red faced from her P90X workout, she was satisfied with what she saw. It pleased her to see that everything was as tight and controlled as it was fifteen years ago when she was seventeen and had just started modelling, even though it was harder to stay in shape these days. She'd had a good run at it, travelled the world, made millions, fucked more famous people than she could remember, before finally getting married to rich boy

Paterson in the society wedding of the year. Falling in love with him was the only real mistake she had ever made in her charmed life.

* * *

In the darkness of the walk-in closet, the perfumed smell of her clothing intoxicated him and he reached out to touch, ever so lightly, the Gucci and Vitton that hung neatly above him. He held the arm of a Vera Wang blouse to his nose and inhaled, long and deep, while he looked through the slats at her. *I smell you.*

She had stopped preening and was looking in his direction. He kept dead still. *She couldn't have seen me.* She looked for a few seconds longer before pulling off her tight, sweat stained top and dropping it on the floor. *I guess not.* She then hooked her thumbs inside her Lycra shorts and expertly peeled them off to join the pile of discards. Completely naked now, she was separated from Walker only by a slatted wooden door and his self-control. *Wait.* Showered and fresh suited him better.

It was strange to see her in the same room as him, the face and body that had featured in so many articles and magazine covers. He had never killed anyone famous before, and the thought of doing so added an extra rush. This was something he would look into for the future. Maybe it could be his niche.

He stared, captivated by this stunning woman with her long willowy limbs that moved so elegantly, at the practiced ease of a woman who had graced the catwalks of the world. For just a second, he hesitated. None of his victims had been this beautiful. For the first time, he felt . . . sexual arousal. It confused him.

Lisa turned and walked off into the bathroom, leaving him in the dark to contemplate. It had all been planned so well. Everything had led to this point, this moment, and he struggled to understand his hesitation. He knew he was on the clock, knew they would figure it out when Trish walked into the police station, knew they would find Paterson, and knew they would come here to rescue her. He wanted Paterson to find her, to see her. He wanted him to pay for taking his wife. He had never before hesitated to kill any of his victims, never shown them mercy or suffered guilt for his crimes and yet without knowing it, this woman called everything into question. He slumped to his knees and pressed the heels of his hands to his ears.

Lisa padded out of the bathroom, still naked except for a towel wrapped around her blonde hair. She sat at her dresser and reached for the hairdryer. Pulling the towel off of her head, she flicked her hair free of the towel and looked into the mirror. Decision time. How to wear it today. Walker stood and stared at her through the slats. Decision time. How to kill her. His heart rate increased, his breathing deepened, his focus steadied. He was ready.

Throwing back the doors, he ran full tilt into the room toward her.

Startled at the sudden noise, Lisa jumped and turned. Walker grabbed her by the hair, dragged her head back and slammed her face into the dresser. Her nose hit the wood with a sickening thud. She went limp and dropped to the floor like another item of discarded clothing. Breathing heavily, Walker looked down at her, unconscious, wet hair straggled across her face, blood smearing her nose and mouth. He went back to the closet for his scalpels.

* * *

He could smell oil. Dirt. Concrete. His face, swollen and cold on one side, hurt. His eyes flickered. Swollen, they also hurt. Seemed to be de rigueur of late. His mouth was dry. He tried to lick his lips but failed. Taped, most likely duct. Still in his garage, still fully bound. Walker. *Caught me off guard.* Suddenly her face flashed into his mind. Panic overwhelmed him and he struggled against his ties. Lisa! The sick bastard was going after her. Of course he was. It all made perfect sense now. He had taken Walker's wife, now Walker would take his. The words jumped into his head: 'I am going to cut her to fucking ribbons. I am going to fucking destroy her.' He wrenched the top half of his body off the concrete, and tried to sit up. *Get up.* He fell back. *Get up!*

'I will take her from you, Paterson, and I am going to rend the fucking whore limb from limb.' *Get up, get the fuck up!* Again, he jerked himself up off the concrete, only to fall once more. *'FUCKING GET UP!'* His voice, muted by the tape, emerged as an angry frustrated squeal as he strained again and again.

'She will grovel and cry and call your name.' He fought to block out the terrifying images of Walker with Lisa that now flooded his brain. What he would do to her. The dead girls rushed in and became superimposed on Lisa. And he couldn't do a thing to stop it happening. He spun around on his back, scraped his fingers across the rough concrete, drew blood. His feet connected with the car, and he kicked out hard. The noise of his Guccis on the metal echoed loudly around the garage. He kept smashing the door. Someone must hear it. Please hear it.

'Ray! Ray? You in there?' For a second or two he thought he was imagining Carr's voice until he heard him bang frantically on the garage door. 'Ray! Talk to me!' Paterson let out a muffled scream, and kicked out at his car again. DCI Carr looked around him, found the side door — locked. He stepped back, and kicked the centre panel until it splintered inward. Paterson squinted in the brilliant daylight that flooded the garage. Half falling through the door, Carr saw Paterson on the ground, trussed up like a turkey, dishevelled, beaten and covered in blood. He ripped the tape off Paterson's mouth.

Paterson turned his head, painfully, toward the light. 'Get me up. Get me up!' Blood flooded his mouth. 'He's going for Lisa. Quick!' Paterson tried again to get himself up. Spotting a pair of wire cutters on a rack, Carr snipped him free of the plasticuffs and helped him to his feet. Paterson wobbled, fell back against the Aston. Another dent was neither here nor there. 'We have to get to my house, Roy. Please!'

'It's okay, sir.' Carr threw the beaten man's arm over his shoulder, to give him some support. 'We know what's going on now. Clocks figured it out. He's on his way to your house right now, and I've called in the shots. She'll be ok, Ray. There's a whole army on its way to her.'

'Hope it's a fucking big 'un, Roy,' said Paterson, spitting blood. He took his weight off Carr and tried to stand on his own. After a couple more wobbles he righted himself, and fumbled in his jacket pocket for his car keys, vaguely surprised that Walker had left them. He chucked them to Carr and opened the passenger door. 'We'll take the Aston. It's a lot quicker than your old heap of shit.' Groaning loudly, Paterson dropped his battered body onto the seat.

Carr calculated that even in a car this fast and cutting through the traffic, it would take a good half hour to get to Lisa's house. He knew Johnny Clocks and the shots were probably already there, and he was hoping that no one would call him until they arrived. If she was alive, then all well and good, but if, God forbid, they were too late and she was dead, Paterson could at least be restrained and taken to hospital under sedation.

Heads turned, as they always do at the sound of a police car's siren, but people took an extra-long look at the sight of a silver Aston Martin DB10 flying past them. More than a few wondered if their community charge money was being spent wisely.

Slowing down slightly at a crossroads, Carr's 'Play that Funky Music' ringtone kicked in. *Shit!* He let it ring.

After the fifth ring, Paterson looked over at him. 'You gonna get that?' Reluctantly, Carr pulled it out of his pocket, saw Clocks's name on his screen and pushed it hard against his right ear, hoping that Paterson wouldn't overhear.

'DCI Carr. Go.'

'Guv. Can I talk? Are you with Paterson?' said Clocks.

Carr picked up on the distress in his voice. *Oh please, no.* 'Go on.'

'Keep him away from here, guv. We were too late.' Clocks was almost whispering. Carr thought he heard a sob. Maybe he just caught his breath. 'This is fuckin' bad, guv. The worst yet. Don't let him see her. Don't.'

'I'll do what I can.'

Paterson looked across at the monosyllabic Carr. This wasn't like him. 'What's happened?' he said, calm.

'Nothing. We have to divert across to Guy's Hospital. I forgot to tell you, Trish turned up. Walked into the nick. She's okay physically, but in deep shock. We need to get over there.'

Paterson stared at him. 'Do we fuck! I'm glad she's safe, but we're going to my house first. Are we clear?' Carr just stared into the road ahead.

'What's happened? Tell me!'

Carr kept looking ahead.

'You fucking tell me now! D'you hear? Fucking tell me!'

'Sir . . . I . . . We have to go to Guy's . . . Trish . . .'

His face contorted, Paterson slammed his fist onto the dashboard. He screamed at Carr's ashen profile, almost causing him to kerb it. 'You fucking get me to my house! Get me to my house now! Fuckin' do it! I'm ordering you!'

They drove the rest of the way in silence, Paterson agitated, drumming his hands, feet, seething. When Paterson turned to look out of the window, Carr dropped his radio down by his thigh and clicked it off. He could do without them broadcasting the details.

* * *

Johnny Clocks had sat himself down on a concrete step outside the mansion. Cold and shivering, he hugged himself, not so much for warmth as for comfort. Only the most observant, had they been interested, would have noticed him gently rocking like a small, frightened child. He was just glad to be out of that place, that room, but it didn't matter whether he closed his eyes or kept them open, he couldn't get the image of what he'd just seen out of his head. Maybe he never would.

* * *

Torn between urgency and the need for a silent entrance to the house, he had killed the lights and coasted the last couple of hundred yards before pulling up outside the main gates. Every light in the house seemed to be on and the place shone in the blackness of the surrounding countryside like a beacon. His first thought was *I'm too late,* followed by, *Fuck! If he's still there, I'm lit up like a stripper in a spotlight right now.* Stealth clearly wasn't an option.

In his earpiece, Inspector Kingston was busy shouting instructions, ordering him to wait for their arrival. He pulled the earpiece out and let it dangle on his shoulder, deciding that the five minute ETA given might be four minutes too long. He reached into his glove compartment and opened up the small box containing his Glock 17. Dave Jordan's murder had prompted the powers that be to give authorised firearms officers attached to Operation Stammer permission to carry. Right now, Clocks was grateful he had taken all his firearms courses. He jumped out of the car and started toward the house, trying to take in everything he saw as quickly as he could, watching for any movement from inside, hoping he'd been wrong and this was all a colossal waste of everyone's time.

He reached the stone steps and looked up at the front door, which was ajar. No sign of forced entry. He weighed the scenarios in his head. *Door open, lights on, not good for Lisa, suspect gone. Door open, lights on, not good for Lisa, mad bastard hiding in the house waiting to jump out and slice and dice me.* Out of the two, the first scenario was the one he most favoured, but he figured that the second was a distinct possibility and likely detrimental to his health. With that thought uppermost in his mind, he kicked the front door wide open before diving in a forward roll entry into an empty hallway, coming to rest in a half crouch, sweeping the gun in a full 180 and back again. Nothing behind him. The hall was devoid of any ornamentation. Ahead of him, a white marble staircase and large crystal chandeliers hanging at the bottom and the top. Nowhere for anybody to hide. He was glad of Lisa's minimalist fetish.

He strained his ears for any sound that might tell him someone was in the house. Nothing. The silence hung like a heavy weight, pressing down. He could hear a faint whistling in his ears, tinnitus? Jimi Hendrix's guitar screamed out from somewhere above, and made him jump. 'Voodoo Chile.' S*till here then.*

He moved fast, taking the marble stairs two at a time, oblivious to the thump of his size tens on the cold marble. 'Voodoo Chile' was hiding any noise he made. He shoved his earpiece back in and began half-shouting into his sleeve mic. Kingston screamed back at him to hold his position. Three minutes away.

Some police officers, particularly those that drive fast response cars, suffer from auditory hallucinations. They can be off duty, walking along a street, when they'll hear the faint wailing of police sirens somewhere in the distance. To some degree, all police officers hear them. All emergency services personnel do. The sound is ingrained in them. Clocks thought he could hear them now, but it was merely wishful thinking.

At the top of the stairs, he held his back against the wall, taking quick glimpses around the corner into a long unlit passageway. The door at the end was open and the music blasted out. Clocks inhaled deeply and stepped into the passageway, gun held high in both hands. *C'mon,*

Kingston. Put'cha fuckin' foot down, son. Breathing deep, he edged toward the room, nerves pulled so tight he could have played along with Jimi, eyes never leaving the door ahead of him. It slammed shut, the loud bang startling him so he almost pulled the trigger. *Fucker's in there!* All coherent thought gone, he ran toward the door and threw his full weight against it.

The door flew inwards, and he crashed into the room, slipped and landed awkwardly on his side. Struggling to right himself, he caught sight of Walker half out of the window, smiling back at him. His face, no, his mouth and nose, were smeared with blood.

Clocks blocked out everything except his target. He raised the Glock, slipped again, steadied himself with his other hand and fired off two wild shots in Walker's direction. Both thudded into the brickwork either side of the window, well wide of the mark. In his second attempt, he put his left hand underneath his right to steady his aim. It slid straight off. His eyes darted from Walker to his hands. *What the . . . is that? Oh fuck!* Back to Walker. Still grinning, Walker gave a little wave and dropped backwards out of the window, crashing into the bushes below.

Clocks pulled himself up and half-slithered, half-ran toward the window. His target was rapidly disappearing into the night, in a manic zig-zag run towards the shadow under the trees. Clocks pulled the trigger over and over, emptying the entire magazine into the dark, knowing even as he fired that it was futile. Walker was gone. In the distance, he really could hear the sound of Kingston's SUV wailing its way up the hill. *Too fuckin' late, mate.*

Holstering his gun, he raised his hand to speak into his sleeve mic and caught sight of his hands again. They were smothered in blood. Hers. It dawned on him that he'd have to turn around. Johnny Clocks closed his eyes, tried to steel himself, knew it was bad, prayed it wasn't, then let out a deep breath before turning.

His legs failed him. He slid down the wall onto his haunches, staring at the carnage laid out in front of him. It took him a moment or two to figure out where she was. He noticed her foot sticking out from behind the bed and realised that when he'd stormed the room, slipped and fell, she was less than two feet away from him and it was her blood he'd skidded on. Focussed on getting his man, he hadn't even noticed her. He stood up and walked slowly, almost reverently, to where she lay, his feet making a faint squelching noise on the carpet. What he saw made him retch, and he jerked his head away with a small cry.

Lisa Paterson was naked. She lay face up, legs and arms spread like a starfish. Her throat gaped wide. Her vagina was gone and so were her eyes, leaving two black holes. A doll from some child's worst nightmare. He stared at the wide gash across her chest and the exposed heart. Written sideways across her stomach was the word, 'Yours.' He'd got it right, wished to Christ he hadn't.

His head started to spin and an ominous blackness, tinged with red, began to creep in at the edge of his vision. He staggered backwards out of the room, screwing his eyes closed tight, fighting to keep the sight from searing into his brain. As he staggered along the passageway toward the stairs, he heard boots clattering on the marble. Kingston and his team ran into the hallway.

'Stay there!' Clocks shouted. 'Don't come up. I lost him.'

Kingston hared up the stairs. 'Where is he? Where'd he go? How long ago, for fuck's sake?'

Clocks waved a hand toward the bedroom. 'He jumped out the window. Ran across the grass into the trees. I emptied my gun. Missed. About a minute ago.'

Kingston spun round and shouted at his men. 'Go! Spread out. Go!' He took the stairs back down, two at a time. And then they were gone. Alone in the silence, Clocks stumbled down the stairs and sat down on the cold, wet concrete steps outside the house. He turned his face up into the rain, let it pound him. He fished out his mobile phone, raked his fingers through his hair and made the call to Carr, telling him to keep Paterson away.

Soon, a carnival of lights and noise approached the house, a procession of assorted police cars, paramedics and ambulances. Kingston's doing. Well, let them get on with it. All he wanted to do was pull his brain out and wash it clean in a bucket of bleach.

* * *

Clocks nodded gratefully to the ambulance man who gently placed an aluminium blanket around his shoulders and handed him hot tea from his own flask.

'Alright, fella. Come with me.' The ambulance man's voice was weary too. He offered Clocks a helping hand and a bit of a smile that said it would all be okay. Taking the hand and getting to his feet, Clocks glanced over the ambulance man's shoulder, just as an Aston Martin DB10 pulled in through the gates. His eyes went like saucers.

Before the car had even stopped, Ray Paterson exploded out of the passenger side. 'Oh fuck! No!' Clocks dropped the tea and pushed past the startled ambulance man, racing to head Paterson off. 'Stop him!' he shouted wildly. 'Don't let him in!' Several uniforms turned toward the running man and attempted to grab him, but he shoved them aside. Clocks kept shouting as he ran. Then three or four of the bigger uniforms grappled with Paterson and managed to bring him to a halt. They held him, struggling, till Clocks rushed up.

'Guv'nor! It's me, Timex,' Clocks panted. 'Look at me! Look at me!'

Still struggling, Paterson turned in his direction. 'Clocks? John? Is that . . ? Is that . . ?' Paterson eyed him, stumbled, legs failing. One of the uniforms shoved Clocks aside, blocking his view and placing himself between him and Paterson, who promptly kicked off again. Furious, Clocks swung an almighty right-hander at the face of his blocker. A big lad, he managed to move out of the way just quick enough for Clocks's fist to scrape his chin. No harm done.

'Woah! Hey, blood! You're covered in blood, you idiot!' shouted the uniform. Clocks stopped dead, realising he'd made an already bad situation even worse. Lisa's blood was all over him. Paterson had seen. The uniform went back to pushing him away, and Clocks went quietly.

In the background, Paterson continued to fight his way forward against increasingly poor odds, until he had no strength left and he was brought to the ground. Clocks staggered back towards the comfort of his stone step, but Roy Carr grabbed hold of his arm.

'Jesus, Clocks. Fancy running at him covered in her blood. What were you thinking, man?'

Clocks shook his arm free and turned, suddenly overcome, hijacked by rage. 'What was I thinking? What was *I* thinking?' he shouted, stabbing his finger at the startled man. 'I'll tell you what I was thinking. I was thinking that I distinctly remember telling you not to fucking bring him here, and yet here he is. Why's that then? Is that my fault?'

'I had no choice,' Carr retorted, puffing his chest up a little. 'He ordered me to come here. What could I do?'

'What you could do,' said Clocks, poking him in the inflated chest a few times. 'Is use a bit of fuckin' common sense. Who the fuck brings the victim's husband to a murder scene? Who does that, eh? Christ! I'm a fuckin' teaboy and I've got more sense than you. Who the fuck's using the Met police brain cell tonight then?'

Carr took a few steps back, maybe hoping it would help defuse the situation. Not tonight. 'He's my senior officer. He ordered me to . . .'

Clocks poked harder. 'Ordered you? He's suspended, you stupid prick! He can't order a fuckin' Chinese takeaway, you moronic knob.'

'Look, I'm sorry, alright? I'm tired . . .'

‘Oh really? Tired are we?’ The punch made a solid ‘thunk’ noise as Clocks successfully re-delivered the one he’d aimed at the uniformed officer just now. It connected with the sweet spot on DCI Carr’s chin, putting him down, and out for the count.

‘Well, you get your fuckin’ head down for a bit then. Hopefully when you wake up, you’ll realise what a dick you are!’ Clocks turned sharply on his heel and came face to face with the ambulance man who, having seen the whole episode developing, realised a lot quicker than DCI Carr that it was going to end badly. He was already on his way over with his medical bag when Clocks knocked out his senior officer. They locked eyes for a second, then side-stepped each other, going their own separate ways.

Clocks heard the rip of Velcro as the ambulance man opened his bag, and suddenly became aware of the intense pain in his two broken knuckles.

CHAPTER FOURTEEN

'What can I do for you, Ray?' Compassion didn't come easily to ACC Young but even he could see that Paterson had been dealt a piss poor hand and felt it appropriate to soften his tone. His chair came out from behind his big desk and he now found himself sitting opposite Paterson with no barrier between them. He'd done the 'open management style' course.

'Come to give you this,' said Paterson quietly, and handed an envelope to his senior officer. 'It's my resignation. I'm done.'

ACC Young looked at his name on the envelope, turned and put it on the desk behind him. 'Not accepted, Ray.'

Paterson bristled. 'What do you mean?'

'I mean I'm not going to accept it. You're in no position to make rational decisions, Ray. For God's sake, man, you lost her ten days ago. You shouldn't even be here. You have to rest. You have to get your head straight. Take as much time as you need. Make sure you see the Met psychiatrist though.'

There was a sharp tap on the door followed by ACC Young's PA, Sheila Mears, carrying a tray of tea. Biscuits too, no less. Pulling out all the stops. ACC Young gestured for her to put the tray down on a table in front of a large plate glass window that overlooked the capital.

'Have you seen your GP?' Young said, rising to pour the tea.

'With all due respect, sir, fuck that. We both know my head will never be straight and all the shrinks in the world won't help with that. We also know my career has gone. You made that perfectly clear at our last meeting.' Young stopped, teapot poised. He nodded, slowly. 'So let's not drag this out, sir. Take my resignation and let me get on with my life.'

Young resumed pouring. 'You can still have a career, Ray. Maybe when the dust has settled a bit we can make you a chief superintendent. Move you off of the CID, give you a nick somewhere a bit quieter. Give it some thought.' Young sat down and pushed a cup towards Paterson.

'Thanks for the offer, sir, but no thanks. I've given it plenty of thought. Not interested.' Young frowned at him. 'There's no point, sir. I am, and will always be, considered a liability, a failure, and we both know that's no good for anyone. So, again, I'm resigning. And whether you accept my resignation or not makes no difference to me. I won't be back, so you'll have to do as you see fit.'

Again, Young shook his head, slower this time, almost condescending, and took a sip of his tea. He looked straight at Paterson. 'We're doing everything we can to catch this bastard, Ray. I want you to understand that. You probably already know that the DCI from Greater Manchester is in place.' He did know. Johnny Clocks, for all his faults, was turning out to be a brick. He'd been round twice a day and run him around to get things done. Shored him up a bit. Both had a lot of sorrows to drown, so they'd smashed their way through a few bottles of whiskey together. Clocks had even crashed on his sofa a few times when things had got a bit too heavy, drink-wise. He'd kept him in the loop and brought him up to speed with how things were going, even though technically he shouldn't have. Said that Walker had gone completely dark, that they were no nearer finding him, let alone laying hands on him.

'Your team is fractured. They're far too damaged to carry out the investigation, certainly as far as the core members go. The Manchester DCI, Caroline Webb, is a good girl, at the top of her game. If anyone can catch Walker, it's her.'

'She sounds absolutely wonderful, sir.' Stung by the thinly disguised and somewhat insensitive suggestion that he'd never been up to the task, Paterson didn't bother to conceal the sarcasm in his voice. 'Do you actually have any idea where he is? Any sightings?'

'No. Nothing at this point in time,' said Young.

'It's been ten days, sir. Perhaps your "girl" isn't quite as good as you thought. Sir.'

Young let it slide. 'It's early days. I'm confident, Ray. Walker will have to surface at some point, somewhere. Even if he's topped himself, his body will come to light.'

'Let's hope he hasn't, sir,' said Paterson and immediately regretted it.

'I'd have thought that's an outcome you'd be pleased with.' ACC Young searched Paterson's face. If it had been his wife, his career destroyed, he'd have wanted the man dead. Paterson shrugged, seemingly indifferent. Young had seen enough liars in his time to realise that Paterson was concealing something and it troubled him. The top ranks had been worried about this, and part of Young's remit was to try to see what play, if any, Paterson had. No point pussyfooting around.

'What are you up to, Ray?' The thought crept out of his head and into his mouth before he could check himself.

'Up to, sir? I don't understand.'

Young shifted in his chair. 'Just a feeling, Ray. I have this,' he waved his hand around in a way that instantly reminded Paterson of the queen waving to her people, 'odd sensation that you're going to do something you'll come to regret.'

'Not planning on doing anything, sir. I'm just going to quit and fade away into the sunset. Spend some of my money wisely. Sit back.'

Young's eyes narrowed. 'Wisely, Ray?'

A faint smile crossed Paterson's lips. 'Yes, sir. I'm going to invest some money.'

'May I ask how you intend to invest your money? Could always use a few tips.'

Paterson sighed deeply and reached for his tea. It was likely cool enough now. Fuck it, he thought, he'll know soon enough. 'I'm going to hold a press conference to let people know that I'm putting up a reward for Walker.'

Young choked on his tea, spilt some on his shirt, grabbed a napkin and dabbed at it.

'I'm thinking a million should shake the tree a bit. Someone knows where he is and they'll give him up. Some people'd sell their firstborn for that sort of money, wouldn't they? Even if it doesn't work, there'll be an awful lot of people looking for him. Quite a few professionals, I would think. I'll up the money half a mil a month until he turns up. Way I see it now, he's screwed one way or the other. He won't be able to stay hidden forever, and once he sticks his head out of his hole, someone will see him and give him up. I'm done being on the back foot.'

Young stood up and slammed both palms on the desk, 'You'll do nothing of the sort, Paterson,' he said. 'This could hamper the investigation. You have no authority to do such a thing.'

Paterson chugged his tea and stood up. Time to go. Poor guy's upset. He looked directly at Young, 'I don't believe it will hamper the investigation, Mr Young. I think it'll open it up quite a bit, and as far as I can see, I'm helping out the new girl. Making her job a bit easier. As for authority, I don't need it.' He stood up and made for the door. 'If you recall, sir, about five minutes ago I quit. As of now, I'm no longer a policeman.' Paterson opened the door and took his first step into the civilian world. 'And don't even try to hit me with any notice period. I'm done with it all.'

Young stared at him, anger written all over his face. He seemed to think for a while, computing the implications of Paterson's plan. He settled on one of them. 'And have you considered the other possibility, Paterson?'

'Do you mean the possibility that once he sees the news and realises the game's up, that he's fucked, he'll come after me? Yes, sir. I have indeed considered it. You never know your luck.' He gave Young a cocky wink. 'Thanks for the tea, sir.' Paterson walked out, closed the door. At last he was doing something positive, taking back some control.

As he left, he heard the sound of a teacup smash against a wall, and for the first time in a long while, Paterson smiled.

* * *

'Put the telly on!' An excited Johnny Clocks ran into the squad room and threw his jacket onto the nearest desk. 'Put it on quick. Paterson's called a fuckin' press conference!' Carrie Gedmine snatched up the remote and flicked the TV on. Everything stopped. Paterson's face filled the screen, healing nicely now but still showing signs of his beating. A small yellow tickertape ran across the bottom of the Sky News report, declaring 'Breaking News. Jack the Gripper cop speaks.'

'Ladies and Gentlemen, thank you for coming.' Paterson, dressed in his best Tom Ford suit, stood on the pavement far enough away to be outside the grounds of New Scotland Yard but close enough so that the revolving logo was in camera shot. He held his hand up and faced the mob of reporters, all itching to fire questions at him. 'I have today tendered my resignation from the Metropolitan

Police Service.' Silence fell. Senior police officers don't call press meetings to say they've resigned. The reporters sensed something better was coming.

'What the fuck is he up to?' Johnny Clocks said, not expecting a reply.

'It is with much sadness and deep personal regret that I admit I have failed to find the killer of two men who were my colleagues and friends, and four women including my wife, Lisa. My inability to find and stop this man, one of my own officers, is something that will haunt me for the rest of my life. I have just come from a meeting with the assistant commissioner for crime, Mr Young, and he has, with some regret, agreed to accept my resignation. I am unable to tell you exactly where the investigation is at this moment in time, but I can assure you that the Met is doing all it can to find Adam Walker and bring him to justice.' A hand shot up, followed by two, then three others. Paterson gestured for them to wait. There was more to come.

'As you know, Walker has gone to ground and cannot, at the present time, be located. Therefore, I am calling on the public and the media to assist the police in locating him as quickly as possible. The need to find Adam Walker is of the utmost urgency and, as we find ourselves in a situation of extreme need, I have decided to take extreme action. Since I am no longer with the Metropolitan Police, they cannot stop me nor can they be held accountable for what I am about to say and do next.' The squad room held its collective breath as did the crowd of reporters. 'As many of you know, I come from a family of independent means, and from my own personal funds I am offering a reward of one million pounds sterling for any information that leads to the detection and apprehension of Adam Walker.' That did it. The crowd of reporters went into a total frenzy. Hands shot up everywhere and they surged forward, firing a barrage of unintelligible questions at him. He held up his hands and waved his arms to quieten them back down.

'Fuck me blind!' shouted Clocks. He nodded approvingly. 'Oh, you clever, clever sod.'

'What the hell does he think he's doing?' asked Gedmine.

Clocks looked at her and grinned. 'What needs to be done. He's doing what we've never been able to do. He's taking back control. He's fucked him.' Gedmine frowned, unsure of how exactly Walker was 'fucked' by this gesture. Clocks looked at the TV. The crowd was settling again. The ticker tape spooled a different message. 'Breaking News — Top Cop resigns. Offers one million pound reward.'

'I want to stress that this man is extremely dangerous, and I urge the public to stay away from him and avoid approaching him at all costs. This reward money is purely for solid information, sightings of Adam Walker that will lead directly to his arrest.' Paterson paused, gauged the crowd. 'Questions anyone?' The reporters exploded again. 'Yes?' said Paterson, pointing to a dark haired man whom he vaguely recognised as a journalist from the *Independent* newspaper.

'Mr Paterson,' he said, thrusting his digital tape recorder forward. 'Why are you doing this? Is it because he murdered your wife? Is that the reason?' Paterson frowned at the man. Why is it, he wondered, that reporters always have to ask the most stupid questions?

'Yes, it is. Of course it is. But it is also for the other girls this savage killed. For the civilian analyst who assisted us in the early days of the investigation and helped identify him. For my friend and colleague, Detective Sergeant Dave Jordan, who gave his life to help us identify Walker. That act of bravery should not be forgotten and will not be in vain. It's for the fact that I couldn't catch him by conventional means. It's because he has to be caught one way or the other.' His face darkened.

'What do you mean "the other?"' shouted a young female reporter.

Paterson checked himself. 'It means that the police cannot do it without the help of the public. All the appeals have come to nothing. He is out there. He has gone to ground. Someone knows where he is, perhaps they're even hiding him, I don't know, but someone, somewhere will see him. Whichever rat-hole this *thing*,' he spat the word out like he had just tasted something poisonous, 'is hiding in, it will have to show its face at some point. I believe the offer of one million in cash will help concentrate people's minds and eyes.'

Clocks was transfixed. He murmured, 'He's goading him. He's dehumanising him. Calling him "Thing" and "It." That's gonna piss Walker off. He won't like that.'

'But let me stress again,' said Paterson, 'I will only pay this money for solid, confirmed *information* that will lead to this monster's arrest. If any member of the public sees him, then please just call it in. Do not make any attempt to tackle him. The money is for information only. There is nothing extra for detaining or trying to detain him. He is a vicious sociopath and will not hesitate for a second to kill anyone if he thinks he is in danger. If there's any vigilantes or mercenaries watching and looking for a quick payday, don't take this as an invitation to hunt him down and kill him. He must be brought to justice.' The crowd of reporters surged forward again, like a pack of hungry dogs baying for more, cameras and recorders pushed forward, desperate to pick up anything Paterson said.

Paterson looked into the crowd and found the Sky News crew. These boys, he knew, would go worldwide immediately. Possibly even live. He stared directly into the lens as if it were a telescopic sight.

'Adam Walker,' he said, his voice calm and steady. 'Give it up now. You have nowhere to go anymore. As of right now, the whole country will be looking for you. And they will find you. You will pay for what you've done. I've beaten you.' He turned away from the camera, back toward the mob. 'That is all,' he said, and began pushing his way through the throng of frenzied reporters who were all shoving and jostling towards him anxious for anything else he might give them. He headed toward a waiting Bentley — a not so subtle display of wealth.

Clocks turned back toward the hushed office, his face suddenly concerned. That bit wasn't so clever.'

'Why not?' asked someone.

'He just used a subtle trick of the tongue.' A few of the detectives just looked at him blankly, waiting for more. Gedmine shrugged, as if to say, well, go on then, explain yourself.

'He just used the word "don't" in front of a command to do something.' Their expressions were blank. Clocks groaned. 'What the fuck do they teach you lot at detective school these days? Carrie, don't think of a pink elephant. Quick! What did you just think of?'

'A pink elephant,' she said, a bit surprised.

'Of course you did. You had no choice. In order for you to make sense of what I just said, you have to "see" it in your mind first. The word "don't" is forgotten. Your mind glosses over it.

'Hold on a second,' said Gedmine, seriously confused at this sudden burst of intelligence from Clocks. 'Where's this pink elephant and pictures shit come from? Since when do you understand language? You only know about eight words, and five of those are "fuck."' The room burst into laughter.

Clocks rolled his eyes. 'It's something Dave showed a few of us a couple of years ago. Said it was an old trick they used to use back in the day to get villains to say what they wanted them to say. Put things into their heads. Saved beating the shit out of them.' Gedmine looked unconvinced.

'Think about what the guv'nor just said: "If there's any vigilantes or mercs watching please don't take this as an invitation to hunt him down and kill him." Take out the word "don't" and he's just said, "please take this as an invitation to hunt him down and kill him." That's exactly what he wants. And he finished it off by saying that he wants him brought to justice swiftly. There will be more than a few ex-servicemen out there who understand exactly what he's just said. On live telly, he's just offered a million sovs to have the fucker hunted down and whacked out.'

CHAPTER FIFTEEN

On the thirteenth day after her murder, Lisa Paterson was finally laid to rest. A long line of black limos snaked their way slowly through the rain-soaked streets towards Honour Oak Crematorium tucked away deep in the back streets of south London. Until her arrival, the most notable residents were Frederick John Horniman, the founder of the world famous Horniman Museum, Freddie Mills the one time world lightweight boxing champion who died in very mysterious circumstances, George Cornell the East End gangster shot by Ronnie Kray, and its most recent occupant, 'Mad' Frankie Fraser, the notorious henchman of the Richardson Gang, arch rivals of the Krays back in the sixties. Paterson really didn't want her here in this company of lowlifes, but her family insisted she come home to south London to be near her family. He had neither the will nor the stomach to argue.

Outside the gates, a large crowd of fans and fashionistas mixed with the press, all jostling to get a glimpse of the hearse bearing her coffin. The youngsters, in thrall to celebrity, pushed their iPhones toward the windows of the lead car, hoping desperately to catch a blurry picture of her coffin to post on Instagram and

Facebook. They knew too, that the place would be crawling with the rich and famous.

The press, of course, were as thrilled as the youngsters to be at the funeral of a TV star, but for a different reason — the money rather than the 'likes.' After all, they needed to pay the bills.

The dozens of undercover police mixed in with the mourners were desperate for a sighting of Adam Walker, whom they never for a moment expected to show. They'd been warned under threat of disciplinary action not to gawk at the celebrities.

As the lead car slid silently passed the crowd of mourners, Paterson caught sight of a group of tearful women of about Lisa's age. He recognised one or two of them as friends of hers from the old days, before she became famous. None of them had worn nearly so well as she had. Lack of money and proper food, three or four kids apiece, ropey husbands that lived in the pubs, payday loans following them around, skincare by heroin . . . that would pretty much do it. As he drove past he gave them a weak smile, a nod and a small wave, letting them know he remembered them, grateful that they'd turned out. He almost thought Lisa'd made it out, was the lucky one, then revised it.

He thought back to the first night he met them all in a pub in Denmark Hill. It was early days for Lisa in the modelling world. She was just beginning to make a mark, still running with most of her old gang, and had only just met him. She was desperate to show him off to her friends and in their turn, they were desperate to meet the man who had won their girlfriend's heart and stolen her from the group. He remembered how, towards the end of that evening, he had been dragged, more than a little drunk, into the ladies' toilet for the chat. One of them, he couldn't remember which, had gone into a garbled half drunken monologue about how lovely Lisa was, how much they all loved her, and how he had better take good care of her. 'If you ever hurt her, I'll fuggin' hunt you down,' said the now forgotten girl. Gillian, was that her name? Yes, Gillian. His eyes teared up behind his Ray-Bans and he turned his head away. *I'm so, so sorry I let you down.*

The car turned through the main gates to begin her final drive. Outside the main chapel, a large crowd of invite-only mourners made up of friends, family and various celebrities were waiting, huddled under umbrellas and bits of building by the entrance to the chapel. Their heads all turned like a shoal of fish as the first of the limos entered the gates and stopped just long enough for the pallbearer to exit the passenger door. After donning his top hat and bowing in reverence to its passenger, the bearer began his slow, respectful walk ahead of the procession. In the distance he saw her parents, her sister and Sebastian Harrison, huddled together outside the entrance. Harrison had his arm around the sister — a bit too low on the back. Careful, Seb, thought Paterson, she'll get you into trouble.

Her parents had insisted on it being a celebration of their daughter's life, and as much as a funeral can be, it was an uplifting ceremony, with family, protégés and friends giving readings and poems. Her favourite music played throughout: 'Somewhere Over the Rainbow' — the Eva Cassidy version — on the way in, Jools Holland's 'Enjoy Yourself (It's later than you think)' after two readings and, on the way out, 'Always Look On The Bright Side Of Life.' Her dad was a big fan, and Lisa grew up watching *Monty Python* with him. She loved it, 'got it' instantly, where none of her friends did. Paterson thought the song was right on the money in summing it all up.

* * *

Funeral over, Paterson found himself standing alone, busying himself by reading the flower cards awash with sentiment. It appeared that no one wanted to be near him and, in truth, he was grateful. He knew that the majority of people there blamed him for what had happened to her, and thanks to the eagerness of the press to dish dirt and speculate, the majority now knew of his fondness for the opposite sex. He felt genuine shame.

'How you holding up, Ray?' He immediately recognised the voice behind him, although he hadn't seen him for a few years. Billy Hitchcock, Lisa's agent. Mister Fifteen Percent himself. Never liked him. He turned to see Hitchcock, umbrella in one hand, other extended in greeting. A short stub-nosed man now in his early fifties, he was wearing a black suit under a Burberry raincoat. The tartan tie spoiled the effect.

Lisa once told him that Hitchcock had discovered her while she was waiting at a bus stop with a friend. He just came up to her, bold as brass, and said, 'You're so beautiful. How'd you like to be a famous model?' Cheesy line, but flattering to a girl just a week shy of her sixteenth birthday. She thought it was just a ploy to get into her knickers, but something about him also told her he might just be telling the truth. So she took a chance. Turned out he was on the level. She would never say, but Paterson suspected he probably did get into her knickers at some point. He recognised the type. All in the past now. 'Billy,' he said, and shook the proffered hand. 'Been a long time. Thanks for coming. I'm doing . . . okay. As well as can be expected.'

Hitchcock nodded. Wasn't much else he could have said, really. 'Good turnout, Ray. She'll be sorely missed.' Now Paterson nodded. Wasn't much he could say either.

'Are you any closer to getting him, Ray, the bastard that did this? Has the reward helped?'

'Not yet,' Paterson said, looking past him toward the crowd of mourners. He saw Lisa's father with her sister. Neither was looking for him. 'But it will. I'll up it by half a mill every fortnight. Something will give eventually.'

Hitchcock instinctively turned to look over his shoulder, where Paterson was looking, and saw the crowd.

He turned back. 'So many people loved her. Lot of tears here today, Ray, not just for Lisa, for all of them. Everyone he's ever killed.' He raised his eyes toward the rain falling in big heavy drops. 'Even the sky is crying.'

Just then the rain picked up pace. Paterson pulled up his collar and said, 'Good seeing you again, Billy. I'm sorry it had to be like this. You take care of yourself.' He turned and walked away.

* * *

Paterson looked up into the flat grey sky that shrouded Land's End. He gazed at a flock of seagulls struggling to make headway against the harsh wind blowing in from the Atlantic. For a full minute, they held their positions, until the pressure changed and they plummeted down, swooping over the heads of the three or four tourists struggling across the jagged rocks.

He had come every day to the same rock to sit and mull over the events of the last month. He struggled to come to terms with the fact that in less than a month what had been an almost perfect life had been ripped to shreds and set on fire, and there was nothing he could have done to stop it happening.

For over an hour now he had sat in the wind and drizzle looking out across the sea, only breaking his reverie to check his phone every few minutes. The cold December wind, carrying with it a miserable sleet, bit into his face, turning his lips mauve, and his nose would have given Rudolph a run for his money. Still he continued to sit, waiting. Johnny Clocks would call eventually, he knew, but after four days of hanging around in London doing nothing, he felt the need to be back here, in the spot where, as a child, he'd found some small comfort.

London was maybe five hours away to most people, but he figured that by the time he got the call, he could make it back in under two and half at the most. The Aston Vanquish he was now using would do it, along with the abuse of the blue light which he should have had removed from behind the grille. It would take the team a good bit longer than that to get themselves together.

His guilt was chewing out his insides. He looked down at the rocks below. The water crashed against the stones, rising high into the air with little broken fingers that seemed to snatch at him. Too easy, he thought, shifting his weight backwards a bit. *I'm not ready.*

Another hour later, head throbbing from the cold, face and hands the colour of plums, he stood himself up, swayed a little in the wind and carefully picked his way back over the rocks toward the shelter of the car. He ramped the heater up to full and felt his head begin to swim as it adjusted from the cold outside. His phone rang. Hands shaking from the cold, he fumbled with the zip on his Goretex and pulled it out from his inside pocket. His stomach lurched when he saw the face filling his screen. Walker.

'Where the fuck are you, you piece of shit?'

'And a good afternoon to you too, Ray.' Walker spoke evenly, sounding unconcerned. 'I'll bet you've missed me.'

'Tell me where you are and I'll fucking show you exactly how much I've missed you.'

Paterson struggled to think. What to do about the call? *Have to trace it. How? Can't. Try to call Clocks. Can't. Record it. How the fuck do I do that? What have I been taught? Think. Think.*

'That doesn't sound very nice, I must say. There's me doing the decent thing and you're getting all arsey with me and *that*, as you well know, can have very serious consequences.'

Paterson took a deep breath. *Calm yourself. Calm.* Another breath, another. It dawned on him that yet again, the situation was out of his control. 'Where are you, Adam?'

'Irrelevant. At least for the moment.'

'What do you want?'

'A few things. First of all, I wanted to say how flattered I am that you consider me worth so much money. I'm almost tempted to turn myself in and claim the reward myself.' He laughed. 'But I won't.' Paterson said nothing. 'What would you like to know first, Ray? How she screamed when I sliced her, or when I fucked her? God, she was a screamer, wasn't she, Ray? Mind you, she had something to scream about this time. A proper man *digging* around inside her.'

Paterson was used to people winding him up. All policemen are. It goes with the territory and usually runs like water off a duck's back. Not this time. Paterson lost it, punched the roof of the car, screamed, 'You bastard! Shut your fucking mouth! I will kill you, you hear me? I will find you and I will fucking kill you, so help me God!'

'God, Ray? I think he kicked us both to the kerb some time ago. I really wouldn't count on him for any help. Deep breaths, Ray. They'll help you more than God.'

Paterson was suddenly too hot. He couldn't breathe properly. The car seemed to be wrapping itself around him, pressing down on him, and he stabbed angrily at the buttons to open the front windows. A blast of freezing North Atlantic wind smacked into the side of his face. He breathed out in short, rapid bursts. 'Why did you kill her? What did she ever do to you?'

'Nothing,' said Walker. 'Nothing at all. But then, the victims of serial killers rarely do anything to piss their killers off, Ray, you should know that. They don't do anything to deserve it. We do it because we have to. It's a need, a real deep-seated, can't control it, have to do it need. But in your case, well, you pissed me off. You fucked my wife, I fucked yours. But you have to admit I did a much more thorough job.'

The guilt washed over him again. He sank back in his seat, exhausted. 'What do you want with me, Adam? You tormenting me, is that it? Is this part of your fucked up serial-killer mentality?' There was no answer for a moment.

'You surprised me, Ray. Good move with the reward money. Made it a bit difficult for me to hide now, hasn't it? I really didn't think you had the brains or the balls, but it seems I may have got you wrong. I got to thinking about things and came to the conclusion that my days could well be numbered. So I thought maybe we should meet up. Sort things out between us. What do you say? Me and you.'

Paterson sat up. 'When? Where?'

'Midnight tonight. Top of Tower Bridge. You up for it?'

His brain handed him a sudden flash of the high walkways above the river Thames and his heart skipped a beat. The bastard knows. 'Fuck, yeah. Wouldn't miss it for the world.'

'It's a date then. I'll leave the door open for you. It's been lovely talking to you. And, Ray, before you go, do your windows up. You'll catch your death.'

The phone went dead.

* * *

The second he heard the beep beep beep of the dial tone, Paterson was out of the car, craning his neck, scouring the landscape for any sight of where Walker might be. He had to be close. He knew the car window was open. Close enough to watch him. There were no other cars in the car park. The only people he could see were those on the rocks below and a couple of old ladies who had rather stupidly braved the conditions against the advice of their coach driver waiting at the top of the road. His first point of call. Slamming the Vanquish into gear, he wheel spun out of the car park and was at the coach in seconds.

Despite the best efforts of the sixty-something driver to block his entry, Paterson stormed the bus like a man possessed. He moved quickly along the aisle toward the back of the coach, scanning the seats, spaces, the faces of the startled pensioners, looking for any involuntary eye movements, shifts in body language, anything that would tell him Walker was hidden down among the seats. Nothing. He searched again on the way back out. He jumped back into the car, punched the redial button again, knew Walker wouldn't answer but wanted his picture up.

The only place left was the hotel at the top. The tyres span furiously under the whip of the V12 engine before they gripped. He tore through the car park and up the hill toward the hotel.

Door open and engine running, he crashed through the reception doors and ran to the desk, screaming, 'Police! Emergency!' frightening the life out of a handful of guests. He waved his phone, with Walker's face on the screen, at the terrified Latvian receptionist behind the desk, and shouted, 'This man! Is he here, is he here?' The girl stood, mesmerised, at the soaking wet, wild-eyed man in front of her. 'Talk to me, woman. This man, is he here? Look at his face, look at it. Is he here? What room?' He spun round, his eyes darting everywhere. Save for the few frightened guests, the lobby was empty.

'Anybody seen this man?' he held out the phone at chest level, spinning around too quickly for anyone to focus. 'Anybody? I'm the police. This man is wanted for serious crimes. I suspect he is here in this hotel. Please, look at his face.' He spun again, slower this time before darting forward to each person, ensuring they got a closer look. 'Please. Look at him. Have you seen him? It's important.' They edged away from him, shaking their collective heads.

'Fuck! Fuck it!' Paterson stamped in frustration.

'Language,' said an elderly gentleman. He had the look and tone of an old-school sergeant major, long since retired but still brave, shielding his wife from Paterson. 'There's no need for that, sir.' Paterson glared at him, then turned his back. The commotion had brought people running into the reception area from various parts of the building. Two men now stood behind the desk flanking the receptionist, giving her protection. Paterson held the phone up again. 'This man. Do you recognise him? He's wanted for murder. Several murders. Please.' The mention of the word 'Murder' sent a ripple of concern through the room. People eyed each other anxiously. 'It's okay,' Paterson said, 'you're quite safe. I'm the police.'

'Your ID, sir,' demanded the retired soldier, and, mustering his last reserves of courage, he held out his hand.

Shit, thought Paterson, haven't got it anymore, have I? 'I lost it in a fight with him,' he said, hoping the lie would satisfy the old boy. It didn't.

'Really?' said the old soldier. 'I'm not sure I believe you. You, girl,' he pointed a bony finger at the receptionist. 'Call the police.'

'Sir,' said Paterson, 'just do me a favour and butt out. I've told you I'm police and that's that. I don't give a toss whether you believe me or not, and I don't have the fucking time to debate it with you right now.'

Paterson turned his back again. 'Anyone . . ?'

'Sir?' A tiny woman, concealed until now behind the two men flanking the receptionist, stepped forward. Room service, thought Paterson. 'I have seen him.'

Paterson's heart jumped. 'What? When? Where?' He moved towards the desk, and the men instinctively closed in. 'Tell me,' he said.

'I see him upstairs. On top floor,' she said. Paterson put her down as East European. 'I finish clean a room and I see a man with glasses.' She circled her eyes with her hands. Binoculars. 'Looking out of the window. I think he is just looking at the sea, the cliffs. He turned around when he heard me and smiled. I smiled back. He walked past me to the stairs and he put his finger to his lips, for me to quiet I think.'

'Are you sure it was him?' said Paterson, holding the phone out toward her.

She nodded. 'Yes, yes. Is him. He left. I think is not normal, and I watch from window. I see him walk towards town.'

'How long ago?'

'Maybe five, six minutes.' Paterson made a rapid calculation. From the time Walker ended that call, it had taken him less than a minute to get to the coach, a minute to search it, a minute to get to the hotel and about three or four minutes here in the foyer.

Eight minutes at most. A two or three minute head start, and he was on foot. Couldn't have got far.

'What was he wearing?'

'A dark jacket. Heavy. Keep out the water. And jeans.'

'Anything else?'

'Yes. He is yellow hair now. Not like picture you have. Yellow hair. Not brown.' Figures, Paterson thought. No one's looking for a fair-haired man. 'Thank you,' he said. Heads turned to follow him as he ran out through the double doors. Retired sergeant major grunted.

* * *

On the drive back to London, Paterson mulled over in his head how Walker had managed to get away from him. He'd been no more than a few minutes behind him, and yet there was no trace of Walker anywhere. What to do next? He was torn with indecision. While he scanned the roads and tourist spots for any glimpse of his target, it crossed his mind that Walker had no intention of meeting him that evening. He was playing with him, tormenting him again.

After a fruitless forty minutes spent driving around, he decided that he might as well go back to London. Walker had got away from him again. He joined the A30, and, sitting in the fast lane, visualised, as he had done every night since Lisa's murder, just what he would do to Walker if he got the chance. He fell into a dream, picturing Walker's face as he broke his nose and crushed his cheekbones with his foot.

Paterson stamped down again and again, feeling the hated face give way under his shoe and the eyeballs pop from their sockets. He was looking down at Walker, watching the life drain out of him when, with a massive bang, he hit the kerb and the dashboard alarm jerked him back to reality. He wrestled frantically with the steering wheel, which had been violently wrenched from his grasp when he kerbed it. Finally, after a few side to side swerves, he managed to get the speed off and coasted into a layby.

He sat still for a few minutes, breathing deeply, and then got out of the car. The tyre pressure monitor had already told him he'd had a blow-out but he had to make sure. The electronics were right. 'Oh no, no, no! You bastard thing!' In helpless rage, he kicked the bumper and stomped around in circles. Then he pulled himself together, and pulled out his phone. Hands shaking, he googled local mobile tyre fitters. He checked his watch. Still time.

He sat in the car to wait, door half open, embarrassed. A number of passing motorists took great delight in the sight of this agitated rich bastard sitting at the side of the road in a broken down Aston.

CHAPTER SIXTEEN

The streets were quiet as Paterson pulled off of the Bricklayers roundabout into Tower Bridge Road. On either side of the road a couple of late night kebab shops were hanging on for the two o'clock pub chuck out time. Both already had a couple of swaying customers, but the big money was in the two o'clock squad.

Ahead, a police car running on the blues and twos took a hard right and disappeared out of sight. Seconds later the area car screamed across the junction in front of him on their way to join their colleagues. Either a large pub fight or some copper needing urgent assistance. He waited for the road to clear, and pressed on. Driving towards him in the opposite direction, he spotted a marked armed response vehicle. These were a common enough sight on the streets of London now terrorism was a constant threat. Paterson recognised the crew and gave a small wave as they passed him. They nodded back and drove on. There was something a bit off about that ARV. He got it. They're usually three crewed. This one only had two. The one in the back was missing. Tucked up with paperwork, he surmised.

Bermondsey antique market had a worldwide reputation. Anybody that dealt with or dabbled in antiques knew this was the place to find the most interesting and unusual pieces and, more importantly, to buy at a sensible price. Officially it opened at six in the morning, but the professional dealers got the jump and bought the best pieces by being there at four when the traders started setting up. That was the difference between dealers and dabblers. A couple of extra hours in bed.

The market staff, or tobies, were already showing signs of activity. A few empty frames had been put in place and a pile of bars and canopies were dotted around waiting for the tobies to return from their kebab break. As Paterson drove past, two young men were squaring up to each other in the market place. One had a bottle, broken by the look of it. A young girl, dressed for a blinding Friday night out, was egging him on to stab the other. He drove on. No longer a cop. Busy anyway. The sight reminded him that he needed a weapon of some sort, but a broken bottle would hardly be sufficient for Walker. A gun was required. Paterson had an idea.

He pulled the car over, got out and looked up. Tower Bridge was lit up against the night sky like a string of Christmas lights. It was good to see it again. Of all the London bridges this one had always been his favourite. As a probationary constable in Bermondsey he had never tired of seeing its bascules rise as it had done virtually every day for the past 120 odd years to let the boats pass underneath. He thought it fitting that it might well all end for him back where he started. Walking toward the bridge, he pulled out his phone and dialled. He checked his watch — eleven fifty-five. *He can wait.*

He looked up, hoping to catch a glimpse of Walker, but saw nothing. He knew he'd be up high, skulking in the shadows behind one of the office windows, watching for his arrival. With the streets mostly empty, Paterson knew he wouldn't be able to hide, and it never entered his head to try. He wanted Walker to see him.

Stepping onto the bridge at a half-jog, he looked over the side, straining to see the faint light coming from the police riverboat station at Thames Wapping. A river cop — river rats as they were known — once told him that when a jumper went in, it took them less than five minutes to scramble a boat and get to the bridge — *if* they were docked when the call came. Chances were they'd be in time to pull the unfortunate jumper out, usually unconscious but alive. However, a lot depended on how high they were when they jumped. If they went over from bascule height, they had a chance. If they went from the high walkways, which many did before they were closed off, they ran the risk of getting trapped in the mud at low tide, or else the current would hold them below the surface, until they were swept downriver. In that case they mostly came to the top at Thames Wapping station, and often a secondary boat would just wait there, scouring the river for a dead pop-up.

Paterson recalled his first night on duty as a uniformed probationer. A stolen car had been chased from north of the river straight towards a road block on the south side, where he was. The car skidded to a halt and the driver, a young lad of about eighteen, bailed out and jumped into the river, thinking he could swim to shore, climb up and leg it before plod realised what he was doing. The driver had stopped the car roughly in line with the edge of the riverbank so at first blush, it seemed like a plan. Not a good one, but a plan nonetheless. However, a forty-foot drop when the tide's on its way out was never going to go well. They found the lad's body when the tide was right out, stuck in the mud up to his thighs. Paterson hoped the river rats found Walker — or him.

The door to the exhibition centre was slightly ajar. Gingerly, Paterson pulled it open and stood in the doorway, trying to adjust his eyes to the dark. He made out a couple of displays and a few TV sets but that was about it. He stepped back outside and pulled out his mobile phone. He hit three nines and waited. A no-nonsense voice sounded in his ear. 'Hello, emergency. Which service do you require?'

'Police.'

There was silence for a moment then a female voice said, 'Police. What is your emergency?'

He started to breathe hard, as if he'd been running. 'This is Detective Superintendent Paterson. I'm in pursuit of multiple murder suspect Adam Walker. I've chased him along Tower Bridge Road where he has forced entry into the building itself. Suspect is armed and highly dangerous. Request the assistance of Trojan units to the scene. Silent approach required.'

'Superintendent Paterson, do you have a description of the suspect?'

Paterson rolled his eyes. Really? 'Yes. He's the same person that's been circulated around every nick and on every TV station for the last month. He's a big bastard waving a gun around and he's the only person waving it around inside an empty Tower Bridge in the dead of night. Can't really miss him, to be honest.'

A beat. 'Thank you for your sarcasm, Superintendent. Duly noted. Stand by.' Paterson allowed himself a little smile.

'Superintendent Paterson, assistance is on its way. You have ARV Trojan Two nearby and on their way to you. Hold your position and do not enter the building until they arrive. Stay on the line, please, Superintendent, and report any sightings of suspect.'

'Will do,' he said, and hung up. He knew it was highly unlikely that the control room would be aware of his resignation, likewise the crew of Trojan Two. Two must be the ARV that had passed him in Tower Bridge Road. He turned and walked north under the bridge, out of Walker's line of sight.

The distant wail of a siren and flashing blues told him he'd guessed right. He stepped out from under the building so they'd see him as they approached. His phone rang and up flashed Walker's picture.

'What?'

'You disappoint me. You've called your friends. Why are you trying to spoil the fun?'

'Don't worry about them. They won't be disturbing us. Listen, Walker, if we're having this out, make sure you don't go hiding in the dark like the cowardly piece of shit you are. You wanted me. I'm here. Bear in mind I'm not a woman. You might just find you get hit back.'

'You seem to forget, Jordan was a man.'

'Yeah, but you never gave him a fighting chance, did you? Surprise is your real weapon. I've figured you out, Walker. Despite the fancy profiles and the poor childhood shit, at the bottom of it all you're just a fucking coward who can't fight unless he's got a knife in his hand.'

'We shall see, Ray.'

'Now fuck off, Walker, and wait for me to come and kill you.' He hung up, grinning. That's wound him up. He might actually face me now. He put his phone into silent mode.

Trojan Two pulled up. Paterson walked slowly towards the back of the vehicle. The operator jumped out, slammed the door and walked toward him. Paterson knew he would have only seconds before the driver was out too.

'Sir, we just got a ca—'

Paterson drove his elbow hard into the man's face, and he dropped like a sack of spanners. Quickly, he unclipped the holster and snatched out the Glock 17. The driver's door opened. Paterson raised the weapon, two handed, over the roof, waiting for the head to appear. As the driver got out, Paterson said, 'Freeze! Show me your hands. Do it now.'

The driver stopped and looked straight down the barrel of the gun. 'What the . . ?'

'Keep your hands up. Do exactly as I tell you. Understand?' The driver nodded. Paterson made his way around the car, his eyes fixed on the driver. 'Take your cuffs out and cuff yourself through the door frame. You understand?' The driver nodded. 'Do it now. Carefully.'

The driver did as instructed. 'What the fuck are you doing?'

'What's your name, fellah?' Paterson stepped toward him.

'Alan Deeks.'

'I'm sorry, Alan. I am truly. But I had to get hold of a gun before I go in there. I've got a date with a pissed off homicidal maniac and I need a leveller. If I'd asked, would you have just given me your weapon?

'Fuck you,' said Deeks.

'That's just why I didn't ask,' said Paterson, helping himself to Deeks's firearm. He flicked the safety off and tucked it into the back of his trousers, then went back to the unconscious policeman, took out his cuffs and secured his hands behind him.

'Do you even know what you're doing with that?' Deeks said.

In the distance, more sirens were wailing their way toward him. He hoped Johnny Clocks was among them. He could use a friendly face. 'More or less. I find which end has the hole, point, and then empty the whole fucking lot into him.' He turned and walked back towards the entrance.

* * *

'C'mon Paterson. Answer your bleedin' phone.' Johnny Clocks looked at his phone to check the signal, even though it was ringing. 'Sod it,' he said, after the tenth ring of the fifth attempt. He tossed the phone, still dialling, onto the seat next to him and shot forwards past the car in front. He kept the accelerator pedal down, picking up speed, weaving in and out of traffic, the back sliding out as he fought for control at corners.

He roared into Tower Bridge approach from the north side and spotted a lone revolving blue light and what looked to be a figure standing by the door. At a hundred yards, he could see it was a uniformed PC and he wondered why he hadn't moved from the spot. Clocks glanced in the rear-view mirror. Sitting tight on his arse was another blue light, and Kingston and his team pulled ahead of him. Thank fuck for that, muttered Clocks.

* * *

Paterson's phone buzzed gently in his jacket pocket again. He left the phone where it was. Right now he really needed to concentrate his mind and anyway, Clocks wasn't going to talk him out of it.

Both vehicles screeched to a halt beside the handcuffed officer and their respective occupants all bailed out.

'Where is he?' shouted Kingston to the handcuffed officer.

Deeks pointed with his chin, 'He's gone in. Other side. He's got our firearms. For God's sake be careful.'

'Where's your crew?' shouted Clocks.

Again, Deeks pointed with his chin, over to the other side of the car. 'I think your man whacked him. I hope that's all the bastard's done.'

Clocks went round to have a look, saw him lying face down, rolled him over and checked his pulse. 'He's alright. Just unconscious.' He turned him into the recovery position.

'He'll be fine,' he said to Deeks. He fished out his handcuff key and released him. 'Call an ambulance and wait with him. You've got other weapons in here, right?' Deeks nodded. 'Good. While you're waiting, tool yourself up and keep an eye on that door. Anyone comes running out of any door and it ain't us, shoot the fucker.

Understand?' Deeks nodded again. Part of him hoped it would be Paterson.

* * *

Straining his eyes and ears, Paterson moved carefully through the gloom amid the shelving of the ticket office cum gift shop. Staring down at him were row upon row of nodding policemen, guarding hundreds of perpetually waving plastic caricatures of HM the queen alongside miniature models of Tower Bridge, souvenir 'gold' coins stamped with images of the bridge, and countless other bits of tourist tat. Ahead of him, he saw a sliver of light coming out of a slightly open door.

He crouched and held the gun out in front of him in both hands. He noticed that the barrel was shaking. Calm down. Breathe deeply. A drop of sweat ran down the side of his cheek and his heart thumped in his chest. Where are you, you bastard? Where are you?

He rose and pressed his back against the wall, and took a quick look through the open door. He spotted two lifts side by side in what looked like some sort of waiting area. The display above one set of lift doors read 'top.' Of course he is, muttered Paterson. Where else would he be? He nudged the door open with his foot and stepped in fast, pointing the gun left, right, up. Clear. *Deeks would be proud of me.* Think, Paterson. Only two ways of reaching the walkway level and whichever one he took, Walker was going to be waiting for him. He opted for the lift, figuring it would save him a bit of energy and get him there before any of his colleagues arrived. He punched the button and the doors slid open. Empty.

Inside the lift, he pointed the gun at the ceiling just in case and kept it there all the way up. The lift dinged its arrival, and he dropped to a kneeling crouch, pushed himself as far into a corner as he could, and held the gun steady as the doors slid open.

Nothing.

Ahead of him was a dimly lit corridor, maybe fifty, sixty metres long. Small diamond shaped windows either side locked behind criss-crossed girders told him he was in one of the visitor walkways. Nowhere to hide here. Carefully, he moved forward, eyes straining into the gloom. Halfway in he looked down at the floor and his heart gave a lurch. His stomach joined in. Nearly ten metres of the floor was glass. The latest tourist attraction. *Oh Christ. You crafty bastard. You know. Of course you do. That's why we're here.*

There was a thin bit of solid flooring either side of the glass which he could sidle along but it didn't matter now, his head was screwed. Once he stepped out there, if he looked down once, even a glance, he was done for.

He'd seen this sort of thing once before on the Grand Canyon Skywalk in the States. He and Lisa had gone on a day trip from Vegas with some friends. He'd waited outside, holding the bags. He watched a party of day-trippers go marching out onto the walkway, all full of themselves, and smiled. Nearly all of them panicked about a quarter of the way round. Some of them made it to the guard rail, where they gripped on for dear life. Others just froze — rooted to the spot. But at least those people had helpers to see them back to terra firma. No such luck tonight.

Crouched low, he peered gingerly over the side, down to the road below. His stomach formed a knot, and terror shot through his body. Some forty metres below him, a few tiny blue lights revolved lazily. As he looked around desperately, trying to figure out his best move, Walker appeared at the door at the far end of the walkway.

'Hello, Ray. You made it then. That's good.' Walker's voice echoed slightly in the empty walkway. Paterson whipped the gun up and pointed it straight at him. 'Smart move. You got yourself a gun. Well played. By all means take a shot, but I wouldn't waste it if I were you. We both know you're highly unlikely to hit me from there.' Paterson looked at his target silhouetted in the doorway, looking exactly like the paper ones at the gun range. He wasn't too good at hitting them either.

'It's difficult to see you from here, Ray, but let me guess. Clammy hands, sweating heavily, mouth dry, shaking, heart going ten to the dozen, pure unadulterated rage at the sight of me.' Paterson stood up, still pointing the gun. His legs felt weak. 'You can come get me, Ray, but you'll have to fly like the birds. Can you fly, Ray? Can you step out onto the glass? Or are you going to stay there, frozen with fear, pissing your very expensive trousers?' Walker took a step onto the glass and looked down. 'It's very high, isn't it? Still, you're a brave man, Ray. Look at you. You have a gun and all.'

'Why don't you come on down this end you piece of shit,' Paterson said, and instantly regretted it. Now Walker knew for sure that he was frightened.

'Ray, you're an educated man. Do you have to keep calling me names? It's very disrespectful.'

'Fuck educated,' Paterson shouted. 'You get your arse down here, Walker, and face me man to man.'

'Man to man? With a gun pointed at me?'

'Fair point,' Paterson said, and threw the gun onto the walkway. His second regret of the night. He hoped it would entice Walker to move towards him. No such luck.

'Oh, Ray. For an educated man you're very stupid. You can't cross the bridge and now you can't even take a wild shot at me. If you keep this up you'll never catch me, will you? Tell you what. How about I meet you half way? Let's meet in the middle. What'd you say?'

Paterson breathed slowly, trying to bring his fear under control. His therapist had given him a few techniques for this. Not the best way to find out if they worked, but he doubted he'd be around to see about a refund. He weighed it up. Halfway. Not so bad, but still high whichever way you looked at it. The gun had slid to a halt about a metre further along.

Walker walked toward him and stopped about halfway. 'It's pretty down there, Ray. Why don't you come take a look with me?' He beckoned to Paterson.

Paterson could feel his blood pump through his veins. His head pounded, his temperature soared and his legs felt like lead. He heard a scream, a loud guttural scream that seemed to come from somewhere outside of him. He was moving. Fast. The scream was his. He ran out onto the glass and began to fall backwards, deliberately. Walker's expression changed from smug to shocked as Paterson hit the glass sideways-on, slid forward, scooped up the gun with his left hand and began firing. The shots screamed for their target and the noise inside the walkway was deafening. Walker stood, helpless, as one shot took him high in the shoulder, punching him around a full one-eighty degrees. Paterson slammed into his legs. The full weight of his body, at the end of its slide, knocked Walker down. The gun clattered away.

Winded, Paterson grabbed hold of Walker, who had fallen face up on top of him. Flat on his back, with Walker's full weight bearing down on him, Paterson threw one arm around the struggling man's neck, and hooked the other under and around his shoulder, in a wrestler's lock. Walker managed to loosen Paterson's grip around his neck just enough to deliver a backward head butt. The back of his head connected with Paterson's nose with a thud. Colours exploded in front of Paterson's eyes and a bolt of pain like an electric shock ran through him. Walker pulled himself free, scrabbled to his feet and began to run. Blood gushing from his nose, Paterson struggled to pull himself up and felt around for the gun. His fingers closed around it, and he picked it up. Dazed and confused and all caution gone, he staggered off after Walker. *Don't look down.*

* * *

Clocks and Kingston heard the shots ring out from somewhere above them. Legs and lungs burning, they took the stairs two at a time until they came to a door leading out onto the walkway. Kingston, in full assault mode, peered cautiously through the porthole window out along the walkway. Empty, as far as he could see. Gently, he pushed the door open and stepped through, moving quickly to the right. Behind, Clocks darted to the left. Secure. No obvious hiding places. At the far end of the walkway they saw an open door. They ran towards it. Nowhere else they could have gone.

* * *

In another dark room, Paterson crouched behind a desk. He wasn't sure, but he figured he had about four, maybe five bullets left. Plenty for what he needed. He shook his head to try to get rid of the pain but it only made it worse. He swiped at his nose. More blood. This was getting to be a habit. Peering over the top of the desk, he saw at least half a dozen places where Walker could be hiding. He'd lost the advantage of surprise. He made out a fire exit sign above a door at the end of the office. For a few seconds he pulled the petals off an imaginary daisy. Will he, won't he have gone through that door? Paterson took the chance and stood up. A feeling of complete calm washed over him. Even the pain across the bridge of his nose seemed to subside. He heard himself breathe. He knew, somehow, that Walker was the other side of that door.

Paterson took a step forward, raised the gun and loosed off another two shots. Both hit the door and wood splintered in all directions. He kept moving.

He heard Walker shout, 'Fuck me!' and then he was off again, up towards the fire exit door at the top of the building. Hearing the shout and the clatter of footsteps, Paterson sped up, focusing on the light through the porthole window, bumping into desks in the gloom, crashing through the door and tumbling out onto the landing. He caught sight of Walker's leg just as it disappeared through the fire exit door and pulled the trigger again — two, three, four. Tiny wisps of dust where they bit into the wall. Click, click, click. Empty. *Pointless. But the fucker knows I'm still coming.* He threw the gun away.

* * *

Hearing the two shots from the room ahead, Clocks and Kingston slowed down and pressed themselves against the wall, taking what little cover they could. More shots rang out, quieter. Further away. Kingston knew that the shooter was now in another part of the building. Clocks edged towards the door and peered through the porthole window. Looked empty. Dead ahead, another door. They entered, covering each other, looking carefully for the slightest movement.

* * *

Paterson reached the top of the stairs and threw himself through the door. A cold blast of icy wind hit him full in the face and it took him a few seconds to realise he was now outside, on the tarmac roof, and one hell of a lot higher up than he wanted to be.

'C'mon, Ray!' Listing to one side like a stricken ship and holding his damaged shoulder, Walker was standing on top of one of the walkways, beckoning to him. 'See if you can take my legs out again. Smooth move, I have to say. Where did that come from?'

Paterson knew backup was coming. He hoped it was Clocks, but he didn't want anyone yet. He cast his eyes around and spotted an old shovel lying close by. He rammed it against the door, jamming the handle. He knew it wouldn't hold them off for long, but it might just be long enough.

He turned to Walker. 'What's the matter, scumball? Looks like you're leaning a bit. I fucking hope that hurts.'

Walker looked at the blood on his hand, then at his shoulder. 'Just a scratch, Ray. You'll have to do better than that, you know.'

'I intend to.'

'Don't think so. You're out of bullets and too scared to come out here after me. You managed to grow a pair downstairs but up here, out in the open, it's another story. Isn't it? I'm guessing that right about now your stomach is in knots and your balls are blocking your throat. A tad windy, isn't it?'

Paterson glared at him and took a step forward. Right on all counts. He took another step, more hesitant this time, and a gust of wind made him stagger slightly.

Walker shook his head. 'Ray. Did they tell you what I did to Lisa? Did you read the report before you resigned?' Paterson stiffened. Walker was about to goad him, freak him out. 'Probably best you didn't really. It wouldn't have been light reading. It all got very messy, even by my standards. When she woke up after I'd smashed her head into the dresser, she started screaming. She screamed the house down, Ray. That was one noisy bitch. I asked her politely to keep it down, but you know what some people are like. They tend to object to having their bodies slashed about. To tell you the truth, all that screaming pissed me off a bit and when I get angry, well . . .'

'Shut the fuck up!' Paterson shouted, the fear giving way to rage.

'Oh I'm sorry, Ray, I didn't mean to upset you. Just thought you should know. Did they find it, Ray?'

'Find what?'

'My saliva.'

'What . . ?'

'On her heart.'

Paterson's face turned grey and his hand went to his mouth. 'Oh God, no . . .'

'When I opened her up, Ray, I licked her heart just as it gave its final beat. I like to think I licked the life right out of her.'

Paterson charged, his face contorted with rage, blood pumping in his ears, all fear forgotten, his eyes locked on this monster dressed as a man. He didn't hear the shots or the fire escape door being kicked open. He threw himself at Walker, hitting him hard in the stomach in a flying tackle that sent them both to the floor. Rolling over and off, Paterson spun around only to find Walker getting to his feet.

'C'mon, scum, get the fuck up!' Walker snarled.

'Johnny!' Paterson shouted. Johnny Clocks and Billy Kingston were out on the roof now, moving towards the two men. 'Stay there! Stay the fuck out of this!' Both men slowed to a halt. Paterson wanted a little alone time with Walker, and they both knew he was entitled to it. Clocks nodded.

'Just me and you then, you sick fuck,' Paterson said. 'Let's have it.'

Walker came for him, straight and fast, his face impassive. Paterson, his years of training forgotten, wildly swung his right hand. Walker ducked fast and easy, came up and grabbed Paterson by the throat, knocking him off balance. Clocks and Kingston raised their weapons. Paterson tried to break the grip, failed, and took hold of Walker's head in both hands and jammed his thumbs straight into his eyes. He squeezed hard. Walker clung on, Paterson squeezed harder. Nothing. Panic rising, he kicked Walker between the legs and felt him lift onto his toes. The grip around his windpipe relaxed slightly, enough for him to shove Walker's arms sideways, breaking his hold. He kicked out again, hard and low to the side of Walker's knee. Walker dropped. He smashed his fist down and into the side of Walker's face. Walker teetered. Clocks and Kingston lowered their weapons. A hard kick to the other side of the face sent Walker sprawling, face up. Walker struggled to sit up. Blood bubbled from his mouth.

'Up,' said Paterson. 'Get up, you cunt.'

Walker smiled, cuffed at his mouth and spat blood. 'You seem angry, Ray. Was it something I did?' He pulled himself to his feet and put his hands behind his head. 'I can see you're upset. Tell you what, I'll put you out of your misery and give up. Like a good boy.'

CHAPTER SEVENTEEN

Paterson stared at him. Walker twirled around. No weapons visible. Surrendered, just like that. After all that had happened, all he'd done. 'Like fuck you do,' Paterson said. 'Not happening. You wanted this. We play it through.'

'Mr Paterson, I said I give up. I have no wish to fight with you.'

'Screw you, Walker. You are not walking away from this.'

'Mr Kingston,' Walker called out. 'I am wanted for several murders, to which I freely admit, including that of Superintendent Paterson's wife. I am unarmed and I am surrendering to your custody. You have a duty to place me under arrest. I am now your prisoner and your responsibility. If this man injures me further in any way, it is a dereliction of duty and on your head. Mr Clocks will bear witness.'

'Will he fuck!' shouted Johnny Clocks. 'Mr Clocks will see exactly fuck all!' It was enough for Paterson, who started to move towards him.

Kingston struggled with himself, undecided. Was Paterson really going to kill him? Would Clocks merely watch him do it? Cover for him? Could he, Kingston, stand by and let Paterson kill a defenceless man? What is the right thing here? Sometimes morals can be a bastard.

He made his decision. 'Paterson! Stand down!' Clocks looked at him, shocked.

Paterson, with his back to Kingston, eyes still on Walker, said, 'Turn away, Inspector. What you don't see won't hurt you.'

'I said stand down. This man is unarmed and has surrendered. He is now my prisoner.' Kingston stepped forward, sure footed and in control of himself. Johnny Clocks followed. The men drew level with Paterson. Kingston holstered his gun, pulled his plasticuffs out and, moving toward Walker, received a blow in the chest that stopped him in his tracks.

Paterson was looking at Kingston, his face a mask of fury. He left his hand where it was. 'I *said,* walk away, Inspector.' The two men stood and glared at each other, locked in a battle of wills. Neither flinched.

The thing about killers, all killers, is that you can't trust the bastards to do as they say. All three men should have known better. Walker worked his fingers deftly underneath his collar and pulled out a small scalpel.

'Get your hand off me now, Paterson, or so help me you'll regret it.' Kingston pointed to Walker. 'He is under arrest. You are a civilian. You are obstructing me. Now get your fucking hand off of me, or there'll be consequences.'

'Consequences? Shove your consequences.' Paterson swung at him.

Kingston saw it coming, ducked under the flailing arm and danced away with his back to Walker. He bounced back a couple of steps, readying himself for Paterson's next attempt. Suddenly he was jerked off his feet. Walker had his arm round his neck. He held Kingston in front of him as a shield, pressing the razor-sharp blade against his throat and drawing a trickle of blood. Clocks stepped forward, pushing a stunned Ray Paterson out of the way, and pointed the gun at both men. 'Let him go, Walker. Do it now!'

'Or what, Johnny boy? You're not going to shoot, are you? Bit risky, I'd say.'

'For Christ's sake, Adam,' Clocks said. 'Just give it up. Where can you go? You're fucked. There's coppers everywhere. Look.' He waved his hand towards the roof edge. Walker looked down to see swarms of police vehicles, ambulances. Even the fire brigade had rolled out of bed, and had their hoses unravelled. In the distance, blue lights glittered off the inky black water of the Thames, signalling the arrival of the river boat police.

'It doesn't look good, does it?' he said to Clocks. 'But, never say die, eh? Throw your gun into the river or I'll open his throat up. Let's face it, we both know I'll do it.'

'Not gonna do that, Adam. You know I can't.'

'Please yourself then. If you're determined to kill me, I might as well take Mr Kingston with me.' Kingston's eyes widened in terror as the blade bit deeper into his throat.

'Okay, okay! I'm doing it.' The Glock inscribed an arc high in the sky, then plummeted into the Thames. 'Now let him go.'

'Fair enough.' Walker stood up and almost casually, pulled Kingston backwards over the edge.

* * *

Clocks and Paterson froze, shocked rigid. Walker looked over the side and watched Kingston fall, arms and legs flailing, desperately grabbing at empty space, until he smacked into the water. From sixty metres up, it was like hitting the pavement. 'Bye, bye, Inspector,' Walker said, and shrugged.

Clocks and Paterson emerged from their daze and together, rushed him.

Walker crouched and swung the scalpel in a wide arc, ready for their attack. Eyes wide, manic, he beckoned with the other hand. 'Come on. Next, please.'

They stopped dead, eyes on the blade.

'No takers? I thought not.' Walker straightened up. 'Well, I'll be going then, gents.'

'Where to?' said Clocks. 'You know there's nowhere to run.'

'Maybe, but if it's going to end for me, I'll take a few more on the way out. Nothing to lose.' He pointed to Paterson. 'That,' he said, 'was your fault. Another one to live with.' Walker turned sharply on his heel and began to walk away.

Two short whistles made him stop instantly, like a dog that has been summoned by its owner. Paterson, his face impassive, stood looking at his back. 'There's a good boy. Come back here. Who gave you permission to go anywhere?'

Walker turned sharply and scowled. 'Permission? That's a joke, right?' He moved back towards him, walking fast, confidently.

'No joke, fucker. Get yourself back here like a good little boy.'

Clocks backed up. Paterson stood stock still, staring intently at the merciless madman bearing down on him, scalpel in hand.

'*I* give permission, Paterson, not you. And now you have my permission to fucking die!' He kept coming, but slightly hesitant, as if unsure as to why Paterson wasn't moving. Paterson was smiling. His eyes widened as Paterson whipped out PC Deek's gun from his waistband and pointed it directly at him.

'Gotcha,' said Paterson with just a hint of a smile. Two sharp reports, two bright flashes and Walker dropped to the floor like a brick. The first shot had struck him in the leg. The second went through his kidneys.

Now Paterson was moving. Clocks followed behind him. Walker writhed on the ground, screaming. 'Oh, Jesus fuck! Jesus fuck!'

Paterson stood over him, impassive. 'Look at me,' he commanded. Walker writhed and swore. 'I said look at me.' Walker looked up, his face contorted in pain and hate. 'Does that hurt, you piece of shit?' Paterson said. 'Oh, I do fucking hope so.'

Walker spat blood. 'Go fuck yourself.' Paterson smiled and pointed the gun directly at his face.

Clocks panicked. 'Guv! Don't . . . don't do this.'

Paterson looked over at Johnny Clocks. He'd grown to like this man. Never thought he would. But that was one of the good things about the police. It was made up of people from all walks of life, all backgrounds, all cultures but all bound together by a code that the civvies would never understand. He was sorry to put Clocks in this position.

He turned back to Walker. 'I have to, John. He can't walk away.'

'If you do, you're no better than him. Don't sink to that level. Please.'

Paterson watched Walker, writhing on the ground, still moaning. He nodded, slowly. 'Hey, scum! Earlier tonight someone asked me if I knew how to use a gun. I said all I have to do is point it and keep pulling the trigger until it's empty. You,' he shook his head, 'are not worth that many bullets.' He let the gun fall to his side, and turned away. Clocks breathed a sigh of relief. Walker slumped.

Turning back sharply, Paterson raised the gun and pulled the trigger. 'Fuck it. One's enough.'

The shot hit Walker above the right eye, killing him instantly. Clocks's mouth dropped open.

Standing in the cold night air, the wind whipping around them, they stood and watched the slowly spreading pool of blood spilling out from underneath Walker's head. Johnny Clocks threw his head back, screwed his eyes shut tight, ran both hands through his hair. He let out a sigh, opened his eyes and saw that Paterson was still looking at Walker.

Clocks spotted Walker's scalpel, dropped when the second shot hit him. He knew what to do. 'Ray. Gimme the gun.' He held his hand out, and flicked his fingers. Paterson handed it over. Pulling out a handkerchief, Clocks picked the scalpel up, put it back into Walker's hand and closed his fingers around it. 'This'll take some writing up, Ray.'

Paterson nodded. The shakes began almost immediately. 'Johnny,' he said holding out his hands, 'get me off this fucking roof.'

* * *

Eleven months to the day after Paterson passed sentence on Adam Walker without the benefit of trial by jury, he found himself once again sitting opposite ACC Young. His fate had now been decided, and ACC Young was going to tell him what that decision was. The past eleven months had been the longest of his life and he was glad that one way or another, it was all coming to an end.

Still slightly tanned from his late summer break, thinning hair bleached by the sun and his full dress uniform pressed to perfection, ACC Young slowly thumbed through the report in front of him. He seemed to be taking his time to study each word carefully and make sure he understood its contents before he spoke. Paterson could see the cover had his name on it and the letter V but he couldn't make out the other name. He presumed it was the Crown. He glanced at his Rolex and checked it against the clock that hung over Young's trophy cabinet. Just a couple of minutes between them. Young, he could tell, was not in a hurry. Playing mind games for some reason of his own. He knew damn well that Young had seen and read the report long before he was called for interview. He also knew that it would have been extensively discussed up, down and sideways along the food chain. Still, he was content to wait. He had nowhere to be. His mind drifted back to the night of his arrest . . .

* * *

As they reached the elevator, Clocks stood in front of the door and pulled out his handcuffs. He looked around at the ceilings, the corners of the room, checking for CCTV, smiled when he found none. 'Gonna have to nick you, guv. Don't want to but for your sake, I have to. I'm the only witness to what happened up there. You're my responsibility and I'm your only hope. They're going to do you for a lot of things, guv, but murder of a murdering bastard ain't gonna be one of 'em. Listen to me.'

Paterson, still shaking, looked directly at him, searching his face for a clue as to what was coming next. 'What I write in my notes is what will be the truth of what happened here. The truth according to us. I'm saying that after Walker tossed Kingston over the side, he then rounded on us both, threatening to kill us and carve us up and all that shit. Which is not a lie. You pulled the gun and told him to stop, to drop the knife and to surrender. He screamed that he was going to cut your heart out and then he charged. You fired two, which put him down but the threat was still high. He still had the scalpel and when we moved in to arrest him, he kept waving it about. He flat out refused to surrender. We moved in again, he made to throw it at you, you feared for your life and popped him one in the nut. You just fired, didn't mean to hit him in the head. That was unfortunate. End of. That's what happened. We gave him ample opportunity to give himself up and he wouldn't. Self-defence on your part, suicide by cop on his. That understood?' Paterson, a little vacant, nodded.

'Good. Now when they pull you in for questioning, keep your trap shut and say nothing to nobody. Play the shock card until we can talk properly.'

* * *

ACC Young cleared his throat. 'Do you know what this is?' he said, flicking his hand at the papers.

'I'm guessing it's a report from the director of the CPS, sir.'

ACC Young nodded. 'That's right, Mr Paterson. It is. It would seem that after very careful consideration and a full examination of the facts and available evidence, there is insufficient substantiation to lay any charges in respect to the death of Detective Constable Adam Walker. Congratulations.' Relief washed over Paterson. He kept his face impassive, but his dancing feet gave him away.

'Nor are there to be any charges or disciplinary action with respect to your action in assaulting two police officers, stealing weapons and using them to end the life of someone who thoroughly deserved to die. That's directly from the commissioner via the PM. Apparently, the DPP and IPCC and any other busybody can go fuck themselves.' A broad smile broke across his face, and he stood up and held out his hand. Paterson got to his feet and shook it.

'Thank you, sir. I don't really know what to say. I'm a bit lost, really.'

'Nothing to say, Ray. Personally, I have my suspicions as to what really happened up there. Pretty much everybody does but, and this is the important bit, nobody cares that much and nobody bothered to look hard enough to prove otherwise. I must say, your little stunt with the cash reward threw the brass into a spin. Publicly they would and could never condone your offer but privately they were clapping the cheeks of their arses together. You've had a result. We've all had a result. Truth be told, I'd have done exactly the same. Let's leave it at that.'

'Thank you, sir.' Paterson choked a little. ACC Young gave a single curt nod. Business as usual.

'Before you go, I know you two have stayed in touch, but I thought I'd let you know that a decision has been made by the chief medical officer to retire Billy Kingston from the met on full disability pension. He won't be back on active duty, I'm afraid.' Paterson had figured that would be the case. Kingston had smacked into the water flat on his back, breaking both of his hips and most of his ribs. Two of those ribs punched holes in his lungs and his head split open at the back, but he'd survived. Depending on your definition of luck, he landed just five feet away from one of the river boats, and was fished from the water, half dead. They were amazed it was only half. The doctors at Guy's Hospital said he hit the water with equivalent force to a Nissan Micra at sixty mph. It sounded feasible to Paterson. It didn't really matter. At the hospital, they induced a coma while they struggled to reduce his brain bleed, and for two months or so Kingston hovered between life and death. It was touch and go a few times, but he recovered. Not fully, but at least he could walk, albeit with crutches. His speech was slurred from the brain injury but he would likely recover from that in time.

'However,' said Young, 'when he's fully recovered he'll be taken back on as a consultant firearms training officer. Better than nothing. I get the impression he wouldn't cut it shoving trolleys around Asda.'

Paterson smiled. 'No sir, he wouldn't.'

'Johnny Clocks seems to have taken to his promotion to inspector. Apparently, he's grown up quite a bit, so no bad thing there. Maybe this case was the making of him, or perhaps he just needed the extra responsibility. Who knows?' Young shrugged. 'And you. Make sure you're back in the office at nine on Monday. Report to DI Clocks and he'll bring you up to speed. You've been off long enough.'

'Sir?' Paterson looked at him. 'I don't understand. I resigned.'

ACC Young opened the bottom drawer of his desk, pushed aside a half empty bottle of Jameson's and pulled out Paterson's warrant card. He slid it across the desk to him. 'I told you I didn't accept it, and I meant it. I put you on gardening leave due to stress. With your money, I don't suppose you noticed your pay going in each month, did you?' Young sounded a tad jealous. 'I want you back. The Met wants you back. It's up to you, Superintendent.'

THE END

Thank you for reading this book. If you enjoyed it please leave feedback on Amazon, and if there is anything we missed or you have a question about then please get in touch. The author and publishing team appreciate your feedback and time reading this book.

Our email is office@joffebooks.com

www.joffebooks.com

LOOK OUT FOR STEVE PARKER'S NEXT BOOK
COMING SOON

25163049R00149

Printed in Great Britain
by Amazon